W9-BLI-650

BIRTH MARKS

Also by Sarah Dunant

SNOW STORMS IN A HOT CLIMATE

BIRTH MARKS

Sarah Dunant

A Perfect Crime Book

DOUBLEDAY

New York London Toronto Sydney Auckland

MYS

A Perfect Crime Book

PUBLISHED BY DOUBLEDAY

a division of Bantam Doubleday Dell Publishing Group, Inc.
666 Fifth Avenue, New York, New York 10103

DOUBLEDAY is a trademark of Doubleday,
a division of Bantam Doubleday Dell
Publishing Group, Inc.

Library of Congress Catalog-in-Publication Data

Dunant, Sarah.
Birth marks / by Sarah Dunant.
p.   cm.
"Perfect Crime."
"A Perfect Crime book."
I. Title.
PS3554.U4626B57   1992
813'.54—dc20   92-14735
CIP

ISBN 0-385-42318-7

First Edition in the United States of America

To Ian and Zoe

BIRTH MARKS

CHAPTER ONE

Mistake number one: I should never have sublet the flat. Mistake number two was letting myself be taken in by appearances. With a job like mine you'd think I would have learnt by now. But she had seemed such a shrinking violet, an anthropology student with so many religious books that she was clearly having trouble with Darwin. Obviously somewhere over the last three months the evolutionists had struck back. The kitchen smelt as if a dinosaur had died there and the bed looked as though it had been used to test out the survival of the fittest theory. Sex and drugs and rock 'n' roll. It had all happened here. And I hadn't had any of them. Ah, these young people. As a woman on the wrong side of thirty I could feel disapproval coming on.

Still, some things were better than others. London looked positively rural after Hong Kong and I would never again have to stand in line while Mrs Adeline Van de Bilt signed another traveller's cheque. God knows why she had employed me in the first place. For a woman in need of security she had enough twenty-one-carat knuckle dusters to lay out most would-be attackers. And what the stones didn't incapacitate the tongue would mop up. Rich women. Maybe they've just never had to ask for anything, so no one ever taught them how to say please. Or thank you. My fault entirely. We never did sort out the small print of extra hours. 'You have to be more business-like, Hannah,' as my father would say when I tried to sell him Mediterranean after I had landed on Boardwalk with two hotels. Come to think of it, Mrs Van de Bilt probably owned the freehold.

Still, no good whingeing. There were things to be done, people to see, bills to be paid. The cleaning firm estimated it would cost a hundred and thirty quid to steam clean the carpets and degrease the kitchen, and with no forwarding address for Margaret Mead the name on the door was the name on the cheque. Work – that was what was needed. Except that's the trouble with service industries. If no one needs the service the industry doesn't work. Like now. The post yielded mild threats from credit-card firms and a billet-doux from British Gas, while the telephone messages that Miss Evolution had managed not to lose were all specific. If I wasn't there they would find someone else. Of course it wasn't the end of the world. There was always Frank. But once you leave a firm it's humiliating to have to go back begging for work. And I had got picky in my old age. I was no longer willing to wheel myself round supermarkets busting women who needed the goods more than the store needed the money. No, Frank.

Two days and one more bill later I called him.

'Hi, Hannah. Back crawling for a job, eh?'

One of the nicer things about Frank is the way he makes you feel so good about your insecurities. I could just picture him, feet on the desk, ash dropping on to the carpet. If the photo in his old CID card is to be believed he used to be quite attractive when he was younger, but too many greasy-spoon meals and a sedentary lifestyle have done for him. He claims it's an advantage – people spotting him straight out as an ex-copper: gives them a sense of confidence. Since most of his clients are white, middle-class or foreign he may be right. I'm still looking forward to the day when the first Rasta walks in through the door and walks straight out again.

'So, my little apprentice, how was high-rise chink island?'

'Tall, short and crowded. Caused any good divorces lately?' Frank doesn't like to see himself as a sewer rat, but it happens. We've all taken rough jobs. Work to fit the times.

'Hitting beneath the belt again, Hannah. And I didn't think you were that kind of girl.'

'Woman, Frank, not girl, and could we stop talking like a bad crime novel for a moment?'

'Let me guess. You're broke, you need a handout and you're praying I've got something I can offload on to you, right?' Funny. When you think about it the only really glamorous thing about Marlowe is Chandler's style. Strip that away and what have you got but sleaze? 'Well, you're a lucky girl – sorry, woman. As it happens, I do have a couple of jobs on the books. There's a jeweller's place up west looking for a lady with sharp eyes.'

'Do me a favour.'

'That's what I'm trying to do. You know your trouble, Hannah? You're too political for this business. You have to side with the client. They're the ones with the money.'

'Till the revolution comes.'

'You see, what did I tell you? I blame myself. I didn't need to employ you. There were other girls. But no, Frank has to pick the only Marxist in the security business. It's an idea that's had its day, you know. We're all capitalists now. But then I don't suppose you're put off by the march of history.'

Dear Frank. Like all ex-coppers, his level of political sophistication leaves much to be desired. A regular diet of the *Guardian* and a healthy cynicism of the Establishment, and hey presto, he's got me tabbed as an instant subversive, and all unemployed Irishmen as members of the IRA. Still, despite his prejudice he's good at his job and for an old boy in blue he has a surprisingly soft heart. Though he still made me sweat for it.

'Just checking through the files . . .' The files, my ass. The only jobs Frank had would be sitting on the desk in front of him. 'OK. How about a missing person? Yorkshire lass comes down to London and stops writing home. Some old lady wants to know what happened?'

'Her mother?'

'Not the same name. But then with our divorce rate . . . So, what about it?'

'How did she come to you?'

'Picked me out of the phone book because she liked my name.'

[3]

Frank Comfort. I kid you not. He's even got his birth certificate on the wall to prove it. I've often wondered whether the guys he busted appreciated the irony. Probably not. 'So, you want it or not?'

Not really. Missing young girls seldom turn up somewhere their mothers want them to be. But if I didn't want it the gas and electricity board did. And I could hear the sound of British Telecom cheering on from the sidelines.

'I want it.'

But did it want me? The lady herself had doubts. 'I don't mean to be rude, Miss Wolfe, but I'm really not sure this is a job for a woman.'

Madam, if I had a pound coin for every time I've heard that remark I wouldn't need to be having this conversation with you. 'Well, I can understand your reservations, Miss Patrick' – I thought of calling her Ms but on the phone it always sounds like a speech defect – 'but in some cases, particularly when the missing person is a young girl, a woman can do a better job.' Listen to me, crawling. Get off your knees, Wolfe. 'But if that's how you feel I won't take up any more of your time.'

There was a long pause. It takes nerves, this game. Then she said, 'Perhaps you're right. Although I should warn you I can't make up my mind until I've talked to you. Shall we say this afternoon? I've consulted the timetables. The eleven o'clock train gets in here at three. Rose Cottage is not far from the station.'

Not far by taxi maybe, but quite a way on foot, especially with a January frost rubbing my nose blue. It wasn't the most promising way to start a professional relationship. Rose Cottage turned out to be a small but immaculately preserved eighteenth-century house on the edge of the village, the kind of place where forty years ago the mystery would have been solved by an old woman with knitting bag and spectacles. But with the social fabric of Agatha Christie breaking down, gracious ladies like Miss Patrick need men like Comfort. And women like me.

[4]

'Milk or lemon, Miss Wolfe?'

'Neither. I'll have it black, thank you.'

She poured, I watched. Augusta Patrick, lady of this parish. She was older than I expected, hovering gracefully somewhere between sixty and seventy. Too old certainly to be the mother. But her body, like her voice on the phone, seemed younger than her years. She sat perfectly upright, her back ramrod straight; beneath a long neck and even longer grey hair pulled back into a neat if slightly severe bun. When I was young and more deliberately feminine than I am now I had dreamt of posture like that as I tripped my way to ballet classes. You don't need to be Sherlock Holmes to tell a dancer from an insurance clerk. And if all else failed there were always the photographs on the piano: an older man rigid with Edwardian values and two dying swans, one recent and colourful, the other fading from chemical imbalance as well as lost love. But elegant nevertheless. She handed me the cup. It shivered on its saucer, the wonderful silver sound of the best bone china. Either she was rich or I was special. Time would tell.

'Her name is Carolyn Hamilton,' she said firmly, sitting back in her chair. 'She is twenty-three years old, and the last time I heard from her was a Christmas postcard from London dated 6 December. I have an address where she lived, and contacts for her last place of employment. I have a number of pictures of her, of course, and her handwriting you will see from the postcards. How long do you think it will take you to find her?'

I met her gaze. Maybe it was her coming so soon after Adeline, or maybe I still wasn't sure I wanted the job.

'Well, that depends on whether she's actually lost: 6 December isn't that long ago. Maybe she wrote and it got mislaid in the Christmas post.'

'No,' she said, as if she and the GPO had already discussed the matter.

'And there's no reason that you know of why she should not have written?'

She stared at me, then said quietly, 'None at all.'

'What about other people? Do you know if she's been in touch with anyone else?'

'Not that I'm aware of. Miss Wolfe, as must be clear to you, I would not be employing the services of a private detective if I didn't believe the matter to be serious.'

'Then perhaps you can tell me a little more about it.'

'What do you want to know?'

'Let's start with who exactly Carolyn Hamilton is, and why you're so eager to find her.'

'I fail to see how . . .'

'In which case, Miss Patrick, let me tell you. Just as you have to employ me, so I have to agree to take on the case. When people call in a private detective rather than the police there's usually a reason. Sometimes afterwards is too late to find out why.'

For a moment I thought she was going to throw me out. Indeed there were times later when I wished she had. But occasionally truth convinces better than bullshit. This was one of those occasions. She stared at me for a moment, then settled herself back in her chair.

'Very well, Miss Wolfe. I've known Carolyn Hamilton since she was five and she first walked into my school. Then she was just like a million other little girls, all eager to be ballerinas, their heads full of fantasy. But I always knew she was different. She was talented, of course, but it was more than that. She was also determined. Her mother and father never really understood that. He was a farmer and she was a local girl from the village. They never had any aspirations for their children short of marriage into the neighbouring farm and a handful of babies by the time they were twenty-one. But I think Carolyn always knew it would not be for her. Of course when I realized her potential I spoke to them, told them they must encourage her, give her the opportunities she deserved.'

She stopped to take a sip of Earl Grey, then paused for a moment, looking down into the cup, tea-leaf-reading the past. 'I was a dancer myself once. Of course you're not old enough to remember, but there was a time when I was quite well known. However, when I was still young my mother became seriously ill. Those were the days before girls officially had careers. My father thought it best that I return home to look after her. When she died, of course, I had to stay on to look after him.'

I shot a glance in the direction of the piano. Certainly he looked a hale and hearty figure, used to getting his own way. It was a sad little tale, retold with a smidgeon too much polish to be spontaneous. Still, practice does not necessarily make things less true, only less painful, and at this stage there was not a lot to be gained from disbelieving a client. As stories go it was a credible if somewhat clichéd one: elderly woman seeks new life in surrogate-daughter figure. It also had the ring of mutual wish fulfilment. Probably if Miss Patrick hadn't existed some dance-crazed little girl would have had to invent her.

'Of course, her parents wanted the best for her, it was just a question of money. So I offered to pay. It was a semi-official adoption. She lived here, I trained her and when I had nothing more to teach, I paid for her to be taught by someone else. She stayed with me until she was seventeen. Then she went to the Royal Ballet School in London. She's been in London ever since.'

Carolyn Hamilton? I'd never heard of her, but then there was a while when I had thought Baryshnikov was a new brand of vodka.

'And has she been successful?'

'She is a wonderful dancer, Miss Wolfe. She's been with some of the best companies.'

I considered my knuckles duly slapped. It was the stuff of fairy tales, the proof that the corn can be green even in the cold black hills of the north-east. So what had happened to stop the 'happily ever after' bit?

'And up until now she has always kept in regular touch with you?'

'Always. Every month, without fail.' My surprise must have shown. 'It was an arrangement we had. She would either call, or more recently write.'

I had a sudden vision of Carolyn holed up in bed with a luscious young man, surrounded by Chinese take-away boxes and a stack of cards addressed to Miss Patrick lying unfinished on the dressing-room table. Maybe she just fell off her points and hit adolescence late.

'Over the last seven weeks I have called her flat at least a dozen times. There has been no answer. The last company she told me she was with informed me that she left a year ago. They gave me the name of another employer. When I rang them I was told that Carolyn had not been there for over six months.'

'And I take it she never mentioned any change of work or any possible trouble?'

'No.'

'Even though you've been in regular contact up until last month?'

'No,' and this time the voice was quiet, directed at the inside of the tea cup. Could this be the first time that her adopted daughter had lied to her? Or just the first time she'd found out?

'And you're sure she hasn't been in contact with anyone else? Her parents, perhaps?'

'Certainly not. And I would prefer it if you didn't disturb them, Miss Wolfe. She hadn't seen her family in years. I am sure she wouldn't go to them now. Not without telling me first.'

'I see. So tell me, Miss Patrick, just what is it you're worried about?'

The question was gently put but it still made her flinch. I waited. In the silence that followed the wall clock ticked like a metronome. I wondered what she had to lose by telling me. Too much, apparently, to take the risk. She shook her head.

Despite her stubbornness I felt sorry for her, but then she didn't seem like the kind of woman who would appreciate charity. She looked up at me, composure regained. 'I'm afraid, Miss Wolfe, that's all I can tell you. Do you consider it enough information?'

More than most, less than some. In the end it's not the case that you take on, but the people. While Miss Patrick was no

[8]

longer a swan, she was still a tough old bird who needed to know where her fledgling had gone. And who wanted me to find out rather than the police. That was my last question. Why me, not them?

'I heard a programme once on the radio. It said that every year 25,000 people go missing in Britain. As you say, Carolyn hasn't been out of touch for very long. I can see if I were a policeman I would not attach very much importance to an old woman's concern.'

She was right. 'Well, Miss Patrick, I'll be happy to take your case if, that is, you decide you want me. I should explain that my fees are seventy-five pounds a day excluding expenses. Obviously I can't tell you how long it will take, but I can give you a report at the end of, say, four or five days, so you can assess my progress.'

When I first started I used to have to practise the bit about the money in the mirror. It seemed so crude, weighing pound signs against someone's loss or anxiety. But talking money, I have learnt since, can often help camouflage the pain. She nodded her head, then stood up and made her way across to an old oak sideboard near the window. Still, after all these years, it was a pleasure watching her move. As she inclined her swan neck to search for something in a top drawer, I imagined her younger, dancing her way through housework, with only an ageing invalid for an audience. Even though I should know better I still think it's a shame that life isn't fair. When she turned she held a grey cardboard file in one hand and a clutch of fifty pound notes in the other.

'Miss Wolfe, I have no idea if you can find Carolyn, but I need help and you are here, so I suppose I had better employ you. You will need an advance, I presume?'

Hannah, I thought to myself as I took the money, you've got to stop dazzling clients like this.

With cash in my pocket I took a taxi back to the station. It left me half an hour to kill. Why sit and daydream when you could work? The local directory yielded up a total of five Hamiltons. From the public phone booth I called them all. 'I would prefer it if you didn't disturb them, Miss Wolfe. She hadn't seen her family in years. I am sure she wouldn't go to them now. Not without telling me first.' So said Miss Patrick. It was not that I didn't believe her, it was more a question of being safe rather than sorry: no point in spending a fortune ferreting around London when the girl you're looking for is sitting by the farm aga learning how to bake bread and re-establish family values. But when I found them, her father – at least I assume it was her father – didn't seem that interested in his daughter's whereabouts.

'No, she doesn't live here, she's in London. I don't know how you got this number, she's not been here for years. What? I don't know, you'd have to ask the wife. I suppose she's got it somewhere. We really don't keep in touch. If you want to see her you should speak to Augusta Patrick. She knows more about Carolyn than we do. What did you say your name was?'

But I hadn't, and there wasn't much point in telling him now. Nothing like paternal affection to set a girl on the right road for life. Families. Either they love you too much or they don't love you enough. No wonder they're called nuclear. Maybe Carolyn was just trying to cut loose from all her apron strings. I thought about the pain and pleasure of leaving home. And how, of course, you never really succeed. Even if you stop writing the letters and picking up the phone.

The train was twenty minutes late, and not interested in improving the situation. We crawled through the edge of daylight into a grey winter evening. I sat and watched till the sheep were eaten up by darkness, then turned my attention to the grey file.

Carolyn Hamilton. Her life story in words and pictures. Not much really when you consider the effort that must have gone into it. A thin black scrapbook retold the news: a series of local cuttings celebrating a young girl's success, first in provincial competitions then in winning medals and lastly in getting into the Royal Ballet School. A blurred news picture showed a delicate

[10]

little fair-haired girl in costume, poised and posed. Then there was another, older, more confident Carolyn, staring straight into the camera, hair scraped tightly back, eyes bright and smiling. Closer to she was good looking, but in that long-haired high-cheekboned way that most dancers are. Maybe bone structure and nimble feet go together. Or maybe they just don't eat enough. Either way I'd be hard pressed to pick her out of a *corps de ballet* at ten paces. I turned over a few more pages. Sure enough there were the line-ups, a bevy of adolescent swans all clamped into cute little white-feather headbands and stiff white tulle, flashing Colgate smiles. About as much help as a mug shot. The final picture was at least out of costume. This time the young woman had her hair down, a great shining wave of it, gushing over her shoulders and down her back, like an ad for conditioner. But the photograph had been taken into the sun and the face was all cheeks and mouth, the eyes screwed up and squinting. At a rough guess she could have been anyone. So much for the visuals.

I moved on to the correspondence, although that proved altogether too grand a word for what turned out to be a stash of postcards. They dated back a year, to the time when, according to Miss Patrick, Carolyn had left her job without telling her patron. Mind you, if these were representative of their communication, then she could hardly have expected a full account. Postcards are usually the way people tell you they don't want to write you letters.

These particular haikus were all much the same, all in the 'Dear Aunt Maud, thank you for the book token. Hope the cat is well, love Hannah' mould. For a 23-year-old Carolyn had retained an alarmingly youthful style. Still, hers was a physical rather than a verbal talent. Why should one expect eloquence? But what about intimacy? Wasn't she writing to the woman who had become her second mother? It must, I realized after I had read it, have been one of the last postcards Miss Patrick had received.

'Dear Miss Patrick, This week I saw a marvellous production of the *Romeo and Juliet* at the Garden. Working hard on a couple of new pieces, music by Rodney Bennett. There is a possibility of a tour sometime in the spring. Will let you know. Yours, Carolyn.'

I turned it over. A Degas dancer bent low over her shoes, the graceful curve of her back inviting admiration. Maybe the words were in the pictures. I flicked through the others. Consistently vacuous. Even the last, postmarked 6 December and sent from somewhere in the West End with a snow-scene stamp and a Christmas franking greeting, was the same anodyne diet of weather and ballet repertoires. Hardly the words of a girl about to disappear. But then that's the point about clues, you have to go looking for them.

Deeper in the folder I found the address and phone number of the last job, a company which I had never heard of. Given my Baryshnikov experience I wasn't willing to stake my life on it, but the Cherubim Studios in the Walworth Road didn't sound like the City Ballet or the Rambert. Could it be that Carolyn's shoulders were flagging under the burden of Miss Patrick's expectations? An image of sexual abandon returned to me, Carolyn seduced from adopted filial duty by orgasm. It didn't quite fit with the identikit angel with the advert hair, but then some fantasies tell you more about the person doing the fantasizing, and it had been a long time. Rule number three. Don't get carried away by your work. After this one I'll take a holiday. After this one.

CHAPTER TWO

As with most jobs you begin at the beginning. Nothing glamorous or dangerous about that. Finding something or someone that is lost usually means checking that it hasn't simply been mislaid.

Miss Patrick was right about one thing. Carolyn wasn't picking up the phone. Neither was she answering the door. It was a big rather shabby house off the Kilburn High Road, with six buzzers decorating the front door. I pushed a few. The woman in the basement was friendly enough, but she'd only been there three weeks and hadn't met any of the other occupants. No one else was in. I looked at my watch. 10.15 a.m. You don't need to be smart to be a private eye but it helps. Once again breakfast had triumphed over punctuality. Those that had work would be there already and those that didn't were either on their bikes looking for it or under the bedclothes with their Walkmans turned up against the day.

I went back to the car and sat it out for a while. I watched a woman with a young child manoeuvring a pushchair full of shopping up on to an uneven pavement. As she pulled it up, one of the wheels caught in a rut and a bag fell out of the underbasket, spewing potatoes on to the paving stones. The toddler whooped with delight and went scurrying off in pursuit, scooping single potatoes up in double hands and tottering back with them like spoils of war. A man in a donkey jacket hurried past, stepping over the child and the potatoes, eyes firmly somewhere else, but an elderly woman stopped to help, and soon all three of them were busy picking up and repacking. What had begun as a chore for the mother had now become a game for the young and the old. The whole operation must have taken five or ten minutes. Another world. I was so engrossed that I almost missed the surly young man in black who came tripping down the stairs of number 22, carrying a large portfolio case and a personal stereo round his neck. He was in an awful rush and didn't have time to answer questions from Carolyn's elder cousin Mary, just down from the north. However, he managed to carve out a little space when I told him I was a plain-clothes police officer. He, now revealed as one Peter Appleyard, student of art at Goldsmiths' College, was even kind enough to look at the photograph which I stuck under his nose.

'Yeah, she lived here. It's a lousy photo though. She was much prettier than that.'

'You say "used to". Has she moved?'

'Search me. All I know is I haven't seen her for a while.'

'Since when?'

'Since when I can remember. Four, five months, maybe longer.'

'But you didn't know her?'

'You kidding? Nobody knows anyone round here. We're just "neighbours".'

'So I'm right in thinking that you wouldn't know where she might have gone?'

'Dead right. So, is that it, or do you want to take me in for loitering in a public place?'

Kilburn, obviously another splendid example of successful community policing, I thought as I watched him disappear round the corner. I closed my notebook on the apparently unpronounceable name of his landlord, given with even less good grace, and looked up at the house. Carolyn's flat was on the second floor. No windows open in the front and to get to the back you'd have to go over a dozen back gardens. I could probably talk my way through the front door. On the inside one there'd be a Yale and if I was unlucky a Chubb. Not impossible, with the right tools, but a lot of time and trouble. And in daylight there was always the risk of being caught. I went back to the car. 12.30 p.m. I had already spent half of one of Miss Patrick's crisp big notes and learned absolutely zero. Nothing like failure to give you an appetite.

As punishment for my late rising I made myself wait for lunch. I headed south, through Marble Arch and Park Lane, then across Victoria and Chelsea Bridge into the hinterland of the south. I ate at a sandwich bar on the Walworth road, slap bang next to the headquarters of Cherubim.

At 1.50 p.m., three young women and a guy came in, all Isadora scarfs and pumping-iron calf muscles. They ordered salads and yoghourt and cappuccinos. The young man paid. They sat themselves down near the window, laughing and giggling, neat lean bodies and bright expressive little hands. It's a great feeling, being on top of your job. I felt giddy with success. Or maybe it was just the coffee. Once my balance returned I walked over to join them.

'Excuse me.' They looked up. And I've seen people more pleased to see me. But then they didn't know how much fun I could be. 'Do you, by any chance, belong to the Cherubim Company?'

You could see they already thought I was a loony. A bag lady in training, or some girl who'd grown too large to dance and spent her days hounding others more fortunate. The Samaritan of the group, a girl on the end with long dark hair caught up in an elaborate French plait, smiled slightly.

'The Cherubim Company? Yes, I suppose you could call us that.'

'I'm a friend of Carolyn Hamilton. She told me she worked here. I hoped I might see her.'

There was a small still silence in which everyone seemed to be looking at the young man without directing their eyes in his direction.

[15]

'Carolyn Hamilton,' said Miss Braid again. 'Well, she used to work here, yes, but she's not with us any more.'

'Oh, what happened?'

'I . . .' She opened her mouth, then seemed to wince, as if someone had kicked her under the table. Which, if you come to think about it, must be one hell of a hint for a dancer.

'She left about six months ago.' It was the boy who interrupted. He had a lovely fawn-like face, with eyelashes that had been stolen from a beautiful girl. 'We don't know where she went.'

'Oh, I see. Do you know why she left?'

'No. I think she just got fed up with the company,' he said, playing mischief with the last word. 'Wanted a change, I expect. God knows it happens to most of us.' And then they all laughed, as if he had said something enormously witty, which of course he hadn't, unless perhaps you were a dancer. Another world. Would Carolyn Hamilton have found it funny? I had no idea. I stood on the edge of their group, not fitting in. Marginal, that's what we private detectives are meant to be. It's supposed to help us keep a sense of morality when all around are losing theirs. Sometimes it works, sometimes it doesn't.

'Would someone in management be able to help me further? It really is very important that I get in touch with her.'

The boy shrugged his shoulders. 'You could try. But they're not awfully good at keeping the ones they've got, let alone following up the ones that got away.' And they all giggled again. Which is how I left them.

You don't have to be in analysis to know that humour is a defence against pain. Once inside Cherubim you could see what they had to be so funny about. Of course, I've read Penny of the Wells, or whatever her name was – I know dance studios are about work rather than glamour, but even without expectations Cherubim was a bit of a sleaze pit. Not so much a company as a second-rate dance school. No wonder they had taken me for a retard. On my way to the administration office I peered in through a couple of keyholes. The class of young women on points looked decidedly shaky and the rest of it was definitely more Fonda than Fonteyn. When I finally managed to find the woman behind the name on the door, she made the café boys and girls seem positively garrulous by comparison.

'She was here, then she wasn't.'

'What does that mean?'

'It means she came in January, taught a few student ballet courses. I booked her in for some spring and summer classes and she let me down. I never heard from her again.'

She picked up a cigarette and held it between pink varnished fingernails. They matched her lipstick. And her track-suit top. Even her blonde hair had a certain strawberry tint to it. Maybe somebody had once told her that the colour suited her. People can be so cruel.

'And that was when?'

'I'd have to look it up. April or May, I think.' I waited. 'May,' she said, having looked it up.

Six hours on the case and I was wallowing in corroborations. Give or take the odd week Carolyn Hamilton had been missing from house and job for almost seven months, but had been writing home for another six. Interesting.

'And you don't know where she went?' I was beginning to feel like a record that had got stuck.

'Don't know and don't care.'

I wondered if she had been this gentle with Miss Patrick. I was beginning to feel bad about the fifty quid I hadn't earned. I hoped I wasn't going to feel worse. I handed her a card.

'Let me know if you see her again, all right? It's important.'

'"Hannah Wolfe, Private Investigator,"' she read. 'Funny. You don't look like one.'

'Yeah, well, disguise is a vital part of the job.'

She turned the card over in her hands, feeling the embossed letters. You could see she was impressed. Just like I was when I first got them back from the printers. 'So this is why everyone wants to know where she's gone.'

'Everyone?' I echoed softly, just in case.

'Yeah, you're the second person I've had asking after her.'

'Who was the first?' Even though I already knew.

'Some old lady who wanted to know if she was on tour.' She laughed. 'Wouldn't take no for an answer.'

'And what did you tell her?'

'Same as I told you. She'd gone and I didn't know where. Why? Is that "important"?' And you could tell she was thinking of all those movies where the detectives have more money than brains.

I smiled. 'Not important enough, I'm afraid. Unless of course you told her anything else.'

It was her turn to smile. 'How about somewhere she might get hold of her?'

'Somewhere other than 22 Torchington Road, you mean?'

And she stopped smiling. You see. Thrift in all things. My mother would have been proud of me. As I was going out of the door I thought of something else I didn't want to pay for. Worth a try anyway.

'One more thing. Who's the young guy with the real fake eyelashes? He was in the café next door buying lunch for the girls.'

But he who laughs last . . . She shook her head. 'You're the private investigator, Miss . . .' By the time she'd glanced down at the card to finish the sentence I was gone.

Outside it was coming on to rain. Someone had snapped the car aerial, but at least the stereo was still there. I managed to dredge up a crackling version of Radio 3 and tuned into something that could have been Brahms but might have been Beethoven. It got me through the rest of the afternoon. Surveillance, Frank calls it. I always found it rather a grand word for waiting. But it has its pleasures. What other job pays you to sit and let your mind graze while your eyes do the working? I found myself thinking of an art teacher I had once had. And how she was so good at her job that for a whole six teenage months I had yearned to become an artist, just to be like her. Somewhere in an attic my mother still cherishes the fruits of my obsession, some

[18]

dreadful lifeless portraits signed with an ostentatious flourish. Role models: as dangerous as they can be inspirational. It set me wondering how charismatic Miss Patrick must have seemed to a young farm girl driven by notions of grace and grandeur. I was wondering so hard I missed the back announcement of the symphony. But I caught the time check: 6.15 p.m. and still no sign of Eyelashes. Maybe he hadn't come back to work after lunch. I gave up. Tomorrow, as someone much prettier than I once put it, is another day.

The rain got harder as I drove north. I had to admit I'd felt more triumphant in my life, but then that was to be expected. It is always hard at the beginning: like finding yourself in a foreign country without the language, it takes time to acclimatize. Especially with missing persons. Who were they anyway but factual figments of another person's imagination? When you did find them they were never the person you expected them to be. If I found Carolyn Hamilton she would be the same as all the others, just different in a different way, if you see what I mean.

I got home and wrote out my report for the day. It didn't take long. That left the evening. If London had been L.A. or Chicago, or even New York I could have hit the streets now and ended up in a dozen places where a private eye might feel at home. I saw myself propped against a bar sipping bourbon and swapping cocktail recipes with the bartender, or dipping French fries into a pool of ketchup while Kirsty, my waitress, refilled my coffee cup. Not exactly images to set the world alight but all part of the myth, and a good deal more convincing than the Holloway Road Chinese take-away where the beansprouts were welded together with MSG, or the local pub where a woman drinking alone after 8.00 p.m. was about as unobtrusive as a fish on a bicycle. And about as comfortable. I thought about going through my address book and inviting a friend round for a drink. But three months is a long time away. Reconnecting would mean recapping and I didn't feel much like talking. To tell the truth there aren't that many people I prefer to my own company, and in the dark, without the grease stains, the flat felt almost cosy. I made myself some pasta with a carbonara sauce and opened a bottle of Chianti. Then I retired to bed with schlock TV and wasted ninety minutes watching a Clint Eastwood movie where people slugged each other to the percussion of natty little fist cracks. The only time in my life someone had hit me in the face the overriding memory was of a thudding crunch of pain and chipped bone, echoing through the caverns of my mind. I couldn't talk for a week and in the right light you can still see the dent. Clint, however, woke up in bed next to a blonde bimbo without a scratch on him. I fell asleep in disgust and had bad dreams.

CHAPTER THREE

Next day I ate breakfast in the car and started the Cherubim vigil early. As every child knows, Saturday morning is the time when the dance schools really do their business. The sight of all of them in their leotards and little adult buns, clutching their shoes and clutched in turn by eager mothers, brought it all back to me. Not that there was much to relive really: a small fat child, smile lost in mounds of cheek, body crammed into white frills with legs like slug pellets poking out underneath. Did someone tell me or did I just get bored? Funny how childhood is meant to be so important, yet we still forget most of it.

By one o'clock I was pretty certain our beautiful young dance teacher wasn't coming. As the last group of kids streamed out I went back in and started poking my head into empty rooms. Eventually I came across one of the girls from yesterday's café. She was standing in front of a wall of mirrors in one of the practice rooms, one leg stretched out exquisitely along the barre – not a breath of a bend anywhere to be seem. She straightened up and stared at herself in the mirror: a long critical appraisal with no hint of vanity. On her shoulders I noticed a glisten of sweat. Then, after a while, she teased the leg even further out and slowly, gracefully curved her torso over until her fingers grasped her toes. I felt a stab of sympathetic agony shoot up my inner thigh into my groin. You can see why most ballet lovers end up in the audience rather than on the stage. Still, no pain no gain. I closed the door noisily behind me and clattered my graceless way towards her.

'You're early,' she said half into her toes without looking at me. 'The next class doesn't begin till two.' And there was, I thought, an edge of frustration to her voice. Cherubim may not be the Royal Ballet School but at least some people were still trying.

Once she'd uncurled herself it took her a while to place me, but eventually we got there. I promised to keep it short so that she could get back to work. Maybe it was my card, or maybe it was the fact that Eyelashes was no longer around to damage her shins, but she became almost talkative second time round. Yes, she had known Carolyn Hamilton. And no, she couldn't tell me much about her. For the few months that she'd been at Cherubim Carolyn, it seemed, had been something of a loner, coming in, doing her classes and going away again. She had made a point of not hanging out with the rest of the girls; indeed she'd given the impression she was rather too good for them, which was a bit of a joke seeing as it was common knowledge she'd been chucked out of her last company for missing performances. On the other hand Left Feet First was a pretty stylish company, and maybe she was just sore at herself for flunking out. Most of the Cherubim girls would have given their eye teeth (I suppose if you were a dancer you could hardly give an arm or a leg) to have been so lucky. But if Carolyn had been feeling sorry for herself she certainly hadn't let on to her.

So if she didn't confide in the girls, what about the boys? Well, as it so happened yes, she had been quite tight with Scott, or Eyelashes as he was known to the private detective fraternity. But then Scott wasn't exactly one of the boys, if I saw what she meant. I said I did and asked her where I could find him now. She laughed and told me he was probably putting on his make-up. After all, it was only an hour and a half till curtain-up. Typical Scott. Luck of the devil. He'd only dropped in yesterday to rub it in. If I saw him I could tell him from her that they'd keep his place open, just in case the routines got too exhausting.

And if they ever needed an understudy . . . When I glanced at her from the door she was back at the barre, muscles screaming, eyes hard into the mirror willing herself into another future, a long way from Cherubim.

Back in the car I revelled in my spoils. Beneath the name Scott Russell was the address of a theatre in London's West End. Even I was impressed. The listings mag I buy every week so that I can fail to see even more films told me Saturday was matinée day. I spent an hour trying to park the car and missed most of the first act, which is just as well since it was standing room only. Not that it mattered much: most cats are grey in the dark, especially in the chorus line. I slipped out during the curtain call and stood in line at the stage door. He was one of the first ones out and you could see he quite liked the attention. I wished I'd brought my autograph book. But as it was, it was mutual recognition. I got the impression he'd been waiting for me to pop up again somewhere.

'I told you, I don't know anything about her.'

'I still need to ask you a few questions.'

'I'm busy.'

'So I'll wait.'

'Look, I don't know who you are, but . . . ' He was standing with his back to the wall, a group of prepubescent girls on one side jostling him for autographs. You could see this was not a conversation he wanted to be having, but I was blocking his path, and ruining his image. He sighed. 'All right.'

The dressing-room, which belonged to him and a few other cats, was cramped and heavy with the scent of bodies and after-shave. Under the bank of wall lights the eyes beneath the wonderful eyelashes looked just a touch bloodshot. Not serious enough to mar the beauty though, which was a pleasure to look at. Evidently he thought so too. As I settled myself his gaze went past me into the mirror behind my head. He flicked a lock of hair back into position, a casual gesture, born as much out of habit as vanity. Who knows, if I was that gorgeous maybe I'd do the same thing. Even without being told you kind of knew that this

[23]

was probably not the type of man to take advantage of the women he danced with.

'I knew you weren't her long-lost friend the minute I saw you,' he said, handing me back my card. 'So who's paying your wages?'

'Her name is Augusta Patrick, she's Carolyn's guardian.'

'Of course, the old bat herself. What happened, did Carrie forget her monthly postcard?'

'Why, did you used to help her write them?'

He raised an eyebrow. 'Well, a regular Samantha Spade, I see. Far be it from me to teach a private dick how to suck eggs, but if you're planning this to be a conversation – you know, as in between two people – I'd recommend a slightly softer approach.'

'Augusta Patrick hasn't heard from her for almost two months. She's worried.'

'Shame.'

'She thought her friends might be able to help.'

'Correction. You thought her friends might be able to help. Well, you're out of luck, aren't you?'

It's one of the important things about this game, knowing when you're beaten. 'Listen, I've got an idea. Why don't I go out the door and we'll start this whole thing again, right? I'll come in, ask for your autograph, tell you what a fabulous dancer you are and then beg you to put aside your dazzling future for a few moments to dredge up memories of a less than glorious past.' I paused and watched as a ghost of a smile appeared, flashed itself into the mirror behind me and then settled, waiting for more. 'I've been to her flat. No one's seen her for months. She hasn't been in touch with any of her family and the Pink Vision at Cherubim couldn't care less if she'd fallen under a tube at Warren Street station. Which means as of now you are the only one who seems to have spoken more than six words to her. And even that's a hunch. So. Will you help me?'

He pulled a pack of cigarettes out of his pocket and spent some time lighting one. People always have a little ritual to get them started. It struck me that the best dancers probably didn't smoke, but presumably he knew that.

'Maybe she doesn't want to be found. You thought of that?'

'I've thought of it. Yes.'

He shrugged his shoulders. 'Or maybe she's having so much fun she just forgot to write.'

'But you don't believe that.'

'Listen, all I know is that she went and didn't leave a forwarding address.'

'But you did know her?'

'Yeah, we hung around a bit. Partners in adversity.'

'What kind of adversity?'

He laughed, 'Come on, you've seen Cherubim. Nobody works there unless they have to.'

'I don't understand. Miss Patrick told me that she could have any job she wanted.'

'Yeah, well, she would, wouldn't she?' He blew out the smoke in a long thin Noël Cowardish swirl. 'I mean no one wants to admit that their protegée might have' – he paused – 'how should we put it? – "feet of clay".'

'You mean Carolyn isn't a good dancer?'

'No. I mean she's a very good dancer. But this is a tough business.'

'And what? She didn't have the ambition?' Determined, that was the word Miss Patrick had used.

'Darling, we all have the ambition, otherwise we'd never get up in the morning.' I think he was waiting for me to laugh, like the girls at Cherubim, but I didn't. 'Put it this way, in my experience the ones who make it are as hard as nails, but all you see on stage is the sparkle. And bright though she was, by the time I met her, Carolyn didn't shine.'

'And she knew that?'

'Yeah, she knew it.' He looked at me with cool grey eyes. 'Most of us do, you know.' He smiled mischievously, 'Lucky boy, aren't I?' and blew out another spiral of smoke. 'Not so much what you are as who you know.' But I was too busy thinking about all the postcards she must have had to make up to keep an old lady's illusions intact. That took a determination, of sorts.

[25]

'So what about all the big ballet companies she was supposed to have been with – the Royal and the City? Are you telling me that Miss Patrick made them up?'

He looked at me for a moment, as if trying to decide how much to tell me. Then he shook his head. 'Boy, the old girl didn't give you much to go on, did she?' He shrugged. 'Yeah, Carolyn was with the big ones, stretching those lovely limbs to get herself plucked out of the *corps de ballet* and become the prima ballerina the old lady never was. Who knows, she might even have made it. The way she tells it, it was all there for the taking. Except somewhere along the way she tried too hard. Stayed up on her points a little too long until her ankles started to give out. I don't expect the battleaxe mentioned that bit, did she? The many and glorious ways in which your body starts turning the dream into a nightmare. Of course at first everyone is all sympathy. Time off for rest, time off for physiotherapy. Even, when it comes down to it, time off for operations. But behind your back you know what they're saying. 'Shame about the Hamilton girl – she had such promise.' When you track down Carolyn take a long look at her ankles. Check out those little white scar veins.' He waited. I felt there was somewhere I ought to have arrived, but hadn't. He snorted. 'Not a ballet lover I see. Tendons, darling. That humble little mesh of tissues that keeps us on our toes. Or off them. And who ever heard of a ballerina on flat feet? Fifteen years of training and then, wham, bam, thank you mam; don't call us, we'll call you. She says she left of her own accord. Others say she got the push, but then this is a bitchy business and you shouldn't believe all that you hear. Either way the only option she had was contemporary.'

The way he said it, it didn't sound like a promotion. 'And was that so bad?'

He shook his head in mock exasperation. 'You really don't have a clue, do you? No, it's not so bad. If that's what you want. And a lot of dancers do. For many it's the only way out of the museum: the companies are smaller so there's more participation, they're always hungry for new choreography, and they get audiences still young and radical enough to think that art can change the world. For others, well they make the switch if they have to, just to keep dancing. But then they haven't grown up being force-fed tales of glory. You know the really sad thing? She could have done worse. Left Feet First wouldn't have impressed the wicked witch of the north but it was quite a hip place to be for a while, till they all partied too much and started falling over on stage. If she was going to make it anywhere it would have been there. But she couldn't shake the monkey off her back. And from there it was a downward spiral. Witness her arrival at Cherubim.' He stopped, made uncomfortable by his own logic. I got a sense that he felt he'd said too much. Or maybe he'd just unwittingly told more than one life story. I wondered what had happened to sour his dream. He went to the mirror again for reassurance. Then came back to me. 'So, now you know. The truth behind the fairy tale. Except, of course, it doesn't help you find her.'

No, but it sure as hell made more sense than Miss Patrick's book at bedtime. What next? 'So where do you think she'd go from Cherubim?'

'You're the private detective. You find out.'

'That's what I'm doing.'

He thought about it. 'My guess is, somewhere where she could earn more money.'

'Why? Was money a problem?'

'Are you kidding? When did you last have enough?'

'Was it?'

He sighed. 'I think so. I mean she joked about it; income versus outcome. But I got the impression it wasn't funny. And Cherubim wasn't exactly the kind of job to pay back an overdraft.'

'So what was?'

'Take your pick. London's full of places where the right girl can earn the wrong kind of money just so long as she's not too picky. Carrie's a good looker. She wouldn't be the first to swop art for entertainment. Though I doubt it's the kind of thing she'd write home about.'

[27]

'And you're sure she never said a word when she left?'

He put up his hands in mock defence. 'Honest injun. I was off for a week with the flu. When I left she was there, when I got back she'd gone.'

'So yours wasn't a close relationship?'

He smiled. 'What do you think?'

I smiled back. 'I think yours wasn't a close relationship.'

'Well, there you go. You are in the right profession after all. Mind you, it wasn't that hard was it?' And he blew out another spiral of smoke. 'Anything else you want to know?'

I thought about it. Most gays don't like talking to private detectives. But then since most private detectives are ex-coppers you can understand why. Bearing that in mind we hadn't done badly. In the paint-by-numbers picture Carolyn had a good deal more colour than before, and I had a few leads to go on. Not bad at all. So how come I was feeling there were still things he hadn't told me? I let the silence hang between us for a while, but it yielded nothing but an absence of words. I took out another card and handed it to him.

'Maybe you could just push it around a bit more. Give it a little thought. You never know – memories.'

Think fast, never take no for an answer and have a good exit line – that way they'll remember you. Comfort by name, Frank by nature, that's him. Some bits of advice were worth following. This time Eyelashes took the card and kept it.

By the time I got back to the car it was nearly 7.00 p.m. and a passing traffic warden had shat on the windscreen. At times like this you have a choice. You can either get depressed or more determined. I decided to see it as an expensive way of parking for the night. From a phone booth in Covent Garden I tried to get a number for Carolyn's landlord. But either I hadn't spelt it right, or the art student had sewn me up. Either way there were no Prozhaslacks in London, let alone in Finchley. On the grounds that there might be a movie playing that I wanted to see I walked through Covent Garden to Leicester Square. But it was Saturday night and a quiet stroll turned into a rush hour of buskers, beggars and fun lovers up from Surbiton. Only tourists could be fooled into thinking London is a cosmopolitan city. Outside one of the larger cinemas a girl was eating fire to the accompaniment of a small string quartet. She had long fair hair scooped up in a ponytail and was wearing a sequinned dress with a black woolly cardigan over it. She looked a little like Carolyn Hamilton, I thought. But then so did a girl in the cinema queue and a young woman standing by the entrance to MacDonald's, waiting for her date for the night. Let's face it, London was full of Carolyn Hamiltons. Most of them happy to be lost in a crowd. My mind was tired with thinking about all the places she could be. I decided to stop thinking and do something.

So I drove to Kilburn and broke into her flat. Why not? After all, it's the kind of thing that goes on all over London on a Saturday night: people talking their way in through the street doors and prising their way in through the top ones. It wasn't even that hard. When I told her I was a friend of Peter, the art student, delivering a canvas which I was frightened to leave outside in case it got nicked, the girl in the basement buzzed me in without a qualm. More fool her. Once in, the other door was amateur's night out; no mortice, just a Yale. I was surprised I was the first.

Inside, a cold little corridor led to two rooms. There was music coming in from the floor above, waves of reggae and the occasional thump as someone provided foot percussion. I took a pair of thin plastic gloves out of my bag and slipped them on. Better to be safe than arrested, even if they did make me feel more like a dentist than a burglar. To the right was a bedsitting-room, off it a small kitchen and to the left a bathroom. I used a torch until I was sure the place was empty, then switched on a few lights. The main room leapt into focus. I had time to register built-in cupboards, bare floorboards, a rug, a sofabed, a couple of chairs and a battered old dining-table with a vase when the overhead light pinged off again. Dead bulbs. How come they always pick me? Still, an impression remained which the torch recreated in segments: an exceedingly sparse and tidy space, no clutter, no excess. Not so much a home as a removals van that hadn't been unpacked yet. Minimalism meets poverty? And cold. That was the other thing. Winter had been allowed to grow here, seeping its way into the walls and up through the floor. I breathed out into the air and watched the smoke curl. One thing was for sure: Carolyn Hamilton hadn't lived here for a long time. Yet her name was still on the bell, which meant that she must be somewhere doing something to pay the rent. But where and what?

I started with the kitchen, where the silence told of a fridge long disconnected. The only sign of life was a small pinboard above the work surface with a few yellowing notices. A milk bill dated 14 April (unpaid?), a poster for a demonstration against animal vivisection in May and another Degas postcard, this time the full face of a young girl gazing out at the artist, passive and lost. I stared at it for a moment. Was this the self-portrait I had been looking for? I took it down and carried it with me into the bathroom where I found a toothbrush but no toothpaste, a tube of hair-removing cream and a half-empty bottle of Valium. I remembered Eyelashes' description of Left Feet First, partying until they fell over. Was this the stash of downers to counteract the uppers or a more sinister way of coping with stress?

Back in the main room a side light cut through some of the gloom. I worked systematically, starting with the cupboards. I had expected clothes. But not so many labels. Certainly not so many that I couldn't afford. Underneath the racks were shelves: blouses, T-shirts, silk scarves and some very classy designer knitwear. Interesting. Clothes may maketh the man, but in my experience they often bankrupt the woman. I thought back to Eyelashes' tale about a girl who had given everything to be Margot Fonteyn, only to discover it was the one thing she couldn't have. Maybe shopping had become a form of depression therapy. As an Oxfam girl myself it was hard to see the attraction, but then I didn't have her body. Or her sense of despair. I went on looking. There was something else. Coats, jackets, woollen skirts and a lot of knitwear, but not much in the summer frock line. In May, of course, when she'd gone she would have needed and taken them. But now summer had gone to Australia and it was time for thermals. Either she had emigrated with the sun (in which case who'd been posting the postcards in London?) or she'd had to go out and buy a whole new wardrobe. I felt a frisson of detective triumph.

Underneath the shelves there was only darkness. I went to work with the torch and fingers and unearthed a shoebox. Inside was a set of ballet pumps wrapped in tissue paper. To the untrained eye they looked new and untouched: just the kind of thing to drive a private eye towards conclusions. Surely these were symbolic of a change of career? Breaking and entering: people only do it because they get so much out of it. Like tomb robbing. As a little girl I had always wanted to be an archaeologist –there was something about the licensed snooping that appealed to me. And that feeling of there always being another layer to uncover. Even with the shoes out it was clear the box was not empty. There it was, underneath the tissue paper, a fat bulging envelope full of papers. Using the torch at close quarters it took only a few minutes to rate the findings. Maybe not the death mask of Agamemnon, but enough economic history to tell you what had made Carolyn Hamilton tick. Bills, bank statements and finally solicitors' letters, the logical conclusion of taste without money. They made painful reading. Her main strategy, it seemed, had been plastic. There were statements from three credit-card firms stretching back for almost a year until last April. Cash withdrawals – a lot of them – clothing and bills that could well have been medical expenses made up the bulk of the expenditure. The statements marked April were for £2300, £1800 and £3000 respectively. By then all the cards had been cancelled and two put into the hands of debt collectors. If you added to those a clutch of outstanding telephone, electricity and gas bills it worked out that at the point when she disappeared Carolyn Hamilton had been in debt to the tune of something like £8000. It made my Hong Kong homecoming look like a celebration. Maybe I was being too subtle. With bills like this maybe I should be looking for her in Newgate debtors' prison. Except nobody had repossessed the flat. I glanced up at the light. And certainly something had mollified the electricity board.

I was on my way to check out the telephone when someone did it for me. The first ring was a bit like Norman Bates' mother coming through the shower curtain with a knife. It took me a while to get my heart back inside my body and realize it was just the telephone. Then I had to decide what to do about it. Seeing as I wasn't meant to be here there was a lot to be said for not answering it. On the other hand anybody who knew Carolyn Hamilton was somebody I needed to talk to.

On the other end of the line there was a lively silence.

'Hello,' I said as quickly and indistinctly as possible.

'Carolyn?' It was a man's voice. Dark, quite rough, even a little forced. It could have been anyone.

'Mmmm,' I murmured, but even as I did I knew I'd blown it. There was a small shocked silence, then the line went dead. I sat for a moment cradling the receiver in the half light of the room, and then for the first time, with my fingers growing numb from the cold, I started to feel a little nervy, as if trespassing on someone else's life might lead you to have doubts about your own.

I stuffed the papers back into the envelope, the envelope into my bag and the shoebox back into the cupboard. Then, casting one last torchbeam around the room, I turned off the other lights and went out. Above me reggae had turned to funk and the house was vibrating. I could probably have broken down her door with a sledgehammer and still not been caught. Back in my car I sat with the engine running, trying to pump some heat into my hands. Across the street a tall man in a grey raincoat and hat was walking in the direction of the house. He turned in through the gate and went up to the front door. He stopped for a second, then took out a key and opened it. The music sucked him inside. Poor guy. Maybe he was thinking about sleeping. I looked at my watch. It was 10.27 p.m. I had been in her flat for nearly an hour. Funny how time flies when you're breaking the law. Back

[32]

home I stuck the Degas postcard next to Miss Patrick's blurred snapshot. I thought they made a good pair. I wished them both good night and went to bed. I was feeling good.

Sunday. And since there wasn't much I could do to earn my living I took the day off. Carolyn Hamilton had been missing since May. Another twenty-four hours wasn't going to make that much difference. I dedicated myself instead to the domestic: hearth, home and sibling duty. I spent the morning cleaning the grease off the cooker and after lunch I went to see Kate.

It was usually that way round – me visiting her – but then sisters are to be forgiven most things, especially two children under three and a husband who thinks he's a newer man than he is. It was a bright freezing day. Islington sparkled, all spruce and upwardly mobile. There were new windowboxes on the two upper floors of the house, I noticed, as I stood with my finger on the doorbell. No doubt come spring there would be daffodils and tulips. Just as when we were kids. Like mother like daughter. If Kate was the chip off the old block I was the sawdust. Who knows, maybe I'd only rebelled because she'd conformed. The door, with its carefully restored Victorian glass, swung open to reveal Kate in a track suit, one arm full of chubby child. My first thought was how tired she looked, my second how lovely she still was, with her thick jet black hair in a long loose cut, and blue-black eyes, against a fair skin. The Irish side of the family. There had been a time when I minded that mine was the English legacy, all mouse-brown and freckles. As the younger it had taken me a while to get out from under her reflection and find my own sex appeal. But you can't really blame your own sister for a trick of the genes, and to her credit she had never used it against me. Maybe I had things she wanted, like eighteen months in hand and a natural mistrust of the world. She grinned and it momentarily chased away the shadows under her eyes. Inside, the baby, who still seemed far too young to be called Benjamin, was exercising his lungs.

'Hannah. My God, when did you –'

'A few days ago. I tried to call you but you were always engaged.'

She made a face. 'Amy. She's obsessed with the telephone. Carries it around with her most of the day. We've bought her a toy one but she isn't fooled.'

Amy, in her arms, squirmed with pleasure at being the centre of the universe. 'Hi, Amy, how are you doing?'

'I'm bigger now,' she announced proudly. Obviously a lot of people had been telling her. 'Wanna see my toys?'

After the obligatory introduction to three dolls and a duck called Malcolm I settled myself in the kitchen, making coffee while Kate changed the baby, and fed Amy, who in turn fed the dog. Domestic bliss. Like living in a circus. I thought about the silence of my own apartment and the empty spaces that made up Carolyn Hamilton's. Single girls of slender means. At least Kate had someone to pay the credit-card bills for her. Even if it did mean he spent most of every weekend working.

'It's a sales conference. In preparation for the 1992 penetration of Europe,' she said with an admirably straight face. 'Apparently it's terribly important.'

'I'm sure. Do the kids still remember what he looks like?'

Only now did she allow herself to grin. 'I know you don't believe me, Hannah, but it isn't as bad as it seems.'

It's an extraordinary thing about motherhood. Like drug addiction. Once you're hooked you want to see others in the same state.

'Don't tell me, you're completely used to living alone amid a wall of noise and constant lack of sleep.'

She pretended to think about it. 'The noise I can live with, the lack of sleep's not so great. Colin says we ought to let him scream, but I can't do it.'

'So let Colin get up.'

There was a small pause. 'Well, he has to go to work. At least I can grab a nap in the day.'

'And do you?'

'Yes . . . sometimes.'

'My God, don't you ever want to kill him?'

She laughed. 'Who? Colin or Benjamin?'

[34]

I shrugged. 'Either. Both.'

'Sure. But it passes.'

'So much for the pluses. What about the minuses?'

'How about a stomach like an empty potato sack and a brain like a sieve? You should be grateful to me, Hannah. I've taken the pressure off you, remember. Carried on the family tree leaving you to go for the career.'

Big deal. Aren't I just what every parent wanted for a daughter – an over-educated private eye who could be earning better money teaching juvenile delinquents how to spell the word 'crime'? Certainly not what I had planned for myself as I burst out of academic training, all shiny with energy and idealism. But then we all get our edges rubbed off sooner or later. Even so I had never intended to stay with Frank. It had just been a temporary job in between the career I had left and the one I had yet to decide on. At the time it was what I thought I needed, thinking about other people's problems rather than my own. Except here I was, two years down the line, still looking for shoplifters and missing persons: power without responsibility, or maybe it was the other way around. No wonder my mother had turned grey. For Kate it ought to have been a tougher decision. She'd spent thirteen years in public relations with a large management consultancy: a good, well-paid job and she'd enjoyed it. They even offered to keep the job open for her. But it was always this that she'd wanted: the man, the home and the patter of tiny feet.

'How's Joshua, by the way?' Good old Kate. Just a little research for the monthly letter home. 'Do you ever see him?'

'Occasionally. He's OK.'

Joshua – otherwise known as the great white hope of Hannah's love life: dependable, solvent and tolerant of unsociable working hours. To be honest I can hardly remember what he looks like. We were, as the saying goes, just good friends who made the mistake of sleeping together and let it become a habit. When it ended it was not so much with a bang as a slow freeze-out: familiarity causing a gradual hardening of the emotional arteries. Almost as soon as he walked out it felt like a long time ago. Once in a while we still see each other, go to the occasional movie together, for old director's sake. And my mother still sends him birthday cards, but then that's hardly my fault. His disappearance completed her vision of daughter Hannah as a surrogate man – a few wild oats and a lady at the laundromat to do her washing. Since it keeps her off my back I have done nothing to disillusion her. And as for the patter of tiny feet . . . of course I think about it. Doesn't everyone? But the older I get the more I realize I'm too young for it. I don't trust my ego. I'm afraid I'd come home one day and find that it, like the cat, out of a mixture of jealousy and the need for more room, had smothered the baby. Kate says I probably just haven't found the right man yet. But then she would, wouldn't she?

After their meal while Benjamin slept I took Amy for a walk in the park and we fed the ducks. She chattered away with all the fervour of a three-year-old for whom conversation is the newest and best toy, and I listened to some of it while the rest of me re-read Carolyn Hamilton's postcards in my mind and thought about how a mother would feel about giving up her child to a dancing teacher, or how the child might feel about being given. And how none of them seemed to know each other well enough to stop eight thousand pounds coming between them. Then I took Amy back in time for tea and when portions of premasticated bread started to catapult around the kitchen I went home and made a list for Monday.

It didn't take me long to get through it. The City Ballet were somewhere in Europe on tour. If I wanted to talk to them I'd have to wait until they got back. The woman who answered the phone at Left Feet First told me that Carolyn Hamilton had left because of a disagreement with the management and that was all she was willing to say. When I told her I was a private investigator looking into Carolyn's disappearance she softened up a bit, but still couldn't help much. Carolyn had been with them for only six months or so. She was a talented dancer who probably could have carved out a successful career in contemporary dance except she just didn't seem to have the motivation. A shame, but there it was. I thought again of those slender little ankles buckling under the pressure of Miss Patrick's unfulfilled dreams. Obviously becoming a female Wayne Sleep wouldn't have sufficed. Or maybe she just got tired of trying. I moved on to her finances, but her building society and the credit-card companies would say nothing at all.

By early afternoon I was reduced to the Polish landlord again, but however much I tweaked he still didn't have a name that directory enquiries recognized. Hardly an encouraging sign, having to go back to pushing doorbells, but then somebody somewhere in that house must have a contact number for the man they paid rent to. And who knows, maybe fate would really smile on me. Maybe this time she'd be there herself, home on a flying visit to pick up the mail and unable to resist the temptation of answering the doorbell just this once. Bingo, case solved thanks to Hannah Wolfe, private investigator extraordinaire.

As fantasies go it didn't last long. I knew it was a police car even before I spotted the other one parked on the opposite side of the road with its Dayglo go-faster stripe. Two police cars in a sleepy residential street on a Monday afternoon? Too bad to be true. I drove past them and parked about fifty yards further down. Then I walked back. The front door was open. And the girl from the basement was standing talking on the step to a patrolman. I walked on, not willing to risk being recognized, then doubled back along the other side of the road. I sat for a while in my car, but the police showed no sign of moving.

Whatever it was it didn't make the news that day. I was beginning to think I had over-reacted and that maybe someone had just complained about the reggae rousers upstairs when Tuesday morning's breakfast TV went local. A young man, well scrubbed and radiating ambition, sat in a studio by a miniature model of Big Ben and told of a threatened strike on London underground, a fire in a children's home in Uxbridge and a body found in the Thames. Then the picture came up. Even then I didn't know her. The blurred smile and bright eyes squinting through from a curtain of hair were still the features of a stranger. I was so busy looking at her that I missed the first few words.

'. . . near Barnes bridge early yesterday morning. She was named by police today as Carolyn Hamilton, a 23-year-old dancer who had studied at the Royal Ballet School and performed with the City Ballet and the modern company Left Feet First. She lived in North London. Police do not suspect foul play.'

I sat for a while watching the weather man count the clouds on his sweater. I thought about the colour of the water in the park where Amy and I had thrown the bread. And the cold. And doctors. I've always had this recurring thought about doctors – how they must feel when they lose a patient, and how you'd have to be a truly arrogant bastard to believe that it really wasn't your fault. It's probably good I didn't go into medicine. From the mantelpiece where I had stuck the pictures, a dead girl grinned out at me, all past and no future. I felt like talking to someone who'd known her. But Miss Patrick wasn't answering the phone. Some cases just never get off the ground.

CHAPTER FOUR

Eventually the client gets in touch. If only to tie up loose ends. I could see how she wouldn't much want to talk to me, so it was nice of her to let me off the hook.

'. . . understand there was nothing you could have done.'

She was probably right. The river police had been called out on Monday morning just after 10.00 a.m. when a man walking his dog had seen something caught up in the weeds. That meant, at the very earliest, that Carolyn Hamilton must have entered the river some time on Sunday night. Even Charlie Chan would have been hard pushed to follow a trail from Cherubim to the river in two days. But honourable failure didn't make me feel any better. Sunday night. I kept putting pictures to the words: a split screen with me scouring grease from the kitchen sink while she floated with the current downstream. Maybe I should have spent Sunday at her place instead of Kate's. Who knows, she might have gone home to pick up her ballet pumps, just to end it gracefully. Either way she must have been carrying some sort of ID for them to track her down so quickly. And the reason Miss Patrick hadn't been answering the phone was because by then she had been in a hotel room in London, recovering from a short car ride to the morgue.

I offered her my condolences. It sounded tawdry even though I meant it. I didn't mention the word 'suicide' and she didn't offer it. She said nothing to explain the death; no talk of motive or even where her surrogate daughter might have been for the last seven months. For all she knew I might even have found out. Though with precious little help from her. Still, this was not the time to bitch about the things I hadn't been told. If it hadn't been for the fact that I owed her, I would have left any talk of money until another day, but I didn't want her to think of me slyly rejoicing in three hundred pounds unearned. As it was she didn't seem to care.

'As far as I'm concerned it's irrelevant, Miss Wolfe. I employed you for the week and we had a business arrangement. I insist you keep the money. You were doing a job. Neither of us were to know you would be too late.'

For a woman who had just lost the thing she loved most in the world she was handling it very well. I could see her, sitting by the telephone, her backbone straight as a die, allowing no curves or hollows for the sorrow to dwell in. If it was a veneer I wasn't going to be the one to crack it. In certain respects private detectives are just like policemen, they're supposed to be tough, but in fact they're just frightened of emotion. It's a form of inadequacy really, though there is method in it. After all, when you get down to it, it's just a job. Employed by someone you didn't know to find someone you'd never met. What's he to her or her to Hecuba, that I should cry for any of them. I'd do better to save my tears for friends and relatives. Since there was nothing more to say I didn't prolong the agony. She sounded relieved when I said goodbye.

But, of course, it wasn't that easy. Inside my head the mouse was already on the treadmill and the faster he went the worse it got. When I had started the case she had been alive. And what had I done? Seen a couple of people, snooped around an empty flat, written a lousy report and watched an even lousier movie. While those who weren't busy being born were busy dying. Bob Dylan should have been a private eye. The mouse began to hyperventilate and fell off the wheel. Let it rest, Hannah, this doesn't help anyone. Carolyn Hamilton went AWOL from life and when it all got too much for her she threw herself off a bridge into black water. I had been chasing a shadow and someone else had found the body. Case closed. If I still felt guilty at the end of the week I could always send the money back in the form of memorial flowers.

I used the morning for loose ends. I would, I had promised Miss Patrick, send back her file with the postcards and photographs, but when it came to putting them into their registered package I found myself taking copies of all of them, just in case. And since it seemed rather callous, just shoving the photos away in a drawer somewhere, I put them back on the mantelpiece, alongside the watercolour view of Venice and sandstone cat from India.

The envelope I had filched from her flat was more troublesome. Technically it now belonged to her next of kin, although more technically it ought at this moment to have been in the possession of the police who were, presumably, busy working out past movements and motives. What if the electricity, gas and telephone had been the only debts she could afford to pay and it was the credit cards that had hounded her to a watery grave? That left Hannah Wolfe guilty of suppression of evidence. On the other hand if I gave it back to them I risked an additional charge of breaking and entering. I decided not to decide yet. It wouldn't take them long to find me anyway, even if Miss Patrick had chosen to keep her own counsel.

Two days to be exact: one to track down the Pink Cherubim, and the other to read the words on my card. When I opened the door there were two of them, but then there always are. Frank used to say that one was the eyes while the other was the ears. And I used to say that left a problem with the brain which explained a lot. In this case all the eyes picked up was a load of dirty washing and a living-room that hadn't been cleaned in an age, while the ears heard everything I had to tell them, except for the bits that broke the law. As far as I remember I didn't actually lie, it was just when it came down to it their condescension and more-knowledgeable-than-thou attitude got right up my nose. If they were as good at their job as they claimed, let them find out

[41]

about the bank statements and the court orders. Frankly they didn't seem interested. No doubt to them Carolyn Hamilton was just another girl from the north who'd discovered that the London streets weren't paved with gold. All they really seemed to want to know was about boyfriends. Or maybe that was all they thought female private detectives were good for. Anyway I gave them Eyelashes and wished them luck. In return they told me the body had been in water since early on Saturday night. That made me feel better about how I'd spent my Sunday. I tried them with a few other queries but they got shy and said I'd have to wait until the inquest. They promised to phone me with the date. In the end they didn't. Untrustworthy buggers. But then, I suppose, they thought the same about me.

But if I didn't go to the inquest somebody did. And somebody told someone else. I would have heard it from the papers anyway, but it was better to hear it from Frank. Ears to the ground, these ex-coppers. Bless his Mr Plod boots.

'Just thought you'd like to know. The missing pieces of the jigsaw puzzle, eh?'

'I don't believe it.'

'Come on, Hannah, even given your warped vision of the police they could hardly fabricate that kind of evidence.'

'So why didn't they say so when they found the body.'

'Maybe they were waiting for the PM.'

'Frank, you don't need a post mortem to tell a woman is eight months pregnant.'

'Well, you know these guys on the river. It's dark and they want to get home for the mug of cocoa. She's just another floater. They probably thought she was fat.'

Frank tells Irish jokes too, usually when there are Irishmen in the room. But credit where credit is due. He notices, eventually.

'Don't give yourself a hard time. Some things you can't do anything about. Obviously the kid got herself knocked up and didn't know how to tell her fairy godmother. It happens all the time. The person who needs to feel bad is the old lady. Maybe if she'd brought you in a week earlier you might have stood a

[42]

chance. As it is no one likes to hear the truth from a suicide note.'

And such a pathetic one at that, although having read the postcards I of all people should not have expected poetry. Even so . . . I got him to recite it twice so I could write it down. 'By the time you read this you will know the truth. I am sorry for all the deceit and the trouble I have caused. Also for all the money which I cannot repay. It seems the only thing I can do is to go. Please, if you can, forgive me.'

So I was right. It had been at least partly to do with money. Somehow she must have scraped together enough to pay off the most pressing bills, then dodged the debt collectors for the rest. But with a baby and therefore no job . . . As sad stories go this was one of the saddest. Frank was right. If I were Miss Patrick I would prefer not to have received it. No doubt that was why she hadn't told me about it on the phone. Or maybe it was even worse. Maybe she hadn't got it then. Maybe it was waiting for her when she returned home to take the photos down off the piano. The last postcard.

'Uh uh. According to the police they found it in her flat. No envelope, no nothing. It wasn't even addressed to anyone. Just tucked under the vase on the table, waiting for someone to find it.'

I reran the film of Saturday night in my head. I walked into the living-room, switched on the light and saw the bare floor, the three chairs and the old dining-table, all flashing on to my retina before the bulb went. Surely if there'd been something under the vase I would have noticed it? Or would I? I made another tour of the room this time in slow motion with the torch beam. Still nothing. But had I really checked the whole table? Then I went into the kitchen and looked around the surfaces. Empty. And the bathroom, just in case. Same conclusion. Yet according to the pathologist her body had been in the water for between thirty-eight and forty hours. Which meant that she'd gone into the river between 4.30 p.m. and 6.30 p.m. on Saturday evening. And since nobody kills themselves until after they've written the suicide note, it must have been there by the time I entered the flat. Shit. I had been so busy with my precious archaeological dig in the cupboards that I'd missed what was right under my nose. For a moment I began to see female private investigators from the police's point of view. But the table? Were they sure?

'Listen, what's the big deal? That's where people usually leave suicide notes. Either there or on the mantelpiece, although I did once come across one in the oven. But that was a demented housewife. Couldn't cope with her husband's affairs because they meant he was always late for dinner.'

I've got this theory about Frank. That he was probably a great detective when it came to clues, but he always forgot to stop talking, so he missed the confessions. Like now. Given half a chance I think I would have told him. But as it was, by the time he was ready to listen, I'd thought better of it.

But it didn't go away. No sir. It played like a cold shiver up and down the spine. I had been there by 9.45 p.m. She had thrown herself in by 6.30 p.m. at the latest. So while I was waltzing round Covent Garden people-watching she had been waddling down some towpath towards the river, the words of the note already becoming fact. Maybe if I had gone straight from Eyelashes to Kilburn . . . Yeah, and maybe if the moon was made of green cheese. It wasn't, I didn't, and she killed herself. And not just herself either. Images of Amy came into my mind, all fat cheeks and self-importance, important enough for Kate to put up with sleep deprivation and a husband who didn't have a clue. And images of Kate, eight months pregnant with the fish inside her butting up against the walls of the tank impatiently. A woman's right to choose. But what could be bad enough to kill two of you? Shame and a stack of credit cards? It just didn't seem right. Just like it didn't seem right that I had been in Covent Garden when I should have been in Kilburn. And I had to stop thinking about that one.

Frank realized it quicker than I did. Just to prove there's an exception to every rule, when it comes to ex-coppers he isn't bad on emotion. But he's a great believer in the healing power of work. I did what I was told – which was four days at the Edgemore shopping mall where their own store detective seemed to have developed a case of myopia. Or chronic boredom, more like. I coped by making it a question of professional pride. After missing the suicide note I needed a little observation practice. On the first day I bust a middle-aged man stealing woman's underwear and two teenagers out for a lark. The next day I struck lucky and found the pros, a group moving anything they could fit under their coats, from VCRs to wristwatches. None of it made me feel any better. At the end of the week I left with tumultuous praise ringing in my ears. I went home, got drunk and sat and re-read her folder. But the postcards were still monosyllabic emissaries from the dead, and she was still just a young woman with good legs, no character and a great gaping hole where the last eight months of her life should have been. Eight months which had led, apparently inexorably, to a riverside bank at Kew or Hampton Court. But why there? Why so far from home? What was wrong with Waterloo bridge, or Westminster? According to Frank, Westminster was the favourite – a little Wordsworth and the odd intimation of mortality. Why hadn't she gone there? Too many questions. I was starting not to sleep for the asking of them. Except in a funny way it was probably what I had been waiting for: the need to know more.

Looking back on it I think I had made up my mind even before Stanhope and Peters, Solicitors, called me. But there is nothing like coincidence to convince one. Not that I realized immediately. At first it just sounded like another job, except that it came direct to me and not through Frank.

'Our client had your name from an earlier assignment.'

'And you don't want to go into details on the phone?'

'Correct.'

Just so long as it isn't Van de Bilt, I thought, as I made my way down the Farringdon Road in the direction of Blackfriars. He said his name was Terence Greville and that he'd be sitting at one of the window tables in a café at the city end of Fleet Street, a place called Chez Roberto. You can never tell with solicitors.

Sometimes they like to impress with the padded leather, other times they just want to be one of the boys. In which case he was too old for the job.

He ordered another cappuccino and started right in there, eye-to-eye contact and intimate delivery over the sugar bowl.

'Miss Wolfe, I have been instructed by my client to ask if you would consider taking on a job for them.'

'Yes.'

'The assignment is to look into the circumstances surrounding Carolyn Hamilton's death.'

And out of all the things I had not been expecting this was the first. 'Carolyn Hamilton's death. You mean above and beyond the verdict of the inquest?'

'I mean the inquest concerned itself only with what took place on that Saturday night. My client would like to know more about the preceding eight months.'

'I see. May I know your client's name?'

'I'm afraid that is not possible. At this stage they would like to remain anonymous.'

I shook my head. 'Sorry. I don't work like that. There are other private investigators who might oblige you, but it has always been my practice to know who I'm working for.'

He paused. Then he cleared his throat. 'I am sure you understand my position, Miss Wolfe. My client is, of course, deeply distressed by the loss. I think it's fair to say that they feel themselves to be responsible in some way for what has happened. These feelings are enormously painful to admit to or talk about. But there is still the need for her to know. My client has asked me to stress that anything you find out will be kept in the strictest of confidence. You may deliver a closed report to myself and I will pass it on to them. No one else will know anything about it.'

Solicitors, of course, do not make linguistic blunders. Seven years of study and a lifetime of earning money from the letter of the law sees to that. Which meant the slip had to be intentional. So Miss Patrick still had the need to know, but no longer the ability to ask directly. Maybe I reminded her of happier times, when the only notes received had first-class stamps on them and talked of dance repertoires and the weather. Grief and guilt. They can do weird things to people. No investigation ever brought anyone back to life, and in the end there are always those willing to speak ill of the dead. I ought to have known that.

But my mind was on other things. Ahead of me stretched the promise of four days picking up carrier bags for a Saudi diplomat's wife in London to buy up Harrod's, then a week at a cash and carry where someone was doing just that. Frank would be pissed off, but he'd get over it. Anyway, I owed Miss Patrick four days' work. I reminded Mr Greville of this when it came to talking money but he, like his employer, wasn't interested. All in all he made me a very generous offer, more than my going rate, and no limit on expenses. We shook hands on the deal and went our separate ways.

I started work in the car going home. First things first. We had a pregnant woman who had disappeared for seven and a half months and turned up in the river. Two questions to start with. Where had she been and who was the father? To help us along we had some dates. According to the PM report Carolyn had been between thirty-four and thirty-five weeks pregnant when she died. Working backwards that took us to the end of April. Which meant she had been on intimate terms with the father of her child exactly around the time she left Cherubim. When in doubt, *Cherchez l'homme*. Any *homme*.

CHAPTER FIVE

I would have gone back to Eyelashes anyway. If, that is, he hadn't come to me first. Funny what dancers choose to do in their spare time. I hadn't figured him for the inquest type. But then I hadn't figured her for the young mother sort either. He rang me in the evening. It sounded like he was calling from the theatre, but it was after eight and I seemed to remember he was in the opening scene. He wanted to know if I fancied a late-night drink. I offered him his place or mine but he didn't like that idea. In the end we met in one of those Covent Garden hangouts which look more like a visitors' book than a restaurant. He was sitting at a table under a signed picture of Tab Hunter. It suited him. In front of him were a number of wine glasses and a dead fish. There was a certain similarity to the look in their eyes.

'I phoned you, you know. A couple of days after. But you weren't in.'

People who don't leave messages on answering machines. I hate them. 'You could have tried again. Or left your name. I would have called you back.'

'Well, wasn't any point, was there? I mean the old lady employed you to find her, not bury her. I didn't think you'd be working for her any more.'

'So what makes you think I'm working for her now?'

'Are you?'

I looked at him for a moment. That touch of red around the

eyes had spread. A thing of beauty is a joy for ever. Well, how would Keats know, anyway? He never stuck around long enough to find out. I kept my fingers crossed behind my back and told him a lie, which was whiter than most. 'No. I'm not working for her any more. I'm working for myself. That's why I'm here.'

He took a swig from an already empty glass. 'Yeah, guilt. It's a killer, isn't it?'

'Is that what you brought me here to say?'

'I didn't know about the baby, you know,' he said, as if I had disagreed with him. 'She didn't tell me.'

'So, she didn't tell you. I thought you said you weren't that close.'

'It wouldn't have made any difference anyway,' he said thickly. 'I mean by the time we talked, you and I, she was already dead, that's what the police said.'

'Not quite. She died some time between four and six thirty. We met just after five.'

He looked up at me and scowled, but said nothing. The waitress arrived, all black fishnet and mini-mini-skirt. He ordered two more drinks. I decided not to rush him. I'm normally quite a good judge of alcoholics, working out the habituals from the anxiety one-offs. Regulars, for instance, never order by the glass; it's a waste of too much time and money. Which meant Scott was on a binge, the old drowning-the-sorrows routine. Guilt, yeah, it's a killer. Except she'd been dead for over a month now. How come he was still crying? Either he was more bi-sexual than he had let on and was facing a paternity crisis or the rest of life was kicking him around too.

'So, how's the show?'

He looked at me. 'Minus a grey cat.' He shrugged. 'Well, I never did like the music anyway. Case of the emperor's new clothes if you ask me.'

'What about your friend?'

'My friend? Oh, he found another friend. Happens all the time.'

'So what do you do now?'

[49]

He shrugged. 'This and that. Auditions, classes, that kind of thing.'

'But not Cherubim?'

He grinned, but there wasn't much humour in it. 'How right you are. Not Cherubim.'

'I'm sorry,' I said quietly.

'No, you're not. Neither am I really. Fucking awful place. All those little boys and girls walking on tiptoe to please their mummies and daddies.'

The waitress sped by the table, depositing two glasses as she went. The wine slopped over on to the cloth. He watched the stain grow. Then he shook his head. 'Shit. I would have told you, you know, I mean if you hadn't been working for *her*. Parents. Jesus, they think they own you. Only they call it love rather than possession. And everything's fine until you do something they don't want you to, or, God forbid, become someone they don't want you to be. Then it's them or you. Simple as that. So she wasn't Marie Rambert. So what? I just thought she deserved the chance to get away. If that was what she needed. Maybe that's why she got pregnant, eh? Cocking a snook at the old dear.'

'Who was the father?'

'I said already – she didn't tell me about the baby.' And you could tell he hadn't liked the question.

'OK. So let's try something else. What about her debts?'

'I told you, she needed some money.'

'Not some money, Scott, a lot of money. What did she spend it on, apart from clothes?' He shrugged. 'Eight thousand quid at last count, which amounts to seriously more than the odd spending spree. What was she on?'

The laugh was more like a guffaw. 'Anyone ever told you that you sound like a social worker?'

'Yeah, all the time. So, d'you wanna talk or just sit here and drink? And if I were you I'd watch that frown. You're going to get wrinkles if you're not careful.'

He sighed. 'A lot of it was above board. Medical bills, physios, that kind of thing. But if you want to believe the rumours, she probably would have been doing some stuff when she was with Left Feet First. Coke, maybe a little speed. But she was clean by the time she got to Cherubim. Contrary to what you guys read in the tabloids there are a number of drugs that you can stop taking. It's just you can't pay back the money they cost.'

Boy, I must be looking my age. Either that or this was just his form of revenge. 'And she couldn't?'

'We didn't talk about it.'

'So what *did* you talk about, Scott? Or did you just invite me here because you've run out of late-night drinking companions?'

I got another scowl, then he sat back in his chair and said, 'I don't know for sure, but I think she might have gone to Paris.'

'To Paris?' And I must say, it's good he mentioned it, because I never would have guessed.

'It was a long time ago, right? So I only remember bits of it. I think it must have been a month or so after she arrived – which would make it some time in February – she saw this ad in one of the papers. And before you ask me, I don't know which paper and I can't remember the date. All I know is what she told me. It was for some job in France. I don't even know what it was doing, exactly, except that it was a temporary post with very good money. Well, she was pissed off with Cherubim, pissed off with not earning enough, pissed off with everything really. I think she thought maybe if she went away, did something different, cleared her debts, got Miss Patrick and her bleeding obligations off her back for a while ... Anyway, she told me she'd applied for it. And then a week or so later she got an interview. I know because it meant going to Paris and I covered for her, her classes I mean. When she got back she didn't say much about it. Just told me it had been some kind of personal assistant business job and that she hadn't got it. I asked her a few more questions but she shrugged them off. I figured she was just disappointed. Then a couple of weeks later she went off again without telling me, just called in sick one morning. I didn't think anything of it at the time, but then the same thing happened a bit later. And I

[51]

knew it was Paris this time, because I saw the ticket in her handbag. I suppose I wondered then if it might be a guy. I even made some joke about how expensive it was, joining the high-fliers' club, and maybe she should just invite him back to her place. But she didn't find it very funny and when I pushed a bit further she clammed up on me. I guess I was a bit surprised. I mean we were quite tight in our own way. I suppose we had some things in common, like we both should have been doing better but couldn't get the expectations off our back. Anyway I figured she just didn't like talking about her love life and I let it ride. Then some time at the end of April I caught the flu. I was off for a week. She never called round or even checked me out. When I got back she had gone. She left me a note wishing me love and luck, but no forwarding address.'

'Just like that?'

'Just like that.'

'And you think she went to Paris?'

'I dunno. All I know is that she was doing a lot of commuting around the time she got pregnant and that Paris was the place she was going. Maybe when he found out he offered to look after her and she accepted.'

'So how come she didn't tell you?'

He made a face. 'Could be she didn't think I'd appreciate the maternal instinct. Or perhaps she thought it would spoil her image. Carrie liked to see herself as more independent than she really was.'

I gave it some thought. Paris? Why not? Except what about the six months of postcards she kept sending to Miss Patrick, all franked 'London'? One thing at a time. I looked at him. He was drawing on the tablecloth with his fork, etching spellbound lines in unconscious homage to Hitchcock. I took it as a sign. 'And that's it? I mean you didn't hear from her again?'

He shook his head. But he still didn't look at me.

'And how much of all this did you tell the police?'

He kept making ski runs in the snow. 'They asked for facts, not opinions. So I told them. I didn't know where she'd gone.

They weren't that interested anyway. They'd already made up their minds. Suicide passed off as accidental death to keep the old bat happy. Either way, she was just one poor fucker less to claim the dole. She was her own witness, they didn't need anyone else.'

'And if they had asked the right questions? Is there anything else you could have told them?'

'What do you mean?'

'I mean you're sure she didn't get in touch with you again?'

'No, I mean yes, of course I'm sure. Shit.' He slammed the fork down on the cloth and you could see he was suddenly very angry with himself. I let him stew in it for a bit. He finished off the rest of the glass and looked around for the waitress, but she was busy with someone more glamorous. He turned to me. 'Anyway, it was your job to find her. You're the one who blew it.'

'Oh yes. And when was that, Scott? At what exact point did I blow it? In the café outside Cherubim on Friday afternoon? Or maybe in the dressing-room with you on Saturday? What was it I should have asked you then that would have got me the information I needed?'

He shook his head in a fury and made as if he was getting up to go, but thirty seconds later he was still there. Behind that gorgeous façade something was crumbling, eaten away by the acid of guilt. I just hung on to the other end of the line. He brought himself in eventually.

'All right. So she rang me,' he said at last, his eyes on the tablecloth. 'Before she died. It was on the Friday, in the morning. She said she was sorry to get in touch so suddenly, but she needed a place to stay, that night or over the weekend.' He paused, then closed his eyes up tight. 'I offered her my flat.'

'And,' I said at last when it was clear he wasn't going to.

'She never turned up.'

So he'd known all the time. Even that Friday afternoon in the café. I saw again the look on their faces when I mentioned her name. And I felt the kick with which Scott had silenced little Miss Motor Mouth.

'Why didn't you tell me?'

'Because she made me promise not to,' he said with a blast of fury and pain that caused eyes to flicker. 'She said it was absolutely vital that no one knew where she was. And that if anyone got in touch looking for her, I was to tell them I hadn't seen her since May.'

'You mean she knew somebody would come looking?'

'I don't know. I think so. When you turned up that afternoon I was sure you were the one she'd been talking about.'

But how could it have been me? She didn't even know I existed. In which case who else could she have been worried about? The father of the child? The same guy who called her flat that evening at 10.00 p.m.? Despite the crushing irony of it all I was beginning to feel better.

'And what did you arrange with her? Were you going to meet her or what?'

'No. She said she didn't know when she'd arrive. I told her I was working and that if it was the afternoon or evening I'd leave the keys at the stage door for her.'

No wonder he'd been so desperate to get me away from the entrance that Saturday after the matinée. She could have turned up at any time. Except she didn't.

'And she didn't say anything about where she was or where she'd been?'

'No.'

'And no mention of the baby?'

He shook his head, more in sorrow than in anger this time.

'How did she sound?'

He didn't need to think about it. 'Anxious. A bit freaked out.'

Even though I could cheerfully have strangled him ten minutes before now I felt sorry for him. 'Listen, Scott. It wasn't your fault. You did what you could. If she'd really needed you she would have got in touch again. In the end people who commit suicide make their own decisions.'

He shook his head and almost smiled. 'Carolyn didn't commit suicide.'

'Why do you say that?'

'Because it's what I think.' He paused and I counted the empty glasses in front of him again. Seven including the one he had almost finished. It didn't seem to have affected his powers of thought up until now.

'What else do you think?'

'I think that in the end it was nothing to do with us. Me, you, her. Any of us. I think it was the old bitch that pushed her into the river. With her stupid ambitions and pressures and fairy stories. All the parental expectation. That's what killed her.' And he grinned. 'Better than the butler, eh?'

CHAPTER SIX

All the way home I had this image of her, standing by the river in the dark with so much weight on her shoulders that she had no need for stones in her pockets: Miss Patrick's expectations, her debts and someone else's baby. Which had proved the heaviest? The eight-month-old foetus? Except that was something else that didn't make sense. If Carolyn couldn't hack it with a baby then why had she left it so long to find out? It's not as if she didn't have any option. She was exactly the kind of girl a generation of feminists had worn out their shoe leather for, marching their way to abortion amendments and the right to choose. If she didn't want her career stopped by one renegade sperm there were places she could have gone, people who could have helped her. She may have been a country girl, but she wasn't a bumpkin. She had partied and played. She knew the score. Which meant either she had ideological objections to abortion (did the animal rights poster on her noticeboard automatically make her a member of LIFE?) or she started out wanting it but changed her mind. Or something had changed it for her.

I was so busy trying to feel what she might have felt that it kept me awake when I should have been asleep. It would have been easier if I could have gone straight from the restaurant to Colindale newspaper library. Searching out one particular newspaper ad from a dozen possible daily and Sunday papers over a period of two or three weeks is not the sexiest part of the job, but it keeps the mind occupied. As it was I got home just past 1 a.m., shattered and with an acute case of insomnia. I dutifully went through the old routine: the milky drink lying in the hot bath with a little night music. It relaxed me, but it didn't put me to sleep. In homage to Carolyn I resorted to drugs.

I rolled a joint and lay on the bed. Old hippies never die they simply go up in a puff of smoke. I could see Frank shaking his head in disgust. What the hell? It's healthier than booze and anyway, how can you uphold the law if you don't know what it feels like to break it? After a while I began to let go. I got up to switch off the light and caught sight of a naked woman in the full-length mirror. I turned to face her to make sure she was me. Yep, there she was, Hannah Wolfe, instantly recognizable from the spiky brown hair and boyish face. *Gamine*, that's what the French call it, except I'd probably be disqualified by the size of my tits. Had the left one really grown larger or was it just a trick of the dope? No problem with the stomach, though, that was definitely mine, a gentle hillock about the size of your average Chinese take-away. And they were my legs too. Not exactly the kind to sell swimsuits but pretty good for walking, sitting and even the occasional sprint. Now we were all gathered together and concentrating I thought about feeling my breasts for malignant lumps but couldn't be bothered. Do men do this, I wondered? Give themselves the quick once over, like cleaning the car and then checking the petrol and the oil? What do you do if you discover you need a respray? If women were cars, what would I be? A Fiat Uno with the road manners of an Audi. Ideas above my station. Kate would be, what, a Sirocco, Mrs Patrick a well kept Bentley, and Carolyn Hamilton . . .? Well, I suppose Carolyn would have started out as a sleek saloon and grown into a Volvo estate.

I tried to imagine what it must be like, blowing up slowly like a ripe melon. When does it start to feel like a baby and not an acute case of indigestion? And when do you start loving it enough to accept the havoc it's wreaking on your body? Especially Carolyn. It must be a particularly weird journey for her, a dancer, someone trained in the ways of malnutrition and boy-like body lines, to have to watch their female curves expand and fill until they become the earth mother with another set of feet practising point work on the inside of their stomach. Maybe I was wrong. Maybe she'd welcomed it, had been tempted by the power of change, a chance to get away from failed ambitions and parental expectations. She might even have been enthralled by the prospect of her own tiny Markova pirouetting around her feet. Why not? What did dancers have ahead of them but old age and aching limbs? Or private eyes for that matter. What would I do when I was sixty, with no one to invite me to Sunday lunch or feed my canary when I went off for my annual fortnight in the geriatrics Club Meditérrané? Put like that it sounded pretty dismal. But then I was stoned and we all know how paranoia stalks those who smoke alone. Just as well Miss Patrick didn't indulge. The picture of her sitting amid her china and sepia prints, out of her skull on dope, did a lot to restore my sense of humour. I fell asleep to images of Paris filled with pregnant women, old dancers and fish that looked like Tab Hunter. I took it as an omen.

Colindale newspaper library is a long way from anywhere, except Colindale. The chairs are uncomfortable, the staff are even more bored than you are and the cheese sandwiches from the café down the road taste like they've been made of old copies of the *Sunday Express*. It does, however, have some things going for it, most particularly its newspapers. I had, of course, no guarantee that tracking down the Paris job would answer anything, particularly since Carolyn's postcards had all been postmarked London. But she had obviously been to France, more than once if Eyelashes was to be believed, and since it was the only lead I had I really didn't have much option. I had a hunch I'd find what I was looking for in the London *Evening Standard*, but hunches come in varying forms of strength, and this one was a little too pasty to risk. In the end it was just slog. A morning and into the afternoon. There were a number of candidates, but when

I found it I knew it was the one. First in the *Guardian* on Friday 4 February, then in the *Evening Standard* 7 February through to the 11th.

> A very particular young woman wanted for a special job. Are you between twenty and thirty? Are you healthy, attractive, intelligent with a love of life and a caring personality? Do you have time to spare and would you like to earn exceptional money living in France for a while? If so, apply in writing, sending CV and recent photograph to: POTENTIAL AGENCY 123 Jubilee Avenue SW1. 071 335 4311.

I called first, but only to check they were still at the same address. Nobody tells you anything on the phone, and I always think of myself as more impressive in the flesh.

The girls manning the Potential desks were a little less stylish than the decor, but they had that air of confidence that comes from one day personnel management courses and operating on commission. There were two ways to play this, the truth or deceit. Why pick one when you could have them both?

'Well, I really don't think I can help you. You'd better see Mrs Sanger, the manager.'

Mrs Sanger was a little older, a little more haute couture and a lot more on the ball. 'I'm sorry, but I've certainly had no communication with the police over this matter.'

'Of course not. I'm just doing some preliminary work to help them with their inquiries.'

'But you're not a policewoman.'

'No, I'm a private investigator.'

'Then I'm afraid I can't help you, Miss Wolfe. All our records are confidential.'

Oh well, brick wall. I thought about all the other ways I could try and get around it. Like joining the police or coming back after dark and breaking in to search the files. Crime had already got me a long way in this case, but Potential would almost certainly have better locks on their doors, not to mention an alarm system. I decided to stick with the verbals. 'You do realise, Mrs Sanger, that this is a murder inquiry we're talking about.'

'But I thought the papers said it was suicide.'

Gotcha. 'The police have reason to believe otherwise. There were certain, how shall I put it . . . "suspicious circumstances".' And I made the last two words positively tactile, like a twirl of the villain's moustache.

'I see,' she said, quietly, meaning, of course, that she didn't. I left a pause.

'So you do remember the girl?'

'Yes, well I read something about it, of course.'

'And she did answer the advertisement.'

'Er . . . yes, I seem to remember she may have done.'

'And it didn't occur to you that the police might be interested in knowing that?'

'It was a long time ago. Almost a year now. Quite frankly, I didn't think it was relevant.'

'Even though she got the job.'

All right, so it was just a flashy hunch. According to Scott, Carolyn hadn't got past the first interview, but then she'd spent years lying to Miss Patrick, why not a few white whoppers to others? There was a small silence. Probably Mrs Sanger's course had been longer than the others. She smiled. 'I still don't see what difference that would have made.'

'Mrs Sanger, according to the pathologist's report it is clear that Carolyn Hamilton conceived the child she died carrying during late April. Obviously any connections she would have made around or before that time are important. I appreciate the rules of confidentiality, but in the circumstances . . .'

Without the make-up and the fancy clothes I would have put her at about thirty-two or thirty-three. Younger than me and less used to this kind of encounter. I wouldn't say that was the deciding factor, but it probably helped.

'All right, Miss Wolfe, what do you need to know?'

'A description of the job and some kind of contact address for the client.'

She tried to look as if she was still making up her mind. Then she nodded slightly.

'As for the job, I seem to remember that it was a temporary post, some kind of personal assistant to a French businessman. We were given a questionnaire to ask the girls, and after some basic vetting we faxed the best results along with photographs of potential applicants to an office in Paris. That was the end of our involvement.'

'And Carolyn was one of the girls whose particulars you faxed.'

'Yes.'

'And did she get the job?'

'I have no idea. We put in the ad, saw the girls and passed on a short list. I don't believe we had any further contact with the client.'

So much for the day's second hunch. 'Isn't that rather unusual? I mean, aren't you usually paid for finding the right girl?'

She shrugged. 'Not always. Different clients use different methods. In this case we were paid for vetting the applicants, not filling the post itself.'

'And you weren't at all suspicious?'

'Of course not. We were employed to do a job and we did it.'

You could see she thought we had reached the end of our conversation. I wasn't sorry to disappoint her. 'Were you given any idea of what the job involved? I mean the ad read a little vaguely for a personal assistant post.'

She looked at me for a moment, then smiled. 'Business is a complex industry these days, Miss Wolfe. A high-powered head of an important firm may have more than one personal assistant, you know; someone geared to office work, another to managing his social calendar, entertaining overseas visitors, the press, that kind of thing.'

She made them sound more like heads of states than producers of steel or sanitary towels. As a child of the seventies I still have trouble adjusting to this new capitalist utopia, where it's not what you do but how much you earn doing it that defines status.

[61]

Speaking of which . . . 'The advertisement also mentioned "exceptional money". Is that true?'

'I seem to remember it was very well paid, yes.'

'You seem to remember a lot of things about it.'

'It was just before I became manager. I was the person who handled it.'

'So you interviewed her?'

And she frowned slightly, 'Yes.'

'How was she?'

She thought about it. 'She was a good candidate. Very attractive, bright, nice personality, a sense of adventure.'

Carolyn Hamilton redrawn as *Cosmo* woman of the nineties: gorgeous, self-confident and afraid of nothing. It has to be said, some people really let their jobs get to them. Still you can't be too careful. I filed this character description along with the rest of them.

'The perfect woman for the job, in fact?'

'I don't know. My memory is that the advertisement attracted a lot of attention. She wouldn't have been the only one they might have seen.'

'So can you give me the Paris contact?'

She nodded and stood up. 'It'll take a minute or two.'

Out through the glass wall Potential was hard at work, busy fitting square workers into round holes. I had been a temp once, pouching money during long winter months so I could spend the summer footloose and fancy free on some exotic Greek island. At least that had been the fantasy. In reality the money earned was never enough and I ended up typing chemical reports for a multi-national while London sweltered outside my window. I watched a middle-aged woman struggle with the plate-glass door, then hesitate in the entrance, wondering which bright young thing to approach. She looked in need of a job and therefore probably wouldn't get one. I tried to imagine Carolyn Hamilton in her place. A personal assistant to a French businessman. It didn't seem quite the thing for a dancer who went to animal rights rallies. Still, she had her own national debt to think about.

[62]

The need to find eight thousand pounds can affect anyone's choice of career. Was it my imagination, or did Mrs Sanger look a little less poised on her return?

'I'm terribly sorry, but we don't seem to have the records easily available.'

'It's not a problem. I can wait.'

'I'm not sure that would help. They don't seem to be in the correct file.'

'I see. What about a copy of the questionnaire and a list of the girls you vetted.'

'All the information would be in the same place.'

'And what about your own notes?'

'It was a long time ago. Some of them I would have transferred to the file, the rest I would have thrown away.'

'So what you're saying is that you have no record at all of the job?'

'That does seem to be the case, yes.'

I registered a small tingle of exhilaration in the pit of my stomach, but didn't let it show. What the body feels the mind doesn't always agree with. And the mind was still working.

'What about your fax records?'

'I'm sorry?'

'You said you faxed details to the Paris office. Wouldn't you have records of that number on your bill covering that quarter?'

Cross fertilization, it's called. Taking information gained in one job to use in another. To be honest it impressed almost as much as it flustered her. Fax records. Telephone bills. This was not the stuff of creative personal management. If indeed such records existed, she would certainly not be able to release them without permission. And permission would mean passing the buck. But not with me in the office.

Left alone again this time I looked the gift horse in the mouth. Why not? I went through the drawers of her desk quickly, one eye on the office outside, the other on the contents. Drawers, I have discovered, are a lot like handbags: they can tell you a great deal about their owners. Mrs Sanger was obsessive about her nails and she had a back-up Filofax just in case life got too full for the first one. Among the many things she didn't have was the file for the Paris job. But there was a separate contacts book. Above her desk was pinned an impressive list entitled 'USEFUL NUMBERS' so it seemed unlikely that she had to keep continually digging about in her drawer. It was small and red and could easily have got mislaid down the back of a filing cabinet or in the lining of a briefcase. Or the pocket of a private investigator. The whole thing took thirty-four seconds. I know because I counted. When I started doing this job I took tips from everywhere, books and bad movies included. Nimble fingers and speed were the lessons learnt. But how do you know how fast you are unless you time yourself? In my experience even the shortest of phone calls takes at least a minute.

Mrs Sanger's took longer. I was sitting reading last November's edition of *Jobs and Management* when she came back in. She didn't look hopeful.

'Company policy, I'm afraid. Obviously if and when the police require it they could get in direct contact with head office and they will process the request, but until then . . . I'm sorry I can't be of more help.'

I got up. 'And there's nothing more that you can tell me?'

'Nothing at all,' she said with admirable speed and efficiency.

I did the 'Well, if you can remember anything that might be of any help' routine, gave her a card and left.

I spent the next hour and a half sitting in rush-hour traffic jams. When I got home it was past seven and I was shagged. I had a dim recollection that there was something I should be doing that evening, but I didn't know what it was. I decided not to bother trying to remember. Instead I made myself a doorstep sandwich and went through her book. As far as I could see there were six French numbers. Four of them turned out to be agencies, with their answering machines on, but then it was after eight in Paris. The fifth, which had the word Etienne next to it, was engaged, no matter how often I called. And the last, which was Jules B something, wasn't answering at all. I gave up for the night and settled down to a little detecting homework.

I'll run it by you just in case you still harbour any illusions about the mystery of the process. The first thing is not to get too excited. After all, every minute of every working day a hundred files get lost in a million highly efficient filing systems; all perfectly innocent human error. But, once in every million there's a mistake that is deliberate. So let's say this was that one in a million. First question – who? Second question – why? Mrs Sanger didn't immediately seem the kind of lady to let conspiracy interfere with efficiency, and anyway why should she want to destroy the files of what was – according to her – a perfectly ordinary lucrative job? On the other hand, why hadn't she released the fax records? Had she really called the boss or just stood with her mouth to the receiver and her finger on the bridge? I thought about that one for a while but got nowhere. So say she was above board. Who else could want to destroy the file? Carolyn Hamilton herself? That one got the detecting juices flowing nicely but it was pure speculation. All I knew for certain was that Carolyn had got pregnant, disappeared, then put a lot of energy into concealing where she had gone. But would she really have gone to such extreme lengths as destroying the file for a job she may not even have got? Or spending seven months in Paris sending postcards home from London. If, that is, she had. If . . . That's the trouble with detecting, it's like travelling round an Escher landscape: you think you're going in one direction only to meet yourself coming back the other. I started to backtrack. To humbler beginnings. Fact: around the time of conception Carolyn had been Channel hopping. And at least one of those hops had been for an interview. Conclusion: even if she didn't get the job I should talk to the people who interviewed her. Which brought me back to the beginning and the little red book.

The phone broke the vicious circle. As soon as I heard her voice I remembered what I'd forgotten.

. 'Christ, Kate, I'm sorry.'

'You're getting as bad as Dad. I thought in your line of work it was important to remember things.'

'I can be there in twenty minutes, will that do?'

'I suppose so. There's food, you know. You haven't eaten, have you?'

'No, no, not a thing. I'll see you . . . Oh, and Kate – I forgot to buy him a present. Is there . . .?'

She laughed, which was pretty sisterly in the circumstances. 'Don't worry, he still hasn't read the copy of *Spy Catcher* from last year. Why don't you stop by an off-licence and make it liquid form. I think he'd digest that quicker.'

It could have been worse. At least I had something to wear. The feel of the Hong Kong silk brought back Mrs Van de Bilt, who had bitched about the half hour it had taken me to do some shopping of my own, but the suit made me look almost elegant, and a generous helping of duty free Chanel dispelled any hint of the Colindale public library about me. I picked up a bottle of Jamesons on the way and arrived twenty-five minutes after I'd put down the phone.

The evening was already in full swing. In the living-room the velvet curtains were drawn and a coal effect fire burned merrily, proud of its ability to fool most of the people some of the time. There were little bowls of green olives stuffed with pimentos and tiny canapés clustered together on lace doilied plates. I had forgotten how grown-ups live. Usually when I visited we stayed in the kitchen and ate off the table with the kids. Despite all the noise the house seemed quiet without them. Caterers slid in and out like well dressed shadows, leaving Kate to play hostess. I'd seen her looking better. The baby had a cold and she'd been awake most of the night blowing its nose, or whatever it is you do for a stuffed-up infant. But she had put on a brave face. And a beautiful dress. Not so much flash as fitting in. I wondered how long I had to stay for my exit not to appear rude. I whiled away a Martini with Colin's partner, a man with a red knitted tie and architect's glasses, who regaled me with some fascinating stuff about the corporate redesign of the Metropolitan Police, and how making police stations more design conscious places would improve relations between the police and the community. I stored it all away for a rainy day when I really wanted to get up Frank's nose. A youngish man with an active Adam's apple joined us. If we thought police stations were bad, we should see the BBC. Talk about Reithian grime. Maybe better office design would give us more balanced programmes. The red knitted tie loved that idea. I thought about trying to introduce a line of weak liberalism into the conversation, but decided I had better things to do with my brain.

Across the room I saw one of the black and white shadows approach Kate. They talked for a moment then Kate left. If I caught her quickly I could make my excuses and slide out before the buffet opened. But when I got out to the hall she was not there. I walked up to the first landing, and called her name. From Benjamin's room I was greeted by a wall of sound: great gulping sobs of indignation and fury as if the world was ending then and there in his bedroom. For a panicky moment I thought I might have woken him. I ran up to the first floor and stood outside the closed door. There were pauses in between the sobs now, but they might just have been gasps for breath. I opened the door quietly and went in. Kate was standing with her back to me, near to the window, silhouetted in the glow of a night light. The baby was cradled over her shoulder, yelling, although already less hysterical. She was talking to him, a river of comfort delivered in a private, sing-song little voice. And he was listening, even through the sobs you could see that.

'There, little goose, that's better, isn't it? See, there's nothing to cry about. Mummy's here. You're all right. Nothing is going to hurt you.' Benjamin shivered in her arms, swallowing tears and air together. He let rip with a few more giant sobs but you could feel that his heart wasn't really in it. 'I know how you feel, little man. It's awful when you can't breathe properly, isn't it? But it's just a cold, that's all, and I'm here to make it better.' He nuzzled his head into her shoulder, and gradually his body grew stiller. The cries turned to whimpers and finally stopped. He slept while Kate rocked on her heels, to and fro, one hand rubbing his back. I felt suddenly uncomfortable, as if I had stumbled across some unexpected sexual intimacy between friends. I moved to go out, but she heard me and turned. She motioned me to stay while she lifted the sleeping baby off her shoulder and put him down in the cot. He whimpered a little as he settled himself, but then seemed to fall instantly into a deep sleep. We stood for a moment watching him. With the crying wrinkles smoothed out he was suddenly the cherub child again, all cushion cheeks and silent-night peace: so powerful and so helpless at the same time. It was the kind of combination that might drive an intellect mad, if, that is, the instinct weren't hooked already. Funny how you can see it all from the outside.

'Sometimes I think sleep is God's way of saving babies' lives,' she said softly, her eyes still on the cot. 'Ten minutes ago I could have murdered him. Now I just want to crawl in and curl up next to him.'

And once again I thought about the great divide between those that have children and those that have not. And about Carolyn Hamilton, who had been so nearly there when she had made the decision not to. And more than ever it didn't make sense.

In his cot Benjamin snored slightly in his sleep. Horizontal again the cold was beginning to flow back into his sinuses, clogging his nose and making him snort out each breath, until for all the world, he sounded like the baby in Alice just before it turns into a pig. Kate smiled indulgently and we tiptoed out.

On the landing she smoothed down her dress and absent mindedly rubbed a grubby nose stain off her right shoulder. The noise of the party filtered up towards us. 'I should go down and supervise the buffet,' she said, but it was clear she didn't want to. 'I don't know. Sometimes I think I spend too much time with children. I can't seem to remember how to talk to adults any more.'

'Maybe they're just the wrong adults.'

She gave a small grin. 'I knew you'd hate them.'

I shrugged. 'We just don't have a lot in common.'

'Like making money?'

'Is that Kate Wolfe or Mrs Colin Chambers talking?'

She wrinkled up her nose, very Kate. As a child I used to call it her bad smell look. 'You always did lose your sense of humour when you were being teased. You know sometimes I wish you'd give him more of a chance. He's not quite the money obsessed nerd you make him out to be.'

I smiled. 'Yeah. Well, you know me. I'm like Dad in such matters. Don't like to admit that anyone could have been good enough for you.'

'You mean you always had a soft spot for David.' David, the only other man she'd brought home for family supper, a university lecturer with a sharp taste in clothes and a sassy sense of humour. A distinctly overblown ego certainly, but, it had to be said, considerably more charisma than Colin. She shook her head. 'It would have been a disaster, take my word for it. You know what they tell you about good lovers making bad husbands and even worse fathers.' Yeah, and Confucius he say all wisdom explodes out of a Christmas cracker. She must have seen my face. 'I know it sounds appalling, but there's some truth to it. Believe me I've met women who are still married to lovers, and it's nothing but heartache. At least I know where I am with Colin. And he really loves the kids.'

Gorgeous Kate, always the woman men lusted after. Maybe she needed relief from the power of sexuality, hers or anyone else's. Maybe that's why she picked Colin. Good husbands and loving fathers. She was right. It sounded almost as exciting as being buried alive. But then where sex is concerned I'm still a teenager at heart. Give me glamour over security any day. Kate would say it all stems from my irrational fear of domesticity, that it would somehow automatically turn me into my mother. I wondered if Carolyn Hamilton had had the same problem. Of course with two different mothers she had had a choice of nightmares. As it was she had clearly gone for the lover who, in the end, couldn't hack it to the husband/father status. Poor Carolyn. Kate was waving a hand in front of my face. 'Excuse me. Anyone there?'

'What? Sorry, I was thinking of something else.'

'It's all right. Don't panic, I've moved away from hearth and home. I was asking about work. I wondered how you were doing with your missing little dancer.'

Like all families we don't see enough of each other. I wondered how much to tell her. Downstairs there was the clink of cutlery and dishes. Colin would be expecting her. But blood was thicker than a couple of bottles of Saumur and I needed someone to talk to. We sat down together on the top of the steps, little sisters eavesdropping on the parents' party down below. And hearing adult tales. She was more upset than I expected.

'Oh, Hannah, what a terrible story.' She was silent for a moment, not looking at me. 'My God, the poor girl. What do you think happened?'

'Who knows. Obviously she felt she just couldn't go through with it.'

'At thirty-five weeks? I can't believe that. It's just too late by then. The baby's ready to be born. You can feel it pushing its way into place, waiting. It wouldn't be just killing yourself, it would be destroying someone else too. I don't see how any woman could do it.'

'Well, this one did. She even left a note to prove it.'

'What did it say?'

I told her. She was silent for a moment, but I noticed a flash of tears in her eyes. 'I'm sorry, I still don't believe it.'

And I thought about sweet Kate, sitting in her Habitat house with her Habitat man bringing her cups of tea and wallpapering the baby's room, while Carolyn sat nursing an eighth-month belly, her dancers' legs lost beneath her and nowhere and no one to go home to. 'Maybe it was different for her. She didn't have anyone. She was on her own.'

'That's not what I mean, Hannah, you don't understand.' And her voice was fierce. 'Earlier maybe, yes, then I can imagine someone being desperate enough to let it all go. But not by then. That's the whole point. By then it's not up to you any more. You're no longer the one in charge. I don't mean you're not scared, I'm sure everyone's scared. But it's not that kind of fear, and even if it is, it's too late to do anything about it. I mean by

[70]

then even the man is irrelevant. It's just you and it. And it wouldn't let you do it.' She stopped, then shook her head. 'I don't know how to explain it, there's a kind of lassitude that comes over in you in those last few weeks, like being in suspended animation. You're just waiting, both of you. I can't describe it any better than that. All I know is, however bad things were, I just don't believe she would have done it, whatever her note said.'

For Kate it was a long answer. I didn't reply. I remember her telling me how, just after Amy was born, she had felt as if someone had stripped away a layer of her skin, so that now everything felt more, and hurt more, but that stories of mothers and children hurt most of all. I felt alienated by her pain. As if she had done all the feeling for me, leaving me no room to find my own thoughts. Elder sisters. Who needs them? But you listen to them all the same. And who was I to say she didn't know more about Carolyn Hamilton than any policemen or male coroner. Or childless private eye. The great divide again.

'Kate?' Colin's voice rose up amid the babble.

She let out a small sigh, and the spell was broken. 'Yes, Colin, I'm here. I'm coming.' She turned to me apologetically. 'Sorry, I can see that instinct probably makes for lousy detective work. But you did ask.'

'Yes,' I said. Because she was right. I had.

CHAPTER SEVEN

Next morning I filed Kate's thoughts filed away under 'intuitive detection' and I went back to British Telecom. This time Etienne answered the phone. Or rather Mrs Etienne. Not so much an employment agency more a private housewife who had never heard of Potential, Mrs Sanger or a personal assistant position. When I asked to speak to her husband she became positively aggressive and starting asking questions back. I began to wonder if maybe a private number didn't mean a private affair between Etienne and a certain English Employment Agency manageress. I decided to think about that one and extracted myself from the conversation, pleading inadequate comprehension of the language, although by now a split French degree and a six-month stint translating EEC business in Brussels were positively flooding back to me.

I went through the Employment Agencies like a knife through melted Normandy butter. I had polished my story along with my teeth: a bureaucratic little tale about how Potential's receptionist had taken a call from Paris yesterday but had been unable to read her own writing. Had they by any chance called and, while they were on the line, could we check a few details on the personal assistant job they had sent us through last February? The answer was the same four times over. Nobody had any record of any such jobs last year. That left one more number. Jules B. It rang seven times before a woman answered.

'Hello. Mr Belmont's phone.'

'Is he there please?'

'No, I'm afraid Mr Belmont is still unwell.'

'I see. Could you tell me when he will be back?' Sometimes I think a parrot could do my job.

'I'm afraid I cannot.'

'It is rather urgent. I wonder, is there a home number where I could reach him?'

'I'm sorry, no. Who is this please?'

So I let her have it with the Potential Employment Agency story.

'I think you must have the wrong number. We are not an employment agency. This is Belmont Aviation and you have come through to Jules Belmont's private phone.' And there was something in the tone of her voice that made me realize Mr Belmont's private number was not the kind you just got out of the book.

On the list in front of me I put a question mark next to Belmont, him and Etienne: still hardly enough to waste a plane ticket to Paris on. I was beginning to feel somewhat bruised from all the brick walls I was running into. I sat for a while pushing mental needles into a wax effigy of Mrs Sanger, then I went back into labour. When I finally gave birth it was a mewling puking thing, not worthy to be called an idea, but it was all I had and better than nothing. According to Mrs Sanger there had been a considerable response to the advertisement. Now what 'considerable response' meant in employment agency jargon was beyond me, but somewhere out there there must be, what – ten, twenty, who knows even fifty attractive, healthy, intelligent caring young women who would have answered an ad, filled in a questionnaire, and in a few cases might even have gone to Paris for an interview. Maybe some of them were still looking for the right job, still checking the employment columns. I phoned through a box advert in the *Evening Standard* for the next week appealing to anyone who had answered the ad last February to contact me. Then I had another idea. Not quite so original but cheaper. When you need help, ask a policeman.

[73]

He sounded quite businesslike until he realized it was me. 'Wait a minute, will you?' In the background I heard the clink of glass and the glug of liquid from a bottle.

'A bit early, isn't it, Frank?'

'And how do you know it's not one of your poncy bottles of mineral water?'

'Let me see? No fizzing sound when you unscrewed the top?'

'Veerry good. Uncle Frank's training is having some effect at last. So, what can I do for you?'

He keeps the bottle of Glenfiddich in the bottom drawer of the filing cabinet. He says it's because it's cheaper than the pub, but I like to see it as a gesture in homage to old heroes. Usually he drinks alone, but occasionally I get an invite. The stories are as good as the booze: tales of metropolitan CID, the busts, the frame-ups, the classy detective work, the ones that got away. Sometimes I think he misses it more than he lets on, but then he keeps in touch. As fraternities go it's probably tighter than Eton. Us girls have nothing like it. Which is why I needed him.

'So you think it was a French bun in the oven. Poor kid. I still don't see what difference it makes. Why don't you let it go, Hannah? Listen, I've got a business woman who needs a smart girl to drive her around London – I daresay you could learn a lot from her dress sense – and a warehouse of shredding to be supervised. You're a pain in the ass but you're the best I've got. Why don't you come back to Comfort? He'll even give you luncheon vouchers.'

'Because I've got a feeling about this one.'

'That's my line.'

'Yeah, aren't you flattered I've stolen it? Seriously, Frank, I just don't think it's as simple as it looks.'

'Don't tell, you think it was a political death. The old "bridge at midnight" routine. "It's the rich what get the money, it's the poor what get the blame." Is that it? She was a modern-day Marxist heroine and you've got to avenge her.'

'Frank,' I said impatiently. 'Do me a favour.'

'Not a chance.'

'I didn't mean it like that.'

'Oh yes you did.'

'All right, I did. But you don't know what it is yet.'

'Yes I do, and the answer is still no.'

'They must have done some work on it. No big deal, all right? I just need to know if anyone else checked out a French connection, that's all.'

'Oh well, if that's all –'

'Come on, Frank. It'll only take one phone call. The old boys' network.'

'Yeah, and you're a girl.'

'Woman.'

'And a bloody nuisance.' There was a sigh, then a pause, then a grunt. 'I tell you, Hannah, it's not so easy any more. A lot of the old firm have gone. And this isn't just a quick dip into the computer to track down a couple of ex-cons and commies.'

I let it pass. He only does it to annoy because he knows it teases. Him and every other ex-copper turned security. They all do it: get their pals to break the law by running a few names through the computer and fishing out the odd record or financial data. It's what those in the know call the freedom of information act. Frank and I had had our rows about it in the past. But even I could see the seduction of it, for friends as well as clients.

'All right. But I can't promise anything. They didn't like you, you know, thought you were too smart for your own good.'

'Frank – I was femininity personified. I even made them a cup of tea.'

'Yeah . . . Well, it'll take time.'

'How long?'

'I don't know. Three, maybe four days.'

'Great. If you can guarantee it's not state secrets I'll take the shredding.'

The advert worked before the insider information. Two days after it went in I came home to a message from a girl with an accent which sounded as if it had just fallen off a polo pony. She said she had replied to the ad and been seen by a woman at the agency. When I called her back she told me she remembered a lot of questions about health and family background, personality, even stuff about boyfriends and moral attitudes. And there had been a kind of aptitude test, the sort of thing she always flunked when she was at school. After that she had heard nothing more.

The next day washed up a girl who thought she might have seen the original ad but it turned out hadn't, and a couple of dirty phone calls from men eager to meet attractive healthy young girls. Then Thursday hit the jackpot. First Frank, then Marianne Marshall.

'Come on, Frank. You're telling me it took four days to find out nothing.'

'Listen, Sherlock, if there had been any real suggestion of hanky panky it would never have got an "accidental death" verdict. It was an open-and-shut case. They had a suicide note, a body with no sign of foul play and a depressed young girl, having trouble with her career and with a bun in the oven that she couldn't tell anyone about.'

'It still doesn't explain where she'd been for the last seven months.'

'So she covered her tracks well. She wouldn't be the first to disappear so she could have the kid in secret. The boys looked. There was no forwarding address, her flat was clean as a whistle, no contact with friends or relatives and no medical trace. Her London GP didn't treat her, and there was nothing at the local hospitals. Which means either she didn't see anyone or she went private. The clinics they checked had no record of her, but then that's hardly conclusive. She could have used another name.'

'So much for the record, Frank. What do they really think happened?'

'Same as you probably. That the father set her up somewhere and paid the bills for a while.'

'In England?'

'No reason why it should be anywhere else. Unless, of course, you have reliable information that should have been given to the police.'

I decided to ignore that one. 'So if there was a guy how come he didn't come forward after her death?'

'Maybe he didn't want trouble. Perhaps he already had a wife and was just paying guilt money to get her off his chest.'

'Yeah, and perhaps he pushed her in the river so his wife would never find out.'

'Hannah, my petal, that's not even circumstantial.'

'Neither are his hand-outs.'

'Ah, sorry, I knew there was something I'd forgotten to mention.' God damn it, Frank. He does it every time. 'Apparently she left a lot of debts behind her.'

'So?'

'But she paid them all off.'

'When?'

'Three cash deposits into her building society account in May, June and July. And from there cheques to all her creditors.'

'Cash?'

'You heard it.'

'Who made the deposits.'

'No one knows. They were made at different branches by someone with an unreadable signature. Could have been her, could have been someone else, the tellers couldn't remember.'

'And you're telling me that no one found that suspicious?'

'So, she got banged up by someone with money and wanted to keep it a secret. You said yourself she was a good-looking girl. We're living in an enterprise culture. Everyone's got something to sell. Maybe hers was silence.'

'God, Frank, sometimes you sound just like a policeman.'

'Yeah, but is it any worse than sounding like a hippie? How many times do I have to tell you, Hannah, you're twenty years out of date. Money is OK now. It's the rich guys who are the heroes. Anyway, in this particular case it makes sense. If he had bought her off it was because he wanted the anonymity. Which would explain why it was cash rather than a cheque and why he didn't come forward when she died. Course, a good feminist like yourself would probably have him lynched, but luckily we still live under a brutal paternalistic legal system, so he can't be brought to justice on purely moral grounds.'

Normally I would have risen to it, just to please Frank, but I was too busy thinking of something else. 'Wait a minute. It doesn't make sense. If someone cleared all her debts, then what's with that bit in the suicide note about all the money she couldn't repay?'

'Well, of course I'm only a man and lacking in female intuition, but if it were my case I'd assume that referred to Miss Patrick. You add it up over the years and she must have laid out a tidy sum on her little protegée. Not to mention all the emotional investment that couldn't be paid back.' Not for the first time I felt more stupid than Frank. 'So. Do I gather from the silence that you've got everything you want?'

'Just one last thing, Frank. Let's say they were right. I mean about the man and the money. If it was cash it could still easily have been converted from French francs into English pounds. If my hunch is correct and the reason they couldn't track her down was because she was in France, is there any way I can check?'

He thought about it. 'Well, no one stamps your passport any more, but technically anyone staying should be registered as a foreigner. On the other hand it's not exactly an enforceable law. So, you really think it was a frog, eh? God, no wonder the kid jumped. At least she picked the Thames.' For some people it goes back as far as Agincourt. For Frank it's more recent history. *Les Misérables*. His wife made him take her as a birthday present and then wouldn't let him fall asleep. 'Do I gather from this that you won't be wanting another job next week?'

I didn't even get the chance to digest the information. Ten minutes later the phone rang again. Her name was Marianne Marshall. She had a dark chocolate voice and a tale about how she had answered the ad and been given an interview in Paris. For a moment I almost got carried away. But nobody gets it handed to them on a plate. She'd been called for an interview, but had been unable to go because she'd got offered another job.

'To be honest I'd only answered as a bit of a joke. I was sick of being out of work and thought it might be a trip on somebody's yacht serving martinis for the summer. Of course I didn't tell them that. I said I was giving up the stage and looking for something more worthwhile. But then this came through, and I must say I wouldn't normally touch rep, but it was such a wonderful season and they were great parts. Added to which it was Sheffield and there was a possibility of a transfer with the musical. Well, I couldn't turn it down.'

Marianne Marshall? It certainly hadn't made a star of her, but she didn't sound too distraught about it. Her memories of the original interview were similar to the polo pony. A surprising amount of personal stuff, family, health, marital status, that kind of thing. As to the job itself, she knew about as little as everyone else. 'Of course I asked, and the woman doing the questionnaire said she hadn't all the details, but that it was some kind of assistant to a wealthy businessman, and I'd know more at the interview.'

'How did you hear?'

'I got a call at home one evening.'

'When was this?'

'February, the 18th or 19th. I know because I had just done the audition the day before.'

'Who called, a man or a woman?'

'Man.'

'Saying what?'

'Could I come for an interview three days later. They would pay all my expenses, a car would pick me up at the airport and drive me to the meeting place then take me back. If I had to take a day off work they would reimburse me.'

'And you told him you couldn't?'

'Oh no, at that stage I hadn't heard from the rep. I said yes. It was all arranged when I got a call from my agent, so I had to ring and cancel.'

'You don't happen to remember the name or the number, do you?' Climb every mountain, leave no stone unturned. I could hear Frank's voice in the darkness. 'It's just like stocktaking, Hannah. The one you miss is the one you'll need.'

'Oh, now you're asking. The name I don't remember. In fact I'm pretty sure they didn't give me one. But the number I've got written down somewhere.'

'You have,' I said casually enough to get an Equity card.

'Sure, it'll be in my Filofax from last year. Next to the interview details. If you hold on a moment I'll get it for you.'

On my pad I doodled around the name Marianne, giving her a cascade of little stars to follow her through life. Then I wrote two names. Jules Belmont and Etienne. I underlined Etienne. She gave me the number for neither. So much for research.

I had a whole story lined up. But I didn't need to do a thing. The apple fell right on my head.

'Good afternoon. Belmont Aviation. Daniel Devieux's office. Can I help you?'

'Yes, you most certainly can. Do you have Mr Devieux there?'

'I think he's in a meeting. Who's calling?'

I decided to be someone else. Someone more poised and groomed. 'My name is Fiona Kilmartin, I'm calling from an employment agency in London.'

Did I register a sliver of hesitation? 'I see. I'm afraid Mr Devieux is a very busy man. Can I ask what it's about?'

'No, perhaps instead you might transfer this call to Jules Belmont's office.'

This time there was a definite blib. 'I'm afraid Mr Belmont is unwell at present. Er . . . If you could just give me some idea . . .'

Brick walls again. Maybe I should try knocking at the door. 'Very well. I'm looking for some information on a woman I believe he might have employed some time last year. Her name is Carolyn Hamilton.'

'I see. Well, if you could give me a number, I'll get him to call you back.'

According to my watch it took her two hours to find the meeting room. In between, Kate rang to find herself talking to the Potential Employment Agency. The phone went again just after five.

'Yes, I've spoken to Mr Devieux. I'm sorry, we can't help. He says he has checked all the relevant files and has no record of a woman called Carolyn Hamilton.'

But then he wouldn't, would he? Not if he had anything to hide. The phone hummed disconnection in my ear. I dialled another number. With luck Andy would still be at the office. Even if I was wrong what else did I have to waste my time on?

CHAPTER EIGHT

Every girl should have one. A man who knows his way around the schedules and the price wars. The only trouble is you have to get up at dawn to take advantage of Andy's cheap flights. And travel to the ends of the earth to catch them. City Airport Docklands, an invention of eighties' capitalism, the art of PR triumphing over reality. Before the fall (real estate not man) it had all seemed glitteringly possible, a new city rising like a phoenix from its nineteenth-century slums with its own airport carved out of the old Victoria and Albert docks, planes taking off where the Empire had once steamed in. Now, with riverside homes being given away free in cornflake packets and developers turning as liquid as the Thames, the airport was already a commercial bad smell. Her Victorian Majesty would not have been amused. Neither was I. The meter in the cab read thirteen pounds.

On the runway a midget plane with Biggles-type propellers sat waiting, the kind of thing a DC10 might eat for breakfast. Inside was a bit like being in the belly of a bomber. I took comfort from the fact that it was too small to warrant sabotage and served free champagne.

Over Brittany I tried my hand at a little storytelling. Once upon a time there was a young woman called Carolyn Hamilton who met a young/older man and didn't live happily after. Fill in the gap. Scenario one: the rich French stranger. Tired with

[82]

London, and therefore tired with life, our heroine answers an ad for a job in France with enough money to mop up her medical and drug debts. She goes to Paris for an interview, doesn't get the post, but does get herself a man. (Who, how and where to be worked out later.) The power of French kisses brings her back for more, the weakness of French letters keeps her there. She tries, with the father's money but not necessarily his support, to make a go of it but the French are so cruel to women larger than a size ten that she is forced to return to London, where she goes dancing one night on the embankment, misjudges her new centre of balance and falls in. Crime fiction: the murder of fact in pursuit of fiction? I had another glass of champagne and tried again.

Scenario two: Carolyn goes to Paris for an interview with Belmont Aviation, either the man himself or one of his legates. What he – or the other he – is looking for is a rather special young woman: healthy, attractive, intelligent with a love of life and the urge to earn exceptional money. An office drudge she is obviously not. Clearly what is on offer here is something more ambiguous, more in the realms of Mrs Sanger's vision: a gorgeous slave to manage his hectic diary, entertain his international clients, maybe even stand in for his wife when she had the occasional headache from shopping too hard. And English? Well, maybe he's already got a reputation for this kind of thing in France and is having to travel a little further afield for fresh meat. He meets Carolyn, likes what he sees, gets to know her better during a series of interviews and, hey presto, before you know where you are he and she are making more than airplane parts. Since she has nothing to loose she decides to keep the child. In the spirit of paternalistic capitalism he keeps her on the payroll for a while and she spends a long hot summer in a Paris apartment knitting a layette and sending postcards home in the diplomatic bag. Then a month before the baby is due Madames Belmont/Devieux find out about their husbands' indiscretion, swoop down on Paris like avenging Chabrol wives and chase our rotund heroine home to London where, rather than face the consequences, she decides

[83]

to end it all in the aforesaid muddy waters. Hmm. I liked that one. It had a certain ring to it. Now I had the story, all I needed was the facts.

Belmont Aviation, I had already learnt from the international operator, was situated in the Zone Industriel at Roissy. As it wasn't far from the airport I thought of going there first, but since according to the map there didn't seem to be a lot more in Roissy than the zone, and it was a long time since I had shimmied down the Champs-Elysées, I decided to base myself in Paris anyway. From Charles de Gaulle I took the train into town and walked from Hotel de Ville across to the Left Bank. I had a memory of a spectacular little hotel just over the bridge from Notre-Dame, all wooden beams and Van Gogh chairs, but it had been a while and the streets all looked the same. So did the hotels, small twin beds and plastic fittings. It had happened everywhere else, why should Paris be immune? I ditched romance in favour of utility, booked myself into the one nearest to the Métro, changed into my nifty little checked business suit specially preserved in tissue paper for the occasion, and set off for Roissy.

It was harder than it looked: subway, train and taxi and even then it wasn't an exciting journey. You've seen one industrial zone and you've seen them all: flat-packed ghettos cutting into the countryside with their steel-clad factories and brightly coloured warehouses. Belmont Aviation wasn't hard to find. It was bigger than most, set back from the road in its own little landscaped park. A tribute to post-modernism, the office building looked like a Mies van der Rohe tower that had toppled on to one side: long clean lines of smoky-brown mirrored glass rising out of a cricket-pitch lawn and dinky flowerbeds. Green peace and industry. Even the taxi driver seemed proud of it, eager to tell me how, while other businesses tried to separate the shop floor from the admin-istration (the bigwigs like to work near home), Belmont had always done as his work force. Hence their presence here at Roissy. Outside the front entrance stood a large statue of a man clasping a bolt of lightning, with a young child at his feet, arms outstretched. It looked like a cross between Rodin and Soviet Realism.

In the lobby a security man directed me to the front desk, where I exchanged pleasantries with a well drilled receptionist. I had decided to go first for the boss. That way they could feel good about fobbing me off with one of his senior executives. I had come to see Mr Belmont. She shook her head. Mr Belmont was not available. Still indisposed, I wondered? You could see she found my choice of words strange. Maybe it was common Roissy knowledge that the guy was off having major bypass surgery. Never mind. Mr Devieux would do. She frowned. Did I have an appointment? Well, she really didn't think . . . I asked her to try anyway and gave her a card. She looked at it, then back up at me. I translated security and private investigation into French. She nodded and told me to take a seat. You could tell from the way she said it she didn't think I had much hope.

The first half hour was fun. You can tell a lot about a tycoon from his employees. They were a smart set, the Belmont babies, all shiny shoes and designer suits: the women in particular all seemed to have the same optician, and the same little ski-run noses with glasses perched halfway down. Their heels clicked sexily across the polished floors, neat little steps constricted by fifties'-tight skirts, tapping out the rhythm of successful business. Even their haircuts looked the same, a subtle touch of Louise Brooks held in place with, no doubt, environmentally friendly aerosols.

Then, just when I was beginning to get bored, I got the brush-off. The receptionist was talking into the phone, but looking at me. She put her hand over the mouthpiece. 'Madame Wolfe?'

I stood up and smoothed my skirt, but the creases had settled for the day. 'I have Madame Claire, Mr Devieux's personal assistant on the line for you.'

Madame Claire and I, of course, had already met, although she didn't know that. She wasn't much more accommodating second time around. Mr Devieux was not available today. If I wrote a letter stating my business she might be able to help me herself or make an appointment for the future. I explained that I had trouble with the future, since I was only in Paris for three days of it. I also told her that the matter was urgent and confidential, that I was investigating the death of a young British woman, one of Belmont Aviation's former employees, and that if Mr Devieux would not see me I would be forced to try and arrange an interview through the Roissy police department. There was just a beat of a pause in response to that one. Then she asked for a number where I could be contacted and said she would be in touch. We left it at that. It was not exactly triumph, but I allowed myself to feel a certain glow of success. I walked out into an early Roissy afternoon.

I spent the journey back working. I had left London too early to check the local library's *International Who's Who*, and the only papers on offer on the flight had been English ones in which Belmont Aviation didn't rate a mention. Typical of the British. European only in name. Now though, as I sat munching my way through the business pages of a clutch of newspapers and magazines from the station *tabac*, it was a different story. Still no photo of the man himself, but the kind of company reports to bring a warm glow to the shareholders' hearts. Boosting exports, encouraging home growth, spawning baby companies; if the press was to be believed the Belmont empire was an economic miracle – not so much a person, more a way of business. The man at the top must be just the kind of chap – in Mrs Sanger's eyes – to need a whole slew of personal assistants. I couldn't wait to meet him.

It was three o'clock when I reached the hotel. No one had called. I sat and waited, but the plastic fittings didn't get any better and outside Paris sparkled in an unexpected burst of sunshine. It was time to pour a libation to memory. I spent the latter part of the afternoon riding the escalators up and down Beaubourg counting the wads of chewing gum that the French had stuck into the heating ducts. Then I walked across the river to the Tuileries and watched squirrels steal peanuts from children's hands. It got colder as dusk came on. I liked it better that way. Paris was different in the winter: there was a kind of cleanness to the city, an unselfconscious quality of life without tourism. When Carolyn Hamilton had arrived here (I should have said 'if' she arrived here, but I was fed up with ifs), it would have been May and Paris would have been already dressed to receive visitors, all new green froth and blossoms spreading coquettish memories of light romance and Hollywood. Of course she would have fallen for it, first time away from home and a whole French summer stretching ahead of her.

I walked back along the embankment, where a dozen plant shops spewed out buds and creepers on to the street, while twc blocks down cages of songbirds serenaded rabbits, hamsters and even the occasional ferret. The Left Bank seemed quiet in comparison. At the corner of my street a man was rolling down shutters on a laboratory shop. The side window was filled with intricate plaster-cast side-sections of the human body: intestines, urinary tracts and oesophaguses, all pink and white and fleshy. And there in the middle sat a cosy round uterus, with a 2001-like foetus curled up on itself protected by layers of tissue and blood. It looked so peaceful in there, waxy and smooth, waiting for B-day. I decided it was more of a sign than any sheep's entrails.

I got back just before 6.00 p.m. to find a message from Madame Claire taken thirty minutes before. It was more or less the right timing. If the world wagged according to my theories then someone, either her or Devieux himself, would already have been on the phone to Potential to check up on Fiona Kilmartin's credentials. And if Mrs Sanger had had her wits about her (and she had in the past) then she would already have put two and two together with the loss of her address book and come up with me. So who should turn up next day demanding an interview but the thief herself? Now came the crunch. If they really had nothing to hide, there was no reason not to see me. And if, by chance, there was something nasty in the woodshed, all the more reason to pretend there wasn't. They obviously saw things my way. When I called back she informed me that Mr Belmont himself would meet me at 8.30 a.m. sharp tomorrow morning in his office. Mr Belmont himself, presumably up, like Lazarus, from his sick bed. I put the phone down and gave just the smallest of whoops of triumph. Nothing so gross as hubris, you understand, just a sense of getting back out what you put in. 8.30 a.m. sharp. That left fourteen hours in which to have fun. I had earned it. My restaurant guide and I went out together. First stop, my local bar for an apéritif.

I think he must have come in about ten minutes later. Certainly he wasn't there when I arrived – I would have noticed. There had been a time, while I was still living with Joshua but already alone in my head, when I developed quite a thing for strangers. That was the point, of course, their anonymity: the perfect antidote to the slow strangulation of domesticity. Looking back on it now it seems rather cold and calculating, but it wasn't like that at the time. At the time just the thought of it could light fires in my stomach: mutual sexual appreciation completely unconnected with real life, a much underrated form of romance. Of course I never told him. I mean it was only occasional and he would have had to take it personally when it wasn't meant so. Later, after we split up, the appeal faded. Or maybe I just got used to the singular comfort of a double bed. Either way it had been quite a while and tonight I wasn't sleeping at home. Who knows, maybe Carolyn Hamilton had been sitting in a bar when she noticed a good-looking stranger.

Actually it wasn't his looks that first caught my attention. It was his suit. It was big and baggy, a touch of the demob with an obvious label to it. He was sitting at the bar reading a paper and playing with the stem of his glass. Hmmn, I thought, interesting. I looked a little longer. It was partly the way he sat, teasing comfort out of a perch designed for posture correction, and partly the body itself, long and loose-limbed as if it didn't quite fit together. Of course we all know that women, like men, go for different things in the opposite sex. Myself, I've never been a buttocks or a powerful-but-sensitive-hands type. I go for the whole torso. His eyes flickered upwards. Women can always feel when they are being sexually assessed, so why not men? The face was slightly older than I had expected, but pleasantly craggy and well lived in. Worth looking at. Hannah, I thought, you're a sexist sow. Well, why not? Men spent their lives studying women.

So tonight it's the other way round. What's wrong with that? What's wrong, said a little voice which for want of a better word I will call my conscience, is that you're working, and business and pleasure don't mix. I listened, gave it some thought, then put a bag over Jiminy Cricket's head.

Nevertheless I kept my distance until it became clear that the interest was mutual. Nothing so crass as direct eye contact, you understand, more a way of not looking. For Jiminy's sake I considered the possibility that this was no mere pick-up, but a deliberate plant by the evil Belmont empire, just to check me out. But if that was the case they'd picked a real amateur. And since when did common or garden tails wear Jean-Paul Gaultier suits? Anyway, there was one way to find out. If I was doing the following the last thing I would want was for my suspect to engage me in conversation. I finished my drink and took it back up to the bar, placing myself deliberately near to him. He kept his eyes firmly on the newspaper, but his heart wasn't in it, I could feel. 'Hello,' I said brightly.

He looked up. 'Hello?' A slight frown, but nothing to worry about. And grey eyes, with a fleck in them. Nice.

'I could be mistaken, but I'm getting the impression that you are watching me.' Christ, said Jiminy in a muffled squawk, didn't your mother teach you anything about the social graces?

He appeared to give the matter some thought, then shook his head, his bottom lip out just a little, very French, attractive. 'Actually, I think it would be more accurate to say that we were watching each other.' He took a sip of his drink. 'The question now, of course, is should we continue?' In my (admittedly) limited experience it was not the level of repartee you found in your average sleaze-bag tail. It registered in the pit of my stomach as well as my head.

'Maybe we should discuss it.'

'Fine. In English or French?'

I will admit to just the smallest twinge of hurt pride. 'It's that obvious?'

'No, but I think I have an unfair advantage,' he said, in

impeccable and very nearly accentless American. And then he smiled, and I have to say it had something of the Tom Cruise about it, although, thank God, a little more mature.

'That's very good.'

He shook his head. 'Upbringing rather than talent, I'm afraid. I had an American father. And I get a lot of practice in my work.' So what did we have here? A war baby no doubt. Mother carried away by a member of the liberating armies. Which made him, what forty-four, forty-five? It wasn't so long ago I thought people that age were brain dead. Which just goes to show how much fun growing older can be. 'How about you, where does your excellent French come from?'

'I think the word is education. Too many years as a student.'

He nodded. 'Not now though?'

'No, not now,' I said, duly flattered by the possibility it should be otherwise.

'Good. So shall we have another drink? Or would you prefer to go back to a more long-distance appreciation?'

I pushed my glass towards him and settled myself more comfortably on the bar stool. I said after a short pause, 'So what do you do that gives you so much practice?' Making conversation, it's called. Like making love, only with words.

'I'm a journalist. I work for an American magazine.'

'Really.'

'It sounds more exciting than it actually is. Mostly financial matters, I'm afraid. I'm their European Business Correspondent.'

And who says that life doesn't come gift-wrapped sometimes? Jiminy Cricket, eat your heart out. I put out my hand. 'On the contrary, I'm sure it's absolutely fascinating. I'm Hannah Wolfe. I work in security. And I'm very pleased to meet you.'

He took it, and I must tell you it was a good clean grasp, like the opening of a boxing match. 'David Mercot. So. Shall I buy this round or will you?'

And thus it began. The chat-up of Hannah Wolfe and David Mercot. I'll spare you (or maybe me) the more excruciating bits of the next half hour. Courtship is, after all, a private affair and not, at this stage at least, directly relevant to the plot. Suffice it to say that as Frenchmen go he had a pleasantly self-deprecating sense of humour and a certain *je ne sais quoi*, as well as what was clearly some tasty insider gossip on the French industrial scene. Jiminy Cricket would have been proud of me after all. To make it look a little less like I was picking his brains, after the second drink I suggested dinner. He accepted. Call it the Mata Hari school of detection. Except, of course, you're not supposed to tell them you're a spy. Over the first course I put some effort into being interested in his job.

'You know it's not often I meet a woman so enthralled by the state of European industry. Is this a professional curiosity or just a hobby?' The food was so good it was hard to think. His choice. I had decided not to look at the prices. Like a tourist I had gone straight for the *moules* poached in wine and herbs and was having trouble keeping a sense of dignity as I dive-bombed chunks of bread into the sauce. I wiped my chin with the crisp white napkin and swallowed. 'Since you ask, a bit of both.'

'Security, I think you said. You selling alarm systems or information?'

Hard to lie to someone with that face. I just smiled.

'I see. All highly confidential.'

I smiled again. 'You've seen the movies.'

'So, do you want to know about the industrial scene in general or one particular company?'

Sometimes it's a fair cop. 'I know what you're thinking, but it isn't the only reason I invited you out to dinner.'

He looked at me for a moment. 'I know. If it had been I wouldn't have accepted. I just hope your client has given you generous expenses. Why don't we agree to eat first and talk later. I can recommend the lamb.'

He was right; suffused with garlic and served on a bed of new peas with a cloud of *le rat* potatoes whipped into a cloud of butter and cream and sprinkled with parmesan it was, as they say in the cookery books, *ravissant*. Later came the lamb's tongue and rocket salad, made sweet by the cut of lemon and olive oil. Simple but subtle. I took it as my cue.

'Belmont Aviation, eh? I feel almost embarrassed about taking your hospitality. Most people on the street could tell you what you want to know.'

'It's that well known?'

'It or him, hard to say which. Jules Belmont. He's one of those original legends in his own lifetime. Built the company up from scratch and dedicated his life to it. Started after the war, a resistance hero building a New France out of the ruins of occupation. The rest is modern folklore.'

'The war. How old is he then?'

'Now? Oh, late sixties, going on seventy maybe. I don't think anyone asks any more. The only figures people quote are his yearly profits.'

Seventy. Now here was a fact to do serious damage to my 'charismatic businessmen seducing gorgeous young ex-dancer' theory. Maybe he didn't look his age. 'What's he like?'

He shrugged. 'Like all successful businessmen, dedicated, a little obsessive, good at backing the right horse.'

'Aviation?'

'Now, not then. I believe he made his first fortune from the newspaper business: a couple of provincial papers that had fallen into collaborators' hands. I think he was given them as a gift for services rendered. Then he went into construction, dabbled in electronics – chasing the Japanese by the tail – and from there the sky was the limit. Most of the airlines you ever flew owe something to Belmont Aviation. And most of them have paid well for the privilege.'

'Is he straight?'

'If he isn't I've never heard about it. Of course, he's got friends in high places. But then so do all national heroes. Nepotism isn't a crime providing you produce the goods. And Belmont produces.'

'What about his private life?'

He raised an eyebrow. 'Who's your client?'

I raised one back. 'You don't have to tell me anything you don't want to.'

'All right. But for dessert I suggest we have a bottle of Tokay. What do you want to know?'

'Married?'

'Let me see. Three times I think. The first wife was killed by the Germans. The second died in a car accident nine, ten years ago. She and their only child, a little boy. It was a big tragedy. This one is number three. I believe her name is Mathilde. I think they've been married for five or six years. It's a common enough scenario, at least in the business world: rich old man, younger good-looking wife plucked from the typing pool. Except the rumour is they're devoted to each other. Against all the odds a happy marriage.' And I heard a crash in the back of my head. It was the sound of theory number three finally hitting the dust.

'Not the kind of man to play around then?'

'His name isn't in the gossip columns, if that's what you mean. Why? Does your client say differently? No, don't tell me. I've seen the movies. Anything else?'

'Not much. How's his health?'

He shook his head. 'Some men age quicker than others. Until two years ago he was indestructible. Then suddenly, pow. Two heart attacks one after the other. The doctors told him to slow down. He didn't. Last year was a third. He ought not to have survived it. But then he is Jules Belmont. I gather he's taking it slower these days.'

'What about the company?'

'It's a family firm. The mantle was meant for his son. When he died ten years ago he started grooming his nephew. He's one of the directors now.'

Seek and ye shall find. 'Don't tell me, Daniel Devieux.'

'Well, at last. I was beginning to wonder if you really were any good at your job.'

I resisted the temptation to bad-mouth him back. Work first, fun later. 'What about him? Is he a worthy successor?'

'You'd have to ask his uncle. Certainly the company isn't suffering.'

'And personal life?'

'Not much to say. Divorced, I think. He used to be a pilot with Air France. Now he just lives for Belmont and the company. A dull man by all accounts. No real personality at all.'

'So not what you'd call a ladies' man?'

'I suppose it depends on your taste. You'd have to ask the ladies. Now, do you think we could look at the dessert menu?'

Knowing when to stop; it's half the secret. I squirrelled away my spoils and turned from work to fun. Not even Jiminy could accuse me of not earning it. The waiter brought the dessert menu. I let him do the choosing. When it arrived it was more an expression of indulgence than hunger: a glass of frozen pink champagne so clear that you could almost count the bubbles. Plus, of course, the Tokay. It was magnificent. So, no doubt, was its cost. What the hell. Intelligence doesn't come cheap.

'So, is this my turn to ask the questions for a while?'

'Be my guest,' I said, with my mouth full of melting bubbles.

He watched me for a moment, then took a long sip from his glass. It crossed my mind that we were both drinking a fair amount. I wondered if it mattered. 'Well, where shall we start? How about the job. Most French girls I know either want to be air hostesses or Ministers of Culture. There's not a lot of interest in security. How did you get into it?'

I had been expecting the usual 'What's a nice girl like you . . .' routine and the question caught me off guard. I found myself giving him something near to the truth. 'I dunno. More chance than vocation I guess. I was in between jobs and I replied to an ad for an office manager, just to pay the rent. I found myself answering the phones for a crazy ex-detective just starting out and ended up joining the firm.'

'He must have been an interesting man.'

'Yes.' I thought about Frank, cleaning his nails with a paperclip while he used the nailfile to show me how to jemmy a desk drawer. 'I suppose you could call him that.'

'What did you do before?'

Before? I had this flash of a rather intense young woman freed

[94]

from the deathly dull arena of EEC politics and out to change the world. In retrospect it seemed like a case of mistaken identity. 'I worked for the Civil Service.' I paused. 'Fascinating, eh?'

'I think so,' he said with an admirably straight face. 'Why did you leave?'

At the time I had had a little speech about this one. Heartfelt. Now it just sounded pompous. 'I got fed up with not achieving anything. Bureaucracy and government policy. The perfect equation for apathy breeding corruption. It got to the point where either I stayed in and kept my mouth shut or I got out.' He raised an eyebrow. 'See. You didn't take me for the moral crusader type, did you?'

He shrugged. I got the impression he was enjoying himself. 'Now you come to mention it ... So how does the security business fit in?'

'Ah well, I think I've probably mellowed a bit since then.' I took another drink from my glass. 'Though you'd be surprised. It's not all going through peoples' dustbins or snapping Polaroids of unfaithful wives. You still get some clients who want to know the truth, even if they don't like it when they hear it.'

All right, Hannah, that's enough. Put down your glass, sweetheart. Remember you're drinking Miss Patrick's money and nobody needs to know your business but you. Jiminy making a cheeky reappearance. Though this time I'd do well to listen to him. I took a long slug of mineral water. What were we talking about? Ah yes, what was a nice girl like me ... I rummaged around in my answers drawer and slipped into something more comfortable. 'Anyway. It's got a lot of rewards. The wealth, the travel, the men ... The chance to be the white knight on the mean streets. What more could a girl ask?'

He was silent for a second or two. Then he shook his head. 'You know, every security agent I ever met always said the same thing. Must be the books they read.'

'Well, ask a mythic question and you get a mythic reply.'

'Shame. I thought for once I was about to get to the truth.'

But I was beyond temptation now. And even if I wasn't

working, confession is an act of faith best kept for the bedroom, and we were still only in the restaurant. 'It'll disappoint you. I don't like travelling in the rush hour. Or knowing where I'm going to be this time next week.'

He smiled, but you could see he didn't believe me. Funny, they never do. Must be the books they read. 'What about money?'

'I don't know about France, but in England it's not polite to ask a lady what she earns.'

He grinned. 'France neither. But remember I'm half American. And a business journalist.'

'Then you already know the answer. There's a lot of dosh in security.'

'Companies certainly. But I've yet to come across a firm where the staff do as well as the management.'

'Yeah, well, this isn't exactly a big firm. I make enough. But then I have modest tastes.'

'So you don't ever get tempted?'

'You mean if the client is loaded do I fiddle expenses?' I smiled. 'Absolutely, utterly, of course not and never.'

'And what about the danger? Do you ever get scared?'

'What is this? You researching an article?'

'I told you, I never met a woman private eye before. This may be my only chance to sort out the fact from the fiction.'

I shook my head. 'No, I don't get scared. There's seldom anything to be scared about. If there is, you're doing it wrong.'

'Is that really true? Even when you go behind enemy lines?'

I shrugged. 'The same rules apply.'

'So what would happen if Jules Belmont turned out to have secrets that he didn't want others to know about?'

Promises, promises. 'Then once I'd found out what they were, I'd have something to tell my client.'

He thought about that for a moment, then laughed. 'Well, let's hope it doesn't come to that. Can your expenses run to a coffee and Calvados or should I ask for the check?'

I used the interlude to go to the loo. In the mirror my face looked ghostly and blurred. I applied a little cold water shock treatment. Jiminy had been right, as always. Although it was as much tiredness as booze. And, if I was honest, a little of something else. We were getting on well. Well enough to ignite a flame for the night ahead. The heat from it burned as well as warmed me. But then ten months is a long time, even when it comes to riding a bicycle. And I had talked to him for too long to make him entirely a stranger. I dug out my bag and started reconstructing my face. When I got to the eyes my hand wobbled and I stabbed myself in the eye with the mascara stick. Tut tut, Hannah, not so much drink as nerves. Or maybe it was cruder than that. Maybe I was just a little unsure how to behave. Who knows. He could be feeling the same. Some men say it's a relief, meeting a woman who's willing to take the initiative. You can see their point really. It gets cold out there, being in control. I would like to have talked about it, but I didn't quite have the nerve. It was the sort of conversation you have after, not before.

Over the coffee and Calvados we talked about him. My turn to get blood out of a stone. He'd been born and brought up in New York. His father had been a lawyer, but more interested in defending the left than the right, which in fifties America might have been good for the soul but was a lousy way of making a living.

'When he died in a car crash I was seventeen and there wasn't much in the bank. My mother's family had to pick up the pieces. She came back to France, her brother put me through business school.'

'So when did you leave the States?'

'Ten years ago.'

'What happened?'

He played with his brandy glass. 'Personal stuff.'

'Does that mean confidential?' He shrugged. 'OK. Let's put it another way. Were you leaving it or going to it?'

And this time he smiled. 'Leaving it. But only because it was about to leave me.'

'And now?'

'Now I work. Like you, I suspect. You want another coffee?'

I glanced down at my watch. It was nearly twelve. Around us the waiter was clearing the other tables. For an exclusive restaurant it was the nearest they would get to a hint. 'Perhaps we should let them go to bed.'

Freudian slip they call it. Ah well, too late to stop now. He was gentlemanly enough to let it pass without notice. 'Yes, perhaps we should.'

There followed a little silence, all full of life. He looked at me. I opened my mouth to say something but the words stuck half-way up my gullet. I have always felt sorry for women who blush. It must be a dreadful kind of exposure. I smiled at him. And he smiled back. And I was sure it was a kind of come on. At least it registered as such in the pit of my stomach. What more do you want, Hannah? I thought. If this reticence turns out to be just social cowardice, you'll be furious with yourself. Go on, say it. All he can do is refuse.

'It's been a great evening. D'you feel like making a night of it?'

And he carried on smiling as he shook his head and said, 'Sorry, Hannah, but there's someone else I have to see.'

CHAPTER NINE

I slept well, considering. I even remembered to drink a pint of water before going to bed, so that when my wrist started bleeping at 6.00 a.m. it didn't take the top of my head off with it. I decided to breakfast in my room, with a river of hot coffee and warm croissant. Food for thought.

So what are you waiting for? A couple of paragraphs about how I'd crawled back from the humiliation of the restaurant and cried all night into my pillow? Sorry. If it's any consolation, if I had done I probably wouldn't tell you anyway. But in the end it wasn't that big a deal. Of course it hurt – I mean nobody likes being told they're resistible – but since when did equality of the sexes mean that women got what they wanted? And when it came to it, sticks and stones . . . not to mention nothing ventured . . . and you can't make an omelette without . . . A poultice of clichés brought down the swelling. It could have been worse. Counting my blessings, the first was all the information I had got, the second was not having to pay the whole bill. If you think about it, you'd have to be a real louse to turn a lady down then let her pick up the check. Of course I offered, but I also gave in. Just as well. I would hate to think of Miss Patrick having to remortgage her sweet little cottage on the basis of one meal. In the end we went Dutch, which saved face and gave me enough for a taxi home. I left him picking up his coat from the cloakroom. I don't entirely remember whether I said goodbye. OK – so I was madder than I let on. It's called sub-text: the art of telling someone what they need to know without using the words. Grown men usually don't have much trouble with it. But among all the things he had let slip I certainly hadn't registered the bit about the settled home life or the steady lover. Now, now, Hannah, remember, God helps those . . . I applied another poultice, got up and headed for the shower. Jiminy was waiting with the towel. I retook my vows of celibacy in the face of duty and we made our peace. Back to work.

I got to the factory just before eight. Roissy was covered in fog, the iron man thrusting his thunderbolt through a pea-souper that might have been weather or industrial pollution. Inside, the Belmont babies were already making things fly. I was impressed. At 8.26 a.m. precisely the receptionist called me over. Would I take the lift to the third floor? Mr Belmont's assistant would meet me there.

To my shame I was anticipating a man. She was standing in the middle of the corridor, slap bang opposite the lift doors, and even at first glance you wouldn't have tried to get past her if you didn't have an appointment; Cerberus at the gates of hell. I followed meekly. At a quick estimate she was at least fifty-five, but her heels were still stiletto sharp and her figure looked as if it had had regular bondage practised on it. According to David Mercot – henceforth to be known as scumbag – Belmont had started his company in the late forties. At which point the dragon would have been just a slip of a girl, eager to make France great again. Maybe she had grown up with the firm. I wondered if she had nursed aspirations to becoming the third Madame Belmont. It might explain her aggression towards women younger than herself.

You couldn't miss his office. The corridor ended at it, a large dark wooden door with a brass plaque on it, big enough for a coffin lid. Inside the sanctum, an outer guardhouse, Cerberus' lair. She pointed to a chair and looked at her watch. When the big hand reached the six she pressed a buzzer beneath her desk. Into the intercom she said, 'Mr Belmont. Your eight-thirty appointment is here.' He murmured something back. She stood up and motioned me to do the same. Then she opened the door, walked in ahead of me and announced: 'Mademoiselle Wuulfe.' I stepped in and the door closed behind me. I looked towards the desk. It was empty.

He was sitting to the side, in a leather armchair, a glass coffee table in front of him. He looked very small, but then the office was very big. I walked across the carpet towards him. He became taller, thinner and older, a strong man felled by an erratic heartbeat. Alec Douglas Home was my first thought – the only British Prime Minister to have a skull for a head and a desiccated manner to go with it. Mummification was my second. He held out his hand. I tried not to grasp it too tightly in case it should crumble into dust. I was looking at a national hero, a man who had carried France out of the ruins of war into the prosperity of the late twentieth century. Three heart attacks later he hardly seemed strong enough to lift his own coffee cup. If it was strange for me, think what it must have been like for him: every morning to find himself lumbered with this body, wondering what happened to the young man with firm hands who laid dynamite tracks across Nazi railroads, always two jumps ahead of the enemy. What did you do in the war, Daddy? And was there really no romance to the suffering? I sort of wished we had the time to talk about it. But we didn't.

'Good morning, Miss Wolfe. You will forgive me if I don't get up to greet you. I am a little indisposed.' No one would argue with that. Except that close to, above the web of lines and sagging skin, the eyes were still bright, the voice surprisingly strong. In fact beneath the frailty, there was a definite brittle energy to the frame. He reminded me of a plant that needed watering. Maybe if you drenched him in Baby Bio all the parchment would fall away and a younger oilier man would appear. But as it was . . .? I thought about him and my lovely lithe young dancer. And I just couldn't see it. All this way on a hunch.

'You are English. But my assistant tells me you speak commendable French.'

'I am reasonably fluent, yes.'

[101]

'So I hear. I applaud you. In deference to an old man then we shall speak in my language rather than yours. I must apologize for not seeing you earlier.'

'I'm grateful you could find the time now.'

'Yes, well, I gathered from my assistant it was important. So, what can I do for you, Miss Wolfe? On your card it says you are a private investigator. I am a rather public man. What do we have in common?'

I kept it simple. In deference to my French and his age. I implied nothing but the knowledge I didn't have. I had been employed to track down a girl called Carolyn Hamilton who had turned up dead, eight months pregnant. Now my client wanted to know why. To do my job I needed to find out who the father was and where she had spent the last seven months. And via the Potential Employment Agency all roads led to Belmont Aviation. He listened intently, his eyes on my face the whole time. And I found myself thinking about Philip Marlowe and his visits to the ailing General Sternwood, drinking the old man's best brandy, but unable to give him back the vitality to cope with his wild erring daughters. *The Big Sleep*. In the end all it brought the General was more grief. And Marlowe never did work out who killed the chauffeur. Private eyes and rich old men: a fatal fictional attraction. Let's hope Belmont wasn't interested in storytelling. When I finished he sat back and was silent for a few moments. 'You may think I'm unforgivably old, Hannah, but believe me I am not stupid' – it had been my mother's favourite retort during a decade of conflict. It would do me good to remember it now.

'Tell me, Miss Wolfe, do I gather from this that it was you who called my nephew's office two days ago?'

Since there was no point in lying I told him it was. 'I'm sorry he couldn't help you. In fact, of course, since Carolyn Hamilton was never technically employed by Belmont Aviation he was absolutely correct in what he told you.'

'But she was employed by you?' I said quietly, while the massed bands of the Coldstream guards played the 'Hallelujah Chorus' in the background.

'Yes, indeed she was. But very briefly I'm afraid, so I'm not sure how much help I can be to you.'

'If you could just tell me what happened . . .'

'Of course. Well, as you already know from your inquiries I – under the auspices of Belmont Aviation – did advertise a post through the Potential Agency in London. As you will probably have noticed, both the advertisement and the questionnaire were somewhat vague on the exact nature of the employment. No doubt you have your own suspicions as to what the job entailed. I think it will probably help you to tell you the truth. It was not a job strictly connected to the company. It was instead a post inside my own family. What I was looking for was, for want of a better word, a social companion for my wife, Mathilde. I think I owe it to you to explain a little more fully. We have been married, my wife and I, for nearly six years now. During that time we have been trying to have a child. My wife is much younger than I but, alas, medical science is no respecter of age. And after a number of tests, Mathilde has had diagnosed certain problems which have, up until now, prevented her from conceiving. And since my health has deteriorated, well, it has become clear over the last year or so that we must resign ourselves to remaining childless. It has been less of a blow to me than my wife. I had to come to terms with the possibility of this with the death of my son some years ago, and I have always had my work to keep me involved. She, however . . . well, she has not found it so easy. Her doctor suggested that she go away, travel a little, but since my illnesses she has been unwilling to leave me. Of course she is much younger than I am, and has a good deal of time on her hands, so I—we—thought that perhaps some kind of companion more of her own age might help lift her out of the depression. She speaks excellent English, indeed she was a translator for the company for many years and is very fond of England. Equally, as I'm sure you appreciate, we were not eager to broadcast the news of her condition all over France. By advertising the post in London we felt we could avoid that. I was sure that if we could find the right young person, perhaps with an interest in the same kind of things . . . Anyway, the response was considerable. Carolyn Hamilton was one of the first we saw. We both liked her right from the start. My wife especially. As a girl she had been very interested in dance, even contemplated it as a career. So, of course, she and Carolyn had immediate things in common.

'You never met her, I assume? That's a great shame. She was a very vital young woman, maybe a little headstrong in some ways, but very charming and full of energy. Not unlike Mathilde herself. She also had a sense of adventure. In many ways she was perfect for the job. She seemed eager for a change, some time away to decide on her own future, and to meet other people. Over the course of the next couple of months we saw her a number of times. Each time we became more convinced. At the end of April we offered her the job and she accepted. She came almost immediately. For the first six or eight weeks the arrangement seemed to work very well. Then, quite abruptly, something changed. She became withdrawn, she complained of being tired and she was sick a number of times. Naturally we were worried. My wife even suggested she see a doctor. In the end that was not necessary. You know, of course, what was wrong. When she told us it came as a great shock. Particularly to my wife who was, as you can imagine, very upset. After all she had been through it was a particularly cruel irony. Of course I offered Carolyn whatever financial support she might need, but it was clear that she could not stay with us, it would have been too painful. Neither did she want to. She left, I think, at the beginning of July. Since then we have not heard or spoken to her. Needless to say we have often wondered what happened to her. Now, alas, I know. I can only say how deeply sorry I am. She was far too young for such a tragedy.'

There it was then, the Belmont end of the story all tied up with a neat red bow. She came, she worked and she left. According to the calendar it all fitted. The only obvious question marks were of my own making. The Belmont marital bed was the main one. A desire for children meant sex, him and her. 'Young, good-looking and devoted' – hadn't those been Mercot's words. It was

beyond my powers of fantasy. Like imagining one's parents fucking. But finally that was my problem not his. No doubt when I
am his age I too will curse thirty-five-year-olds for believing they
have a monopoly on desire. It was certainly no reason to disbelieve
him. And I'd had such great hopes of this one. Tough shit,
Hannah; since when was it ever handed to you on a plate? So,
start working.

'She didn't tell you who the father was?'

'We didn't ask and she didn't volunteer.'

'Did she give you any idea as to whether she was intending to
go through with the pregnancy?'

He was silent for a moment. 'All I can say is she gave us no
reason to believe otherwise.'

'And she didn't say where she was going?'

'No.'

'Can I ask you about money? I gather from her family that she
was quite badly in debt before she left England. Did she talk
about that at all?'

'Not in so many words. But we had got the impression that
there may have been some money problems, yes.'

'And did you give her money?'

'Of course. She was our employee. We paid her in full for the
eight weeks she worked for us, and I also gave her six weeks'
salary when she left. I offered more, but she would not accept. I
got the impression that the father, whoever he was, could provide
for her and I did not like to intrude further.'

'So how much would you have given her, in total?'

'Hmmn. Offhand I can't tell you an exact figure. But I believe
we had talked about an annual salary of around three hundred
thousand francs. So three and half months of that would have
been what – something like a hundred thousand.'

Or ten thousand pounds. Somewhat more than had been deposited in her savings account over those three months, but then
she could always have kept some back for rainy days to come.
Give or take a few thousand it still added up to a hefty salary for
what sounded like a fairly easy job. I said as much and he smiled.

[105]

'Miss Wolfe, as you have probably realized by now, I am a wealthy man. I am used to paying for what I want. And I wanted the right girl. I was willing to make it worth her while.'

'Do you have any idea what she did with the money?'

He frowned as if the very idea of asking would have been distasteful to him. 'No, none at all. I simply paid it into a Paris bank account as she requested. From there it was hers to do with as she wished.'

'And when she left in early July that was the last you heard from her?'

'Yes.'

'And you didn't find that rather strange? I mean you had been very generous. Didn't you hope she might keep in touch?'

'I'm an old man. The ways of young girls are something of a mystery to me. As I mentioned to you, Carolyn had a strong personality. I never for one moment believed that she wouldn't fall on her feet. To be honest I think I was grateful for her silence. Any news could have only further upset my wife.'

'And you're sure that Carolyn never got in touch with her either?'

'I'm sure. She would have told me if she had.'

'Does she tell you everything?'

'I don't think I . . .'

'I just thought . . . well, you said how fond of Carolyn she had been. I wondered if they might have exchanged words, I mean without your knowing.'

'Miss Wolfe, I understand your need to find out what happened to this poor girl, but I have told you everything I know. Everything *we* know. Carolyn Hamilton left here in June and we have heard nothing since. That is the full extent of the help I can give you.'

It was also the first hint that the old man in front of me was more than just Maurice Chevalier on a diet. I left a second's pause then said quietly, 'Would it be possible for me to have a word with your wife about all this?'

He smiled. 'Alas, I'm afraid not. As I'm sure I have made

clear, my wife is not a well woman. I wouldn't want her upset in any way. Particularly since I have kept the news of Carolyn's death from her.'

'Of course, I wouldn't need to tell her. I would just —'

'I'm sorry, Miss Wolfe, the answer is no.'

I accepted defeat, keeping my bad grace to myself. 'One other question. Your nephew, Daniel Devieux. He presumably knew about all of this?'

'Of course.'

'Was he involved at any stage?'

'Once again, I'm afraid I —'

'I gather from one of the applicants that she was in touch with him. I just wondered . . .' I let myself trail off.

He smiled. 'You have been busy. I hope they are paying you what you deserve. I was taken unexpectedly ill during last spring, just after the original advertisement was placed. My nephew stepped in to help with the arrangements.'

'So he met Carolyn?'

'Yes.'

'Did they get on well?'

'Miss Wolfe, I appreciate you have a job to do, but if you're asking me whether or not my nephew could possibly have been the father of the child, then the answer is categorically no. And in response to your next question I'm afraid the answer is still no. Daniel flew to Tokyo on business last night. Although no doubt when he returns in ten days' time he will be only too delighted to tell you all this himself. Now, if I can be of no further assistance . . .'

The audience was most definitely over. As if by magic the door behind us opened and Cerberus bounced in. Belmont offered me his hand again, the same cold dry touch. Like shaking hands with an iguana, I thought, even though I'd never done it. I was still on reptiles when the lift deposited me downstairs. No problem with pregnancy there. Just lay an egg and get on with it. Madame Belmont could even have done the sitting.

Outside, the weather had taken a turn for the worse. I know

how you feel, I thought, as I stood underneath the outside awning, watching the man of iron being pummelled by a sheet of rain. Fat lot of use his thunderbolt. Needless to say I had no umbrella. Back inside I called a taxi and wondered what to do next.

Mild schizophrenia took over. If Belmont's story was correct then I had just fallen down the longest snake on the board. All I had to look forward to was a plane ride home and a week throwing the dice to get the six I needed to start playing again. So much for schizo. Phrenia, on the other hand, had other ideas. According to her a story was only a story until it was verified by at least one other source. And since Devieux was airborne – a good deal too coincidentally for my liking—and Cerberus clearly wasn't the gossiping type, that meant tracking down Madame Belmont to hear her version of English companionship and fertility. It was just a question of finding out where to look.

The girl at the reception desk told me my car had arrived. I picked up my bag and left Belmont Aviation behind. Outside it was still lashing down. I wondered how much it would cost to take the cab all the way back to Paris, but after last night I didn't have the chutzpah to charge it to Miss Patrick. I gave him the name of the railway station and sat back and watched the rain.

CHAPTER TEN

I've always been a great believer in free will over destiny. I mean even if you fuck it up occasionally, making your own decisions has to be preferable to the idea that it's all been agreed already and you're just playing out the moves in someone else's game plan. So I'd like to think of what happened next as an example of positive nihilism; an act that had absolutely no meaning except what others, or in this particular case, I, chose to get out of it.

The car must have been parked in front of us all along. You'd think I would have registered a shiny black limo big enough to sublet, but it was pissing down, I was worried about my suit, and I had just decided to stop being a detective for a while. But even I couldn't miss the sight of the entourage that now emerged from the Belmont foyer. First came a security guard holding a huge black umbrella. He walked to the back door of the limo and stood there, umbrella poised above his head, waiting. Then came another man, hidden behind a hat and wielding another equally large umbrella. He positioned himself outside the foyer door. For a moment nothing else happened. It looked like a freeze frame before a musical sequence bursts into action: Americans in Paris dancing in the rain. Alas, the star of the show couldn't hoof it. He was a little too old. But he certainly wasn't an invalid. In fact for a man who just fifteen minutes before couldn't get up to shake hands he was pretty nifty on his feet. He was wearing a smart black raincoat, belted, with the collar turned up and an even smarter trilby. It took him maybe thirty seconds to make the journey from the door to the car with his henchmen providing a roof of umbrellas to save him from the smallest raindrop, and during that time nobody else either entered or left the building. I got the impression that the rest of the staff were all lined up behind the glass doors watching him go, like the servants at Manderley wishing goodbye to the master. No doubt Mrs Danvers was even now ordering them back to their posts.

The door to the limo slammed shut, leaving the security guard standing in the rain. The show was over. I was so busy wondering when to applaud I almost missed the next act. In front of me the taxi driver had been equally mesmerized. Now the spell broke.

'Where d'you say you were going?' he asked over his shoulder, as the limo started its engine and signalled to pull out from the forecourt.

You will, I hope, forgive me if I admit to a certain shiver of vocational pleasure at my next remark. 'I've changed my mind. Follow that car.'

Of course, it was touch and go. I mean he could have told me that he didn't do stunt work, or asked to see the colour of my money before showing me his finesse with the gears. In my experience taxi drivers are a bit like first dates, either they work out, or they're an unmitigated disaster. Still, after last night I deserved a romantic break. He shot me a fast frowning glance and said with more than a hint of professional pride, 'Do you want it obvious, or shall I keep my distance?'

'Keep your distance,' I said, trying to make it sound like the sort of decision I made every day. 'That is, if you can do it.' He offered me up the kind of look which a Frenchman reserves for legless frogs, swung back to the wheel and let out the clutch.

The first ten minutes or so went strictly according to the movies. The limo was so large and so fast that it didn't have to boast and it took the cruise through the industrial zone at a quiet pace. Monsieur cabbie, who had evidently seen the same films as I had, lit up a cigarette and relaxed back into his seat, keeping at an easy distance. The zone ended on the outskirts of Roissy. Left took you back into town, right was signposted to the autoroute. The limo turned right and started to pick up speed.

The autoroute sorted out the men from the rally drivers. The limo slid straight into the fast lane and never looked back. The gap between us widened. In the back I could feel the palms of my hands getting moist. The taxi driver moved into the middle, wound down his window and tossed away the cigarette butt. Then he put his foot down. For the first few minutes I still thought we were going to lose him. But for a little car it had a big engine and gradually the distance between us began to diminish. I wondered vaguely about a speed limit, and how an important businessman such as Belmont would probably like to be seen as someone who upheld the law, in little ways at least. Anyway, why should he rush? He didn't know he was being chased. The gap between us was constant now, the limo well within our sights. The French countryside zipped past looking much like any other landscape in fast forward. I felt a certain exhilaration at the smell of the chase and the pleasure of a cliché come true. We'd been going for another few minutes and had just passed the turn-off for Charles de Gaulle airport when I first thought about the meter.

The big hand was already reading 197 francs and the little dial on the right was whizzing round fit to bust. I had a sudden horrible thought, too horrible to share with the cab driver. I slid my handbag on to my knee and felt inside for my wallet. I had cashed a hundred pounds at the airport, but it had been a lousy rate and I had intended to change more at a bank in town today. One hundred minus yesterday's cabs, lunch, drinks and my half of dinner must have come to at least fifty-five. I fingered through the notes. Delacroix's revolutionary flag-carrier flashed her breasts at me, four times. Four hundred francs. Plus some small change, which I was too frightened to count lest he hear me from the front and realize the problem. I looked back at the clock: 215 and rising. Funny how you never come across this one in the movies. In front of us the limo was cruising confidently. What had the first taxi driver told me that morning in Roissy? While other tycoons live close to the office Belmont goes where his work force is. Oh Christ.

I timed the meter against the second hand of my watch. The centimes positively raced by. At 150 kph we were clocking up nearly a pound a minute. At this rate in less than twenty minutes I would run out of money. Great. How come everyone else's classic moments were always my most shabby? I began rehearsing an eloquent little speech about personal cheques and the value of the English pound, while the meter spun round in joyful abandon. We were hovering on 300 when the driver cursed and braked swiftly. I looked up in time to register the limo cutting across us ahead of us into the far right lane and signalling its intention to take the next slip road. A sign flashed by announcing a place beginning with S, but I couldn't make out any more. Wherever it is, please God make it close to the autoroute.

The rain had turned to drizzle now. The taxi driver cut into the slow lane four or five cars behind. Sure enough, the limo took the right fork off the autoroute. We followed, but at a distance. For the first time since I had started practising maths I noticed the countryside. It was flat, with long rolling fields, and pockets of quite dense forestation against the horizon. The taxi driver pulled back; we were the only cars on the road now and to be too close would only draw attention to ourselves. The road curved and we lost the limo in the folds of the hedgerows. I went back to the clock: 347 and rising steadily. We slowed right down to take a sharp descending bend, passing a small stone cottage, half derelict, on the left and a sturdy handsome farmhouse opposite, all coloured bricks and freshly painted shutters. And then, as we came out of the long curve a pair of iron gates flashed by on the right with a glimpse of a long gravel road and a large building at the end of it. The road ahead was straight for the next fifty, maybe hundred yards, but the limo was nowhere to be seen. The driver put his foot down and we ate up the gap between us and the edge of the immediate horizon. Another long slice of road greeted us, dipping and meandering, but still visible

[112]

and still deserted. He slammed on the brakes, said something deeply disparaging about the Virgin Mary and did a three point turn in two.

Twenty yards before the iron gates he stopped again and turned to me, glancing at the meter on his way round. It was flashing a triumphant 368. 'You want to get out here or do you want me to wait for you?' he asked abruptly and the half-naked French women in my bag shivered in anticipation. Fuck it, I thought, I don't know.

'How far is it to the nearest town?'

He grunted. 'Senlis? Three, maybe four kilometres.'

I took a deep breath. 'Look, I've got four hundred francs in my bag. If you waited for me, just for a few moments, then drove me there would I still have enough money to pay you?'

He stared at me for a moment then said darkly. 'And what would you have done if the meter had said 410 now?'

I smiled. 'I suppose I would have got out 10 francs ago.'

He shrugged his shoulders in one of those extravagant, ir-refutably French gestures which bad English actors love to copy. And then he laughed. Thank God for the Second World War, I thought. Who says history doesn't count? 'OK, I wait. But you make it quick. And' – I was halfway out of the door already – 'you leave your handbag here.'

Even seen at a distance through the gates it was the kind of house which made you understand why the French had had a revolution. It wasn't so much its size as its arrogance. Look at me, it said with utter confidence, aren't I more beautiful than the landscape? And so it was: perfect symmetry and a simplicity of elegance that was dazzling. I counted ten windows on the top floor and four from the top down to the bottom. What did they do, the Belmonts – rotate slowly through the year, or keep the odd wing in splendid Miss Haversham-type decay? Certainly the place looked deserted, and but for the limo, lying like a large well-groomed black cat near the doorstep, you might have been fooled into thinking there was no one at home. What would happen if I creaked open the gates and crunched my way up the gravel to the big front door? Having come so far, would he really refuse to let me see her?

I put my hand up to the gate, to see if some faithful old retainer would come shuffling out from a concealed gatehouse to take my calling card. I rattled the lock. The retainer, it turned out, had friends. They came bounding out from the bushes to the left of the house, yelping and yowling, three streaks of black pedigree muscle built out of the French equivalent to Alpo and the odd leg of trespasser. I forced myself to walk and not run back to the car. Inside, the driver started the engine. In the mirror I watched him trying to keep a straight face.

Senlis took ten minutes. I was too busy with the meter to give it a lot of attention, but the square where he dropped me was old and cobbled, though the vehicles more Renault than *Jean de Florette*. The clock read 427 francs. I counted out the four notes and then added three ten-franc coins that had grown warm in my palm as I clutched them over the last mile or so. He took the money and looked at it. Then up at me. 'Is this it?'

I registered a small ripple of panic. 'I told you,' I said. 'I only had four hundred francs and some coins. Unless you're willing to drive me to a bank and wait while I try to cash some foreign notes, that's all I have.'

He made a face and pocketed the notes. Then he gave me back the three coins. 'You might need to buy yourself a coffee while you wait for the bank to open,' he said, grinning broadly. He started the engine. 'Oh, and if you want to find the house again, tell the taxi driver you're looking for the Belmont château, near Villemetrie. Everyone knows it.' And he chuckled to himself as he pulled away into the traffic. I looked down at the three coins in my hand and thought idly about what could have been the bus fare from Roissy to Senlis. 'Hannah, my darling,' Frank's voice said in my left ear, 'how many times have I told you, expenses are expensive and there's usually a cheaper way to get what you want.' Oh, get stuffed Frank, I said out loud as I turned and started looking for the bank.

By lunchtime I had money in my purse and a place to stay.

[114]

More a guesthouse than a hotel, but clean, quiet and cheap enough to assuage my conscience about a hundred quid frittered away on meals and a taxi cab. I called the hotel in Paris and told them if they needed the room they could have it. I would be back in a day or so to pick up my things. Then I followed the landlady of the pension up ever-narrowing stairs to the top of the house. From my window I could see a pattern of old roofs rising up to the spire of the cathedral. Exquisite. I told her so. She nodded approvingly and hovered behind me in the doorway. I used it as an excuse for conversation. I asked her about local colour and historic houses and it didn't take long to get on to Villemetrie and the lovely château hidden behind green gates. Oh yes, everyone knew the Belmont estate. Built in the mid seventeenth century it had belonged to minor aristocracy whose descendants had survived the guillotine only to go slightly batty through inbreeding. Belmont had bought it twenty years ago and gradually refurbished it, room by room, back to its former glory. That much was civic knowledge; but not much else. The Belmonts, it seemed, were not a sociable couple, especially the new Madame. She kept herself very much to herself, except for the times when she was in Paris buying her way through the department stores. Senlis was evidently too small and too provincial for her. She delivered this information with a certain curl of the lip. Two hundred years after the revolution the nouveau riche, it seemed, were no more democratic than the old first estate. So much for politics, what about transport?

Three p.m. saw me out on the road to Villemetrie, my skirt tucked up under the saddle and my bag, with a bottle of wine and a baguette, clipped to the back panier. It was not the kind of model to tour France in, but the gradients were gentle and according to Madame, who had hired it to me for the day, it had been around long enough to know the roads of its own accord. In the old days, she said, like an advert for the French tourist board, people had cycled everywhere, and the countryside was better for it. After the first couple of kilometres I stopped feeling like something out of the French resistance and got into my stride. Even the physical activity felt good after so many days spent grubbing around in the inner recesses of my brain. The rain had long stopped and the sun had come out. Some way outside town I had to stop to take off my jersey. Thanks to the destruction of the ozone layer the air was definitely too warm for March, but as a Friend of the Earth I was able to take pleasure from it without being crippled by guilt. I passed two other cyclists on the way, an old man and a younger woman with a baby on her back. We greeted each other with a wave. For a while I saw no one. I began to feel as if I were travelling through time. Maybe when I arrived at the Belmont château I would be met by aristocrats in shepherdess gowns playing at poverty, and Carolyn Hamilton would be just a memory in the future. Carolyn Hamilton, my client's adopted daughter: a young dancer who had pirouetted off a river bank with a baby inside her struggling to get out. The mystery. The reason I was here. I had not thought of her since this morning and already this morning seemed a long time ago. Now, as a form of discipline, I imagined myself following in her footsteps, whistling down country lanes to the sound of French crickets and the occasional carrion crow. Had she been happy here? For how long? And whose seed did she have sprouting in the summer sun? Maybe I was riding on the edge of an answer. I could almost feel it, ripe in the bushes of the Belmont estate, waiting to be plucked. The road dipped and the bicycle flew towards the bottom of the hill. If there was ever a moment of invincibility it was now.

Villemetrie was so small I must have missed it. No longer a village, just a scatter of houses and then on out into the country-side again. In front of me a straight stretch of road opened out, ending in a long slow curve in the distance. It was somewhere here that Batman and I had lost the car and turned back towards the iron gates. I slowed down and sure enough, over a line of trees I caught a glimpse of the rooftops of the house, square and rhythmical like a chessboard. I felt a small frisson of nerves in my stomach. Why don't you drive on past, whispered a traitorous voice in my bowels, so low I thought it must be the wind in the fields. Lie in a wood, eat your bread and cheese and drink the wine, then fly home with a bottle of Calvados and memories of an early French spring. No lunch till after work, Hannah, boomed the rest of me. Get off your bike and get in there.

I searched around for a suitable place to leave it. Senlisians were no doubt salt-of-the-earth types, but living in London breeds a certain paranoia when it comes to stolen bikes and among the many possible scenarios imagined for this particular afternoon a three-mile hike back to town was not one of them. In the end I stuck it and the rucksack in a ditch by the edge of a field and covered it over with a few brambles.

The dogs were nowhere to be heard. I rattled the gates. Nothing. Maybe they were sleeping off the effects of a French peasant caught earlier in the day. In my bag were two kilos of best horsemeat wrapped up in polythene, just in case. The car from this morning was gone too. An afternoon take-over bid meeting or a garage? Hard to know. At the end of the drive the house shimmered in the sun. The gates seemed to be the only way in. Is this where the tradesmen came, marching milk and toilet paper up to the main house in full view of a score of blinking windows? Since I had most definitely not been invited, and I had nothing to sell, I decided not to risk it.

I followed the wall for maybe a quarter of a mile up the other side of the long hill until I found a place where the conjunction of trees and branches let me climb in. It was a five- or six-foot drop down the other side, but the ground was soft. I landed with a muffled thud. The forest closed in around me. No dogs, no birds, nothing. I stood for a while getting my bearings. The house was somewhere off to my right. I struck out in that direction. The land graduated downhill. Eventually at the bottom, slicing its way through a shallow valley I came across a small river fast running. The walk had made me thirsty but the water running through my fingers was none too clean and bitter to taste. I let it slide away. I climbed across a strategic bridge of stones and pushed my way along the valley floor. As the trees cleared I was rewarded with a sudden spectacular sight: a long rolling lawn punctuated by huge chestnut trees rising up until it reached the back façade of the house, grand and solid. Next to it a semi-circle of stables where horses had been long since gazumped in favour of houseguests or servants, and halfway across a sheet shimmer of light, the sun playing games with the surface of a long kidney-shaped lake covered in weeds and lilies. You could see how for your average aristocrat it was the kind of view that might lead you to forget the plight of the third estate.

I skirted around the edge of the lawn and approached the main house from the side. And as I did so the romantic gave way to the realist. Not before time. Running down the back walls of the house through the ivy I could make out at least a couple of alarm systems. I had cut my teeth on urban bedsits and the occasional locked car. This was not exactly the kind of challenge I was looking for. Even assuming Madame Belmont had a story to tell, how the hell was I going to get in to hear it from her?

For the second time that day fate interrupted. It made one hell of a noise. Maybe someone had just let them loose, or maybe they'd recently been fed and were lazy from full stomachs, but once they realized I was there they didn't let up. They covered the distance between the side of the house and the back lawn in less than twenty seconds (or maybe it was ten, to be honest I wasn't counting). At that speed they looked like hell hounds rather than dogs: not the kind of animal to check the name on the card before they started chomping. The stables were less than fifty yards to my left. In my bag my fingers squelched on raw meat. I pulled it out, ripping it from the paper and flinging it in a long arc across the grass. I didn't stop to see if they were still hungry. I sprinted my way round the back of the stables and went for anything with a handle on it. There was a merciful pause in the sound effects, then from a long way away I heard a man's voice calling out. The door wouldn't budge, but the little window just above to the right rattled comfortingly. I gave it an almighty thump with my right shoe and it swung open. The sound of the dogs was closer as I hoisted myself in.

[118]

How come it's always the loo? 'Ventilation versus security' – a short monograph on the pleasures of breaking and entering. I closed the window behind me and lowered myself on to the loo seat. I could hear them, somewhere outside the walls exhorting me to come out and lay myself between their teeth. I sat stock still. The man's voice was louder now. 'Come on, come here boys, leave it alone. It's gone. Come on.' Hannah Wolfe, not so much a secret agent as a rabbit, run to ground. I stayed with my whiskers trembling for a while longer. Then when my heart had returned to its normal relationship with the rest of my body I got up and opened the door.

The first thing that greeted me was the stillness, an ocean of it, deep and dark. It humbled as well as reassured me. Houses that have been shut up for the season have a particular charged quality to the air, as if the silence had built up gradually over time until there is too much for the house itself and it starts pushing at the doors and window-frames, trying to get out. A wave of it hit me now as I stood there. I stepped aside to let it past. It's one of the skills of the job, establishing a good re-lationship with silence. In my experience you can waste a lot of energy being frightened by things you haven't heard. I waited for my eyes to reprogramme. In the dim light I picked out a quarry-tiled hall with three doors leading off. I picked the nearest. It was a large room, gloomy with light filtered through closed shutters. I made out a sofa and two easy chairs on a polished wood floor. Simple, nice. In high summer with the sun streaming in it must have been magical. I turned and went out.

The staircase led up into darkness. The banister was cold under my fingers. I counted seventeen treads in a wide wooden spiral. Then at the top more darkness and the impression of a landing stretched out like a girls' dormitory, doors, like beds, in neat rows. I picked my way along the wall till I hit the first door. For my sins it was another bathroom, but at least in this one there were shutters not quite closing out the light. And the door in the wall at the end had to lead somewhere.

It was like entering a secret garden, a bedroom, but big enough to be its own world, decorated by wide zebra stripes of sunlight slicing in through the half-open shutters. They flattened everything in their path; the double bed with its patchwork silk quilt, the chair, and the teak chest of drawers with a single art deco vase on it. My footsteps made sharp music on the wooden floor. Almost immediately I heard another sound in my head. That of dancers' feet tapping out points rhythm on a rehearsal-room floor, their bodies reflected to infinity in a trap of wall mirrors. Maybe it was the light playing games, or the association of treading wooden boards, or maybe there was something about its sparseness and simplicity that reminded me of that other room so far away. Whatever it was I had this sudden sensation that this was it; that I was standing in a room where Carolyn Hamilton had been before me. I went to the window and eased open the shutters. The afternoon sun came streaming in and I looked out over a view of gardens and forest. But there was no sense of her out there. Only in here.

I had been waiting for this. I began to search. I went through the dresser and the bedside table. But all I found was soft lining paper and a clinging odour of pot pourri and mothballs. I upturned the vase and looked under the bed. If she had lived in this room for a while she would have left something of herself behind, however small. I went back into the bathroom. But here again everything was scrubbed clean. There was nothing: no tissues, no nail clippings, no safety pins, not a single sign of human detritus. Either I was mistaken or someone had cleared up too well. In the end I admitted defeat. I closed the shutters and left.

Downstairs I had left the door to the sitting-room open. I moved in to close it and as I did so something caught my eye. On the wall near the half light of the window hung a picture, a figure in the middle. I went closer. It was a dancer, delicately painted in watercolour, standing on a stage, her chin held high into the spotlight, drinking in the light. Signs. They come in all shapes and sizes. If she had slept in a bedroom she would also have sat in a living-room. I slid off a shutter catch and propped it open a fraction. Outside the magic circle of the sofa and rug were now revealed a bookcase and a small desk. It was locked. On top there was a cut-glass paperweight and underneath it, two small keys. One of them fitted the lock. Inside it was just a regular writing desk, paper and envelopes in neat little stacks. And two small drawers. It was in the second I found them: a small stack of Degas dancers waiting in the wings, bent low over their shoes, caught like animals by the eye of the artist. I had seen them before, in a pink folder which I had studied on a train journey in the rain a million years ago. I picked them up. There must have been seven or eight of them. I was almost too scared to look at them. One by one, like the wrong playing cards in a game of poker, they turned over blank. Until the last. That one had an address on it: Miss A. Patrick, Rose Cottage, it read. And on the opposite side a simple message. It was so boring it made my fingers tingle. 'Saw the Christmas Nutcracker at Covent Garden. Disappointing. Tour has fallen through. Plan to visit some time in the spring. Hope you are well. Happy New Year, love Carolyn.' And in the corner a date. '14 January.'

CHAPTER ELEVEN

'He is not in.'

Whooppee, 'I see, then I wonder if you'd tell Madame Belmont that I'm here.'

'Who are you?'

You could tell even from the way she had opened the door that they didn't get many uninvited visitors. Not surprising really, considering the dogs. I had sprinted the distance between the stables and the front and arrived mercifully unsavaged. We had already taken a cordial instant dislike to each other, she and I. For her part no doubt it was my dress sense: too much denim and decidedly muddy boots. For me it was her face, long and thin with a mouth that probably hadn't smiled since the suppression of the student riots in 1968. I gave her my brightest little grin, usually reserved for traffic wardens. 'If you just say I'm a friend of Carolyn Hamilton, from England.'

I suspect if it hadn't been such obvious gross bad manners she would have shut the door in my face and left me on the doorstep. As it was she told me to wait in the hall, while she pitter-pattered her way off down the corridor, disappearing off through a door at the end like the white rabbit in search of the queen. I admired the decor, counted to ten then followed her.

Where I had anticipated eighteenth-century chintz I found greenery, acres of it. I was standing just inside a large conservatory, the sun streaming in through glass panels on to a jungle of plants. In the middle like a temporary safari camp was an elegant white cane three-piece suite and a wrought-iron table on which stood a pot of coffee and a satisfyingly large cup. The air was heady with that sticky warmth that comes from too many plants and too few people to use up the oxygen. The word sanatorium came to mind. I caught sight of the housekeeper, a flash of dark hair amid the foliage, talking intently. Somewhere in the tropical rainforest the mistress was listening. I cleared my throat. The housekeeper turned, shot me a murderous look and hurled herself in my direction. I was getting ready to step aside, when a woman's voice, cool and commanding, stopped her in her tracks.

'Leave it be, Agnes. Since the lady has come all this way, of course I will see her.'

When she stepped out from the jungle I had trouble keeping my eyes in my head. If money can't buy you love it can certainly get you beauty. Tall, maybe five nine or ten, with long slender limbs and a cap of short shining fair hair, Madame Belmont was a real stunner. She was also, I realized with a shock that was almost physical, very like somebody I already knew. Or at least felt I knew. Grow the hair, stick her in a pair of ballet shoes and an acre of tulle and what would you have but a second Carolyn Hamilton. Funny Belmont hadn't seen fit to tell me. But then, of course, he wasn't intending us to be introduced.

She walked forward smiling and offered me a hand. Close to she wasn't as young as Carolyn, mid thirties, maybe older, but she was one of those women for whom age holds no terrors. Her bone structure had seen to that. She smiled, and it struck me that for a woman reputedly severely depressed she looked a picture of health. Even her skin glowed. Either she was on a miracle medication or someone had been telling a whopper.

'Good afternoon. And are you . . .?'

'Hannah, Hannah Wolfe.'

'I'm pleased to meet you, Miss Wolfe. We don't get many unexpected callers these days. Would you like coffee? Or maybe you'd prefer tea?' Her English was good, the accent light and charming in an Isabelle Huppert kind of way. She had probably been good at her job, although it must have been clear to everyone that she was destined for higher things.

'Thank you. Coffee would be fine.'

She translated my preference to Agnes who clearly thought it was beneath her to wait on someone like me, but couldn't quite bring herself to revolt. She snorted her displeasure then turned on her heel in the manner of a Prussian guardsman and flounced out of the room. I had the feeling I hadn't heard the last from her. But for now it was just the two of us. I felt the sense of occasion upon us. I smiled at her. She beckoned me to sit down, then settled herself opposite, drawing her long silky legs up under her. I found myself staring at her. It didn't seem to bother her. She was obviously one of those women who was used to being looked at. I was still working out which approach would best undermine her apparent sense of confidence when she said, 'Were you a close friend of Carolyn's? You must have been devastated. I still don't quite believe it. She was so energetic. It seems almost impossible to accept that she's dead.'

I slipped my hand underneath my chin just in case my mouth had fallen open involuntarily. 'I wouldn't want her upset in any way, particularly since I have kept the news of Carolyn's death from her.' The very words. For a war hero Jules Belmont may have gone for beauty but he had scant commitment to the truth. I decided not to model myself on him.

'Actually, Madame Belmont, I'm not exactly a friend of Carolyn. I'm a private investigator. I've been employed to look into the circumstances surrounding her death.'

She stared at me for a moment, as if assessing the likelihood of my success. 'Goodness. You look rather young for such a job,' she said, then smiled. 'But then I expect people always tell you that.'

I nodded. The same could be said of you, oh third wife of an ageing war hero, I thought but did not say.

'How did you find us?'

I told her briefly, leaving out the bits which involved theft. It sounded quite impressive.

'I see. And now you want to ask me about Carolyn?'

'Yes.'

She nodded. 'Well, I'm not sure I know what to say. I think you'd be better off talking to my husband.'

'I already have.'

And something flickered behind the eyelids. He must have warned her, surely. What else could they have talked of over lunch? 'Well, I really don't know what more I can add . . .'

'He told me that you employed Carolyn Hamilton as a companion back in May. That she stayed for just over eight weeks, and then, when she discovered she was pregnant, she left.'

She held my gaze. For a moment she said nothing. I had a fleeting impression of something, a quality of concentration in her, the sense that she was watching me as hard as I was watching her. Then, suddenly, she dropped her eyes. 'Yes, I think that's more or less right. I'm afraid I'm not very good on dates.' And above her head a banner unfurled. It read: 'I am lying.' Softly, softly, Hannah.

'I wonder, Madame Belmont – during the time she was here did Carolyn ever ask you or your husband to post any letters or cards for her? From England.'

She appeared to think about it. 'As far as I can remember, no. But you'd have to check with Jules. Or perhaps Daniel. Daniel often travels to London for work. If she'd wanted something posted he could have taken it for her.'

'I see. But I gather Daniel is away at the moment. On business.'

'Is he?' And this time she looked up, evidently surprised. 'I didn't know that.'

'Why did she leave, Mrs Belmont?'

'I thought my husband told you. She was pregnant.'

'And you didn't think of asking her to stay?' I said this time in French.

The change of language threw her for a second. She frowned, as if she had not completely understood the question. I didn't give her time to think about it.

'Madame Belmont, I gather you and your husband have been trying for some years to have a child.'

Still she said nothing. Then she looked me straight in the eye. And I could tell she knew what I was thinking. 'Yes,' she said in a firm voice. 'Yes, we have.'

'But with no success.'

'No.'

'That must have been painful for you both. I mean especially since your husband's only child died in the accident.' It was so easy I was beginning to feel sorry for her.

'My husband wanted a child very much, if that's what you mean.'

'And you?'

'Me?' And now we were really volleying, both our eyes firmly on the ball.

'That must have been very important for you too?'

This time she hesitated. 'I wonder how old you are, Miss Wolfe? Haven't you ever thought about having a child? Don't all women of around our age?'

And coming as it did, right out of the far court slamming on to the baseline, I had to let it bounce twice. As I looked back over the net I thought just for a second that I saw her smile. And just for that same second I wondered who was baiting who. She was the one to break first. She looked away. But then, of course, she didn't have Carolyn Hamilton's postcards nestling like a warm gun in the bottom of her pocket.

'Forgive me, Madame Belmont, but the reason I mention it is because I just wondered why, when Carolyn told you she was pregnant, you didn't think of a way in which you could all benefit from this "accident". I mean there she was, a talented young dancer with a career before her and a baby that was evidently not planned and there you were, a devoted couple desperate to have child. I wonder why you didn't offer to adopt it.'

To give her her due she treated it as a serious suggestion. In fact she appeared to give it a good deal of thought. Then she said, softly, 'I'm afraid that could not have been possible. You see, my husband would not have been interested in having someone else's child. He only wanted his own.'

'You mean his and yours?'

'No, I mean his own.'

And once again I had this strange feeling that, against all the odds, this was all some kind of game between us. A game which she was enjoying as much as I was. His own? Well, why not? I mean what is it they say about all cats being grey in the dark, especially fair-haired ones? No way of putting that tactfully.

'Forgive me, Mrs Belmont, but you are absolutely sure that the child Carolyn was carrying was not your husband's?'

And if she was shocked, then it certainly didn't register. She held my gaze and shook her head slowly. 'Yes, Miss Wolfe. I am absolutely sure. Sadly, it was not.'

Sadly? the word hung between us, enjoying the attention it was getting. But inside my pocket the postcards were burning a hole in the palm of my hand. I took a deep breath. 'Madame Belmont, I think I should tell you I know that Carolyn didn't leave here last June. I know, in fact that she stayed much longer. As long as January of this year.'

I left a dramatic little pause. But she didn't fill it.

I pulled out the cards and held them up towards her. 'I know because of these. I found them in a room in the stable house. They are identical to the ones Carolyn's guardian received throughout last year. As you can see, the last one, which was never sent, is in her hand writing and is dated 14 January.'

You know I really think if we'd been given the time, she would have told me. As it was she was still staring at me when Agnes marched back in. It was, of course, far too much of a coincidence to be such. I wondered where she had been standing that had allowed her to hear it all. She placed herself firmly between Mathilde and me. I pocketed the cards quickly.

'Madam, I'm sorry to interrupt, but there's an urgent phone call for you in the drawing-room.'

I bet there is. Belmont tracked down in his limo, racing home towards a wife incapable of keeping the family secrets. I could see his point now. If I were her husband I wouldn't let me within a mile of her either.

She stood up, and now, I thought, her eyes seemed rather glazed. She gave me a big bright smile, a sort of parody of a social occasion. 'I'm sorry. If you'll excuse me, Miss Wolfe.'

As she went out of the door he came in. I wouldn't have called him overgrown, but there was definitely something about him that made you take him seriously. The bane of my life, heavies. It's at times like this I always regret the fourteen years I didn't spend in discipleship to a Tibetan martial arts master. Of course Frank has given me a couple of tips. But that and the self-defence class at the Holloway adult institute just doesn't do it. I got to my feet and picked up my bag.

'Well, I'd better be getting on my way. If you'd be so good as to show me the way out?' I passed Agnes, hovering. She was so pleased she almost smiled.

They saw me to the front door. Then he saw me to the gate. The next bit was more tricky. The bicycle would give me away as living too close to home. On other hand how else had I got there? I went for the hired car parked in Villemetrie, taking a risk that the mile and half was more than he wanted to walk there and back. I was right. He did however accompany me part of the way and when I turned around on the brow of the hill he was still there in the middle of the road, legs planted firmly apart, arms crossed. I gave him a jaunty wave and continued on my way. This time I kept walking. I was almost into Villemetrie when I stopped and looked back. The road was empty. I counted to three hundred, then doubled back, uncovered the bike, took a long swig from the carafe of wine and headed for home.

CHAPTER TWELVE

Now I knew, of course, it had been obvious all along. The weather, the odd dance performance, a bit of chat about this and that – there had never been anything in any of Carolyn's postcards which couldn't have been gleaned from any English newspaper or magazine. A copy of the *Guardian* two days late regurgitated on to a card in Senlis and posted in London and, hey presto, Carolyn Hamilton was alive and well and living in Kilburn.

It had its own satisfaction, like finding the last piece in a jigsaw puzzle. The January postcard now sat reunited with its sisters, laid out on my bed in front of me. So Carolyn had been here all along. And the cards proved something else. They proved beyond a shadow of a doubt that the baby was meant for someone else. Why else go to all the trouble and deceit of pretending she was still working in England, single and most definitely not pregnant? And if it was meant for someone else, then who could that possibly be but the childless, wealthy Belmonts? So, according to Mathilde, it wasn't his flesh – strangely, even though I know I shouldn't, I had believed her. That didn't mean it still couldn't be in the family. The flying nephew had yet to be discounted, although he would hardly tell me the truth even if I could get to him. Either way it didn't really matter that much. They were desperate for a child and she had one to offer. This way everyone got what they needed, she enough money to get her out of debt – no doubt there would have been more cash promised on delivery – and they a little Belmont to take on the family name.

So far so symmetrical. Except, of course, for the unhappy ending. What could have happened between 6 December and 14 January to propel her back across the Channel and into the river? And what could have been serious enough to have everyone treating it like a national defence secret guarded by dogs, housekeepers, French postcards stamped in England and Belmont's smokescreen of lies to anyone who came asking awkward questions? Certainly nobody wants a suicide on their hands, particularly not someone of Belmont's national prominence. But it was hardly his fault. And what makes the headlines in England probably wouldn't raise an eyebrow in France. Tough business, this detecting. A couple of answers and what do you get but more questions. When in doubt put yourself in their shoes. I conjured up an image of Belmont, old, dry and angry, sitting at his big desk while his secretary tried to raise my Paris hotel on the line, only to be told I had checked out that very afternoon. What would he do next? Wait for me to get in touch, or try to find me? After all, I had to be staying somewhere, and somewhere near enough, presumably, to get to Villemetrie. Put like that it was child's play. Only a question of time, and not long at that.

In my little room the sun had dropped behind the rooftops and it was getting chilly. It would be dark within the hour. I pulled the window closed and put on the bedside light. Rather than wait to be discovered, I decided to take the initiative.

It was almost 6.00 p.m. Not late for a workaholic. But I got Cerberus again, barking her way down the phone. The boss was not available.

'Then maybe I can leave him a message. Perhaps you'd tell him I will meet him tomorrow morning outside the main entrance to the Louvre. Let's say 10.00 a.m.?'

'That is absolutely impossible. He is in meetings all day.'

'Fine. But perhaps you'd tell him anyway. I think he'd like to know.'

'But –'

I put the phone down. To my surprise my hand was shaking slightly. 'And you never get scared?' Scumbag's teasing question slid into my mind along with a picture of a tasty man in a good suit. Frank, never a man to respect privacy, joined in. 'You know what I say, Hannah. It's only as dangerous as you're stupid enough to make it. Why do you think coppers always go out in pairs? So someone's covering your back. You get into trouble – how do I know where to look for you if I don't know where you've been? Boy Scouts' motto. Be prepared.' Thanks, Frank. Who needs friends when you've got employers?

I didn't have the right change to call England, so I reversed the charges. 6.30 p.m. in France, 5.30 p.m. English time. Frank would be cleaning his Smith and Wesson and thinking of all the pubs he could be in. Or he could, of course, be in them already. Since answering machines do not accept reverse-charge calls the operator informed me that I would have to call again. I gave her another number. At the other end I heard a high-pitched little shout before they cut me off. Amy, guardian of the telephone. A few seconds later Kate's voice broke through.

'Hannah? Hello there. What's up?'

'Oh, not a lot. I'm here for a few days and I thought I might pick up an outfit for Amy, but I couldn't remember her size.'

'Where's here?' She seemed so close I wondered why they needed a Channel tunnel. Why couldn't we all just drive along the telephone lines?

'Senlis. A little town to the North East of Paris.'

'You working?'

'Ahah.'

'Your sad pregnant little dancer?'

'Yep.'

'Find the father?'

'Not yet.'

'You all right?'

'Fine. As I said I just called to get Amy's size.'

'I think they might be different in France, though you could always say three years. But I wouldn't bother. She'll probably

[131]

have grown out of it by the time you get back. Why don't you bring her something for later. How about a poster of Johnny Halliday? By the time she's ten he'll probably be a cult hero again.'

'Johnny et Sylvie. *Vers une nouvelle séparation?*' Headlines from a dozen *Paris Matches* came back to me, found lying in the dusty corners of Brittany guesthouses and painstakingly translated on the beach while the wind whipped sand in our seven-stone weakling faces. Family holidays, we used to call them. *In loco parentis*: for years I thought it meant a form of madness brought on from spending too much time with your parents. No wonder I preferred to work. But some things are never forgotten, especially by sisters. On the line Kate was talking.

'What?'

'I said are you sure you're all right? You sound strange.'

'No. I'm fine. Just busy. I'll be back in a few days.'

'OK. Listen, I'm sorry to cut this short, but Benjamin's howling, it's Amy's bathtime and Colin isn't home yet . . .'

'No problem. It's your phone bill anyway. I'll call you when I get back.'

'OK. Oh, wait. Just say goodbye to Amy.'

I put down the phone with the little voice still chattering brightly in my ear. It was only then I remembered I had never given Kate my number. I thought about calling back, but it seemed absurd. She would only worry, and anyway, the sense of threat had slipped away with the baby talk. At least she knew where I was, and I could always call Frank later at home.

Upstairs twilight had turned to darkness. I lay down on the bed and thought about supper. But sleep kept getting in the way. I recognized the syndrome: too much adrenalin in one day. Once it goes there's nothing to keep you going. I would take a nap now and eat later. A nice little local restaurant with the patron personally introducing each course. Even if Belmont was seriously looking for me he surely wouldn't risk drawing attention to himself by making raids on his local bistros. I set my wrist-watch for 8.00 p.m. I don't remember lying down again.

The door woke me. For an old lady she packed a hefty punch

– even the frame was rattling. I was up and talking before my brain had caught up with me. There was someone on the phone for me. A man. He said it was urgent. You could see I had taken a dive in her estimation. Men calling me after 8.30 p.m. Shit. So much for the alarm. Since I didn't have any option, I took the call. It hadn't taken him long to track me down. I girded my loins.

'Hannah. Is that you?' Well, of all the bars in all the towns . . . Scumbag. I wondered how I felt about it. 'It's David Mercot. Remember me?'

'Barely. How did you find me?'

He laughed. 'With some difficulty. The clerk at your hotel in Paris told me you'd asked the way to Roissy the day before. I figured if you were Belmont hunting you'd have to end up at Villemetrie. And Senlis is the nearest town. From there it was easy. Although I must admit for a woman on expenses I had expected something a little more chic than a pension.'

'Yes, well, I've been spending rather a lot on food lately.'

That one hit home, not so much what he said as the pause before he said it. 'I rang to tell you I've been doing a little digging on your behalf. And I've come across something I thought might interest you. About the Belmont family.'

'Really,' I said, but with zilch enthusiasm.

'Yeah, something to do with a girl they employed last year. I gather there was some trouble. I thought you might like to know.'

Deep inside, the juices began to run. Only this time it wasn't just sexual. Work before pleasure. Except sometimes with botñ it's wise to play hard to get. 'Yeah, I probably would.'

Another pause. At the other end he sighed, but it didn't sound too guilt-stricken. 'OK. So I also rang to apologize. I know what you must have thought. I didn't intend it to sound so . . . brutal.' I was still trying to think up something clever for that one when he said: 'Oh come on, Hannah. Don't go all cold and English on me. I realize it was a lousy thing to do. And I don't blame you for being mad. I just didn't have any option. At the time, I couldn't tell you about it. It was a professional appointment. In confidence. Something you should know all about. But if you'll let me buy you dinner I'll come clean.'

Bloody cheek. Tell him to stuff it, said the bruise in my ego, now turning from purple to yellow. 'No problem. I'll be back in Paris next Easter. I'll call you then.' But we both knew my heart wasn't in it.

'I can pick you up in about three-quarters of an hour. There's a new restaurant I've heard about, just outside the town. My treat, of course. Shall I wait by the hotel?'

'You know you could always just tell me over the phone. Save yourself the time and money.'

'Hannah, give me a break. Don't make it harder than it is. I'm trying to say I'm sorry. And that I want to see you.'

I took a deep breath. 'OK. I'll meet you in the square by the cathedral at nine thirty. But if you're more than a minute late I'll assume you've stood me up.'

Swallowing pride; sometimes it tastes better than you expect. I took a bath and washed my hair – not so much vanity as cleanliness. Under torture I might admit to a little mascara, but just to make my eyes look more open. Then I set about unpicking a couple of inches of stitching from the inside of one of the pillows on the bed. When the hole was big enough I slid the postcards in. Since I didn't have a needle and cotton I put the open end back into the pillowcase first. Eventually the feathers would start to escape, but not yet. Should anyone come looking they would have to be willing to cause considerable damage to find them. As far as I remember it was an action of instinct rather than intellect – I don't think I had seriously considered the possibility of coming back to find my room ransacked – but sometimes you do things anyway. This was one of those times. Then I put on my coat and went out.

It was a beautiful night, colder now, but clear with a half-eaten moon and a few choice stars. The square was right behind the pension. On a bench at one end two teenagers were huddled over the lights of their cigarettes. That's one of the few things to be said for adulthood: it's no longer adolescence. I walked past them over towards the façade of the cathedral and its huge rose-petal window. The stone glowed ghost-white under the street lamps, not so much welcoming as imposing. The doors were closed. What happened if the faithful suffered spiritual crisis after 10.00 p.m.? The devil take them until morning. I looked at my watch: 9.28 p.m. I heard him first. Footsteps on cobbles. I turned and watched him walk towards me. He was wearing a trenchcoat, belted in the front, and dark shiny shoes. Very Jean-Paul Belmondo. It suited him. He stopped a few yards in front of me. I wondered if I should hold out my hand but I don't think either of us felt like touching.

'Hello. I'm glad you came.' And there was no doubt that he was just a little embarrassed. Guilty is as handsome does. I enjoyed his discomfort. 'Shall we go? I parked the car a couple of streets away.'

We walked but we didn't talk. The car was bigger than I had anticipated, shiny and new. He opened the passenger door for me. Inside it smelt of new leather. He noticed I was noticing. 'Sorry. It comes with the job.'

He slid in beside me. The key in the ignition started off a slow swell of cellos and violins. Vivaldi. He turned to me. 'Maybe we should leave the talking till we get to the restaurant. It's not far. What do you say?'

And once again for a man so poised he felt surprisingly nervous. I thought it was rather touching. 'OK.'

We purred our way out of town, past closed doors where the good burghers of Senlis were no doubt drinking their wine and water and watching yoghourt ads on the television. A mile or so out, darkness engulfed us, the car headlights piercing a narrow shaft through country roads. I stole a glance. He was concentrating on the road, but he felt the look. He smiled back. It said, 'I'm glad you're here.' But did it also say something else?

It's always hard to tell the levels at which one knows something. I mean when I think about it now it strikes me that I always knew, or at least from the minute I heard his voice at the other end of the line. Why else would I have gone to such trouble to hide the postcards? But that's when I'm being kind to myself. The rest of the time I think I just blew it, allowed myself to be fooled into believing what I wanted to believe, rather than what was in front of my eyes. In the end it was the long slow winding curve that gave it away. I had such a powerful memory of it from the bike that afternoon: wind whistling through my hair, freewheeling towards those big green gates. When it happened it was the nearest I've come to what I imagine to be a religious revelation: that absolute sudden knowledge of something descending like a shaft of light to dazzle the unworthy chosen one. Except that this revelation had a sound effect to accompany it: the metallic click of the automatic lock on the car doors going on. And this time the look that shot between us was the truth and nothing but the truth.

I suppose I could have gone for the wheel. At the end of the gradient the gates were already open. If I had grabbed it I could probably have brought us off the road, maybe done some serious damage to the car. But even if I had managed to concuss him and not myself there was nowhere to run to. And anyway, just for that second, I was too distracted by the slide show in my head: a quick succession of *tableaux vivants* from recent history. Number one: the half hour spent at Belmont reception while someone studied me on the security-screen scanners. Number two: a man called David sitting in a bar trying to look as if he was trying not to look at me. Number three: that same man allowing me to take him to dinner so that he could tell me everything he wanted me to know and then sliding his way out of what could have been a compromising situation. And number four, the unkindest cut of all, the return of the conquering hero when his prey proved a little more stubborn than anticipated. The show ended on a close up: a woman with newly applied mascara standing in a village square, her mind momentarily muddied by carnal desire. How would I ever tell Frank?

The car glided to a halt outside the château. From the house a man was already running towards us, light on his feet despite his size. I kept my hands clasped tightly in my lap.

In the car the ex-pilot clicked off the automatic lock. Then he turned to me. He registered my hands welded together, and also the fury they controlled. You could see he was grateful I had decided against violence. 'Look at it from my point of view, OK? You wanted to see Jules, Jules wants to see you. This was the quickest way to arrange it. But you would never have come if I'd told you.'

It was one of those times when one is thankful for small mercies. As a woman who you already know not to be a blusher, I used what I'd got. 'On the contrary, David, or should I call you Daniel Devieux, I'm grateful for the lift. Especially considering how shattered you must be. Tokyo and back in less than thirty hours. For a man of no personality it must have been a super-human effort. Or maybe it's just another miracle of Belmont Aviation.'

CHAPTER THIRTEEN

They put me in the stables, in her room. Deliberate, of course. Across the bed someone had laid out a towel and on the chest there was a small vase of fresh flowers. I imagined thin lips arranging them, checking all the surfaces for dust, humming a little melody under her breath as she prepared for my imprisonment. I thought about picking up the vase and smashing it against the door, but didn't want to give them the pleasure of my anger. They would expect me to be upset: I would be calm.

Practicalities first. Now I was in here, how could I get out. Start with the obvious then improvise. Outside the bedroom shutters a tiny balcony gave way to a drop of twelve, maybe fifteen, feet on to concrete below. If I was willing to risk a chipped bone I might make it; a pregnant woman, it struck me, would not. In the bathroom the opening was smaller and just as high. Both doors were, of course, locked. I called out, just to be sure. A voice grunted: Mr Muscle Man, no doubt. Maybe when he came in to deliver my cocoa I could tickle his biceps and escape when he was laughing.

I sat down on the bed and waited. It was just after 10.00 p.m. What now? Could they really be planning to leave me for the night? In their shoes I might have been tempted. Let me fret a bit, stew in my own helplessness, so that by the morning I would be softened up for whatever was to come. OK, I would play it their way. If I had to wait until the morning I would sleep.

I moved myself into a crosslegged position on the bed and focused on the wild flowers in their cutesy little vase. Stop the mind and the body will stop itself. I took some long deep breaths. But images of Modesty Blaise kept seeping into my mind and distracting me. I've always been suspicious of women who keep weapons hidden in their hair and who manage to get through rape by meditation. By now she would probably have picked the lock, incapacitated the guard and scaled her way up into Devieux's bedroom to castrate him and leave his balls on Belmont's breakfast plate. I rather liked that idea. It was somehow more soothing than flowers. I lay back on the bed and watched the ceiling. I thought briefly of Kate who had no number for me and of the white-haired landlady who I had paid in advance and who would, presumably, not even know I had gone. Then I closed my eyes and thought of England.

It must have been after midnight when the key turned in the lock and the door opened. To be honest I was surprised to see him. If it had been me I would have given the job to somebody else. As it was he didn't look happy. I have this theory about baddies. That they are, in fact, troubled by conscience, but that like toothache it makes them bad-tempered rather than repentant. I got up to meet him. Through the open door I saw the bodyguard take up a position behind him. Protection for whom? He walked towards me. Despite myself I took a step back. He stopped. 'Well now, Hannah, you surprise me,' he said in English. 'I thought you told me you didn't get scared.'

'I lied. But then I was in good company.'

He moved his body slightly to one side, as if to let the jibe slide past him. 'Jules is ready to see you.'

'Jules,' I echoed, marvelling at our first-name terms so soon into a relationship. 'I'm surprised he's still upright. But then, of course, he may not be quite as ill as he looked.'

'I thought you and I should have a talk before you met him.'

'Why? Is there some other piece of whitewash you forgot to tell me? A few orphanages or hospitals he's endowed, third-world children he's sponsored?'

He shook his head. 'I didn't lie to you, Hannah. Any business journalist would have told you the same story.'

'Really. A dull man with no personality at all,' I said in French so that Muscles could hear us from the back of the room. 'And certainly not a ladies' man. Come on, Daniel, you probably get into the gossip columns on your dress sense alone. Maybe I should ask the ladies about you. Except, of course, there's one who isn't around to answer. Was getting her pregnant a present for your uncle? Strange. Given your place in the family tree I would have thought you might have preferred to see him remain childless.'

'Don't be snide, Hannah, it doesn't suit you.' But you could see he didn't like it. On the other hand neither did I. He was right. It was snide. It was also cheap and showed how angry I was. So much for meditation. I sat down on the bed.

'So. What would you like to talk about? I should tell you now I don't have them. But since I assume you've already been through my bag you probably know that already.'

'I know you're angry, Hannah,' he said, moving back into English. 'If it had happened to me I would be too. But I'd also be smart enough not to let it affect my judgement. We needed to know more about you. You could have been anyone. I had to find out.' He paused. 'I didn't expect to enjoy your company as much as I did. You'd feel worse if I'd accepted, you know,' he said quietly. 'I al– '

'Save me the confessional, Daniel, please. Every Catholic I ever knew lied anyway. Let's just call it business and leave it at that, OK?'

'OK. Then if you're ready I'll take you to Jules. You can hear the rest from him.'

'And what guarantee do I have that he'll tell me the truth this time?'

'None at all. Does that make you feel better? If it's any consolation, Hannah, I warned him not to underestimate you. We could have all saved ourselves a lot of trouble. Shall we go?'

It was, of course, not the kind of offer one could refuse. I stood up. He was standing between me and the door. I would have to walk around him to get out. I stayed deliberately close, just so he would know I didn't care. So close that I could smell him, feel him. Why not? The world is full of men that you're glad you didn't sleep with. Since when was it a problem? Fuck you mate, I thought, as I walked past him. And as I did so he shot out a hand and grasped my wrist. I whirled round to face him and we stood for a second, both of us rigid in confrontation. Behind me I felt the Muscle Man take a step forward.

'Let me go,' I said between my teeth, but even I could hear the tremor in my voice. He didn't move. My skin began to whimper with the pain of his grasp. He must have seen it in my face. He lessened his grip, though not enough to free me, and it was then, underneath the anger, I recognized something else. It hit me so fast I didn't have time to protect myself from it. It ignited like a line of petrol between us, my stomach turning over with it, sweet and sour at the same time. I felt fury and shame. But I also felt excitement. Mind and body, best friends and arch betrayers. By the time I smashed it down the damage was done. Only this time the confession had been mutual. And he knew I knew it. He dropped his hand, and his voice when it came, was almost as shaky as my own. 'I want you to remember that we're both just doing our jobs, Hannah. And you were the one who said you could handle it behind enemy lines.'

Without looking at him, I moved towards the door. The guard blocked my path. 'It's all right, Maurice, let her go.' The big man moved aside, and I strode past him, down the stairs, and out of the door.

Outside it was suddenly cold. The three of us walked in crocodile formation as far as a side door in the main house. There the faithful retainer left us, no doubt scurrying to the kitchen to get his mess of potage and mug of ale. A corridor stretched ahead. He waited. I walked, then he followed. At a staircase I stopped. I was already lost. He took over and led the way. We went up two flights, and along more corridor. Then outside a door he stopped and knocked. A voice grunted from within. We went in.

Restored to its former glory, that had been the landlady's phrase. I was standing in a library, high windows looking out, presumably, over the formal gardens towards the back. But now the shutters were drawn, and the room was bathed in quiet concealed lighting. The books made up the walls, stacked floor to ceiling, their spines cracking like skin from old age and bad ventilation. Good company for the owner of the house. He was sitting in a winged armchair near a fireplace which had a huge arrangement of dried flowers where the flames would once have been. After office hours he was out of his suit, dressed in a pair of corduroy pants a little too large for him and an open-necked shirt with a cravat. Last year's clothes and a body that had lost too much weight. He looked like a frail old man. I wondered how many Germans he had killed in the war. Holy warriors against the infidels. Except everyone knows that not all the crusaders were good guys.

'Good evening, Miss Wolfe, I hope you had a pleasant journey. Won't you sit down?'

Someone had done some strategic furniture planning. There was one chair to the side of him and one opposite. I kept my distance and picked the one with a view. Among the things in vision was a table with my bag sitting open on it. And lying next to it a small collection of Degas postcards. I had an image of an attic room caught up in a snowstorm of feathers, and a figure bending over the bed. But who? And how had they talked their way in there? Or maybe it was simply *droit du seigneur*, a feudal leftover by which the lord of the château was also the lord of the people. No doubt I would find out eventually.

'My secretary informed me that you wanted to see me. I'm sorry to have kept you waiting. I mislaid something that belonged to me and had to get it back.' He paused. I kept my eyes off the postcards and said nothing. 'Can I offer you a drink? I have some excellent Cognac. I, alas, am no longer allowed but it gives me pleasure to see others enjoy it.'

I would like to have said yes, just for the myth of it all. But it was late and I was tired. I was also a little scared and I needed my wits more than I needed a drink. 'No. Thank you.'

[142]

'Fine. Daniel, would you ask Mathilde to join us now?' We both watched him go. Then we sat and watched each other. After a moment he said, 'I think it's important for you and me to start by clearing the air, don't you? So I must tell you I don't respond well to being bullied, Miss Wolfe. Neither do I like people trespassing on my property and stealing my possessions.'

I swallowed. 'And I'm not crazy about being conned and lied to either, so maybe we should call it quits.'

He stared at me and I held the gaze. Then he nodded. I registered a ghost of a smile. 'Very well. I can see I should have listened to Daniel. He advised me to tell you the truth yesterday, suggested that you wouldn't be fobbed off with stories.' He moved his body slightly in the chair, as if already he had sat for too long and bedsores were developing. 'So. Where shall we start? I have decided to ask my wife to be here because it would be insulting to you to pretend any more that she is too ill to talk. Also I thought you might take what I am about to say more seriously if there was another source to corroborate it.

'However, before she comes I will say one thing. I would prefer even now not to have to tell you the truth. As a public man my private life is very important to me, and since this matter is most certainly a private one I would under most circumstances not disclose it. However, you have forced my hand. You and your client. She is, I gather, an old woman with no children of her own. I can see how Carolyn's death must have affected her. In that respect, at least, we share something. Now, if you don't mind, we shall wait until Mathilde arrives.'

He sat back in his chair and laid his arms on the long leather armrests. He reminded me of a Giacometti sculpture. Did he know about Miss Patrick or was it just an educated guess? It wouldn't have taken a genius to work out that she was the one who would need to know more, just to help her to sleep at night. I thought of her: the bone china tea service and that tough, stoical grace. He was wrong. They had more in common than he thought. But sexual politics divided them. Rich old men can buy beautiful young wives. Old women have to see it through alone.

The silence grew around us. He did not seem uncomfortable with it. On the mantelpiece a large ornate clock counted off the seconds. I consoled myself with the thought that I was younger than him, and could afford to let them go. Assuming that is, I still had a long life in front of me. I decided to be optimistic. The truth would have to be pretty spectacular to warrant killing people.

A few moments later she made her entrance. She was wearing a long silk dressing-gown and satin slippers. On her it looked like evening wear. She nodded towards me, a half smile, then bent over her husband and kissed him on the forehead. It felt like the gesture of a daughter rather than a wife, obedience rather than love. She settled herself in the seat beside him and, after a brief glance at me, kept her eyes firmly on the floor. It was a pose which didn't suit her. But I didn't have time to give it much thought. When he started to speak his voice was strong, that of a man used to being listened to.

'I should begin by correcting the lies. Of which, I suspect, there are fewer than you think. As you already know, Carolyn Hamilton did not leave here in June as I first told you. She left in mid January. Secondly we did not ask her to go. She went of her own accord. Indeed it would be fairer to say that she went against our wishes. Those are the two central discrepancies. The rest is more a case of things you were not told.

'As must be clear to you, Miss Wolfe, I am not a well man. In fact, although I fully intend to outlast the expectations of my doctors, it is common knowledge that I have only a limited time to live. As you also know I have no children. I believe Daniel has told you the facts of my son's death, and we have already spoken of my present marriage. It is a grave sadness to us both. My wife and I had both wanted a child very much. For me, of course, it could never replace the son I lost, but I had allowed myself to believe it might in some way make sense of the tragedy. I wonder if you can have any sympathy or understanding of what that means: the desire – or maybe even the need – to leave a little of yourself behind, to give life to something when you are so near to

[144]

death. Maybe not. You are young and still have it all in front of you. I, however, have not.

'Of course, there were things we could have done. Adoption was a possibility, although my age would have counted against us. No doubt influence could have been brought to bear but it would still have meant an inevitable amount of bureaucracy and publicity. And more than that, it would have meant a child that was not biologically my own. I am an old-fashioned man, Miss Wolfe. I'm afraid notions of paternity mean a lot to me. I wanted a child to carry on the family line. My child. I would have given everything I had to make that child also Mathilde's, but there are some things that even my money cannot buy, and for us time was running out. However, there was one alternative, albeit a some-what complicated one. I am talking, of course, of surrogacy.'

The word exploded into the air like a bunch of trick flowers, so colourful, so damn obvious that the audience can only marvel at how it could ever have been concealed. For the audience read me, me and my dull, stubborn imagination. Surrogacy. Old him and young her. I had been betrayed by my own sense of aesthetics. I tried not to show it.

'You have an admirably impassive face, Miss Wolfe. It is impossible to tell whether what I am saying is a revelation or simply the confirmation of your suspicions. Anyway, now you know. Of course, surrogacy is a delicate business. It needs careful thought and preparation. It is not every woman who is willing to rent out their womb and then walk away from the baby they have created and carried for nine months. It is also not every woman who is allowed to. That, as you may have realized, is why we went to England. Here in France they are in the process of drafting laws to make surrogacy illegal. By finding an English woman we, at least technically, avoided some of the problems. It was also a way of trying to guarantee secrecy. Had a similar advertisement appeared in a French newspaper something would almost certainly eventually have leaked its way into the press. Here I am a national figure. In England I am unknown. Neverthe-less we were still very circumspect. As you know the question of surrogacy was not even suggested in the original advertisement. All applications went through an agency (who knew nothing either) and once they had screened the replies we picked a few, and only a very few, women to interview. It was only when we felt we had found the right girl that the word surrogacy was even mentioned at all.

'As it was we were very fortunate. Or so it seemed then. Carolyn Hamilton was our first choice. She was young, healthy and intelligent. She came from a large family and was obviously fond of children, although had not thought of having a family of her own. She had lived for many years with a woman who could have none of her own so she had some understanding of the pain childlessness could cause. Also, as you no doubt know, she was at a difficult time in her own life. Her career was going badly and she was even contemplating giving it all up and trying something else, perhaps going back to college or even beginning her own business. But to do this she needed money, and, as you also know, she was very heavily in debt. Last of all there was something about her that none of us could have predicted – her extraordinary similarity to Mathilde. It seemed to us that she had been delivered by fate. Assuming, of course, that she would be willing.

'Of course we made it as tempting, and as easy, as possible. Needless to say there was never any question of intimacy between her and me. Conception would take place by means of artificial insemination and she would be paid for each attempt, regardless or not of whether she conceived. If and when she did conceive over the course of the first few months she would be paid a sum of ten thousand pounds. Then at birth, when the baby was handed over, a further fifty thousand would be added. Yes, it was a lot of money. Deliberately so. On the other hand I don't believe it was an easy decision. Indeed to be frank with you I still don't quite understand why she agreed. It is, believe me, something I, we, have thought about a great deal over the last few months. Certainly she was genuinely moved by our plight, that much was clear right from the start. Also she and Mathilde liked

[146]

each other, got on very well. And, of course, she needed the money. But more than that I can't say. Mathilde herself has another theory. She believes that Carolyn felt in some way trapped, that all through her life other people had made decisions for her, and this was one chance for her to take control, do something for and by herself. How far that is true I cannot say. All I can tell you is that she did agree and almost immediately.

'We drew up a contract. The terms were simple. Aside from the money, and of course a promise of complete secrecy, our only other stipulation was that as soon as conception had taken place she should come and live with us here so that as far as possible we could be involved in the pregnancy of what would be our child. In return she asked that we keep on her flat in London and arrange for communication between her and her guardian to take place as if she was still living there. It seemed that she was as concerned as we were to keep the matter absolutely confidential. We agreed and, as you know, her correspondence was all duly posted in London. No one knew where she was.

'In the event conception took a little under three months. During that time she travelled to France on a number of occasions for artificial insemination. At the beginning of May pregnancy was confirmed and she came to live with us at Villemetrie.'

He paused. It had been a long speech and he seemed to have run out of saliva halfway through. I could hear a sticky dryness in his voice. She had heard it too. She looked up at him and frowned, then leant over to the table and poured him out a glass of water. He took it without acknowledging her. As he gulped it down I found myself staring at the ski runs of old flesh stretching between his chin and his neck. He seemed to have become scraggier as I watched. I had an image of an old man sitting in his glass and steel tower rotting away, his skin flaking and dropping off while a foetus ducked and swam in an ocean of fluid. Such a story. The old king and the barren young queen; a fairytale filled with the magic of gynaecological science and the goodwill of a graceful peasant girl willing to sacrifice her body in return for riches. I could almost hear Frank chortling in the background.

[147]

Didn't I tell you, Hannah, everyone has something to sell? But you know what they say about supping with the devil . . . All in all a Grimm fairy tale, and so weird that I could find no immediate reason for not believing it. I wondered briefly why he had decided to tell me. Certainly if I had been him I might have gambled on another lie: an informal adoption of an accidental baby would have made equal sense and, although he wasn't to know it, might have given me equal satisfaction. Except, of course, either way we would have reached the same point. And the same question. What happened to spoil a happy business arrangement?

'I don't like mysteries any more than you do, Miss Wolfe. If I knew I would tell you. All I can say is that for most of the pregnancy everything went absolutely according to plan. After some initial sickness Carolyn was well and active. She lived here in the summerhouse which gave her privacy when she needed it. She walked and visited Paris and the countryside around. She and Mathilde spent a good deal of time together, involved in the process of the pregnancy, reading, talking about it. Miraculously for us, it seemed, she felt able to share it with us. In short she was in excellent spirits, content, indeed I would say almost happy with her decision. There was certainly no hint of what was to come.

'Of course, as the pregnancy progressed and became more obvious it became advisable for her to spend more time here. At first she didn't seem to mind. Then, towards the end of the year, something changed. Having spent long periods of time with Mathilde she now actively avoided her company and she spent more and more time on her own alone in the summerhouse. Thinking that perhaps she was becoming anxious about the birth we didn't impose. On the contrary we let her be. Our doctor assured us it was only natural for her to feel unsure, perhaps even overwhelmed by what was happening to her. She had at times during the pregnancy suffered from intermittently high blood pressure, not enough to cause any serious worry, but enough to force her to rest. Bearing this in mind he warned us against pressurizing her. We did as he suggested and gave her more space. We spent an uncomfortable Christmas together: we preparing ourselves for the birth of our baby, she now apparently equally distressed by the prospect. Then in the middle of January she came to me and asked to be released from the contract. She said she would find a way to pay back all the money and would never divulge the identity of the father, but that she had decided that she couldn't go through with it, it was her child and she wanted to be its mother.

'You may or may not understand when I tell you that I refused. She was over seven months pregnant. The baby, my baby – or rather our baby as we'd come to think of it by then – was almost ready to be born. It was clear from my deteriorating health that this would be our last chance. I offered her more money. I told her I would set up a trust fund for any other children she might have in the future. That she and they would be financially secure for the rest of their lives. I éven offered her visiting rights, so she could see the child at certain times every year. And when I had nothing else left to offer I threatened. The contract she had signed was legally binding. She had understood that when she signed it. If she tried to break it I would take her to court and force her to give up the baby. Of course I would never have done it. The contract would never have stood up in a court of law and the scandal would have destroyed us all. She knew that.

'She asked me to give her a week to think about it. That was on Sunday 11th. For the next six days we waited. She said nothing. On the next Saturday morning she asked Maurice, the driver who I believe you have already met, if he could take her into town to buy a present for her guardian's birthday. I admit I was concerned, but I felt that a refusal would be an admittance of mistrust, and would make things even worse between us. Of course he had instructions to accompany her everywhere. Which he did. Except in the changing-room of one of the big department stores. She was a long time inside. And when he made inquiries . . . well, there was another exit and she was no longer there. So simple. Anyway, once she had gone there was nothing we could do. Given the situation we could hardly call in the police. She knew that as well as we did. We checked the airports and the train stations, but she was nowhere to be found. We waited all afternoon, hoping against hope that she might come back. After a while we called her London apartment but there was no answer. Finally on Saturday night Daniel flew over to try to find her. But, as you know, by the time he arrived it was already too late. Two days later we heard the news.'

He was silent for a moment. 'Obviously what happened between Saturday morning and Saturday night we will never know. For a while I think we hung on to the hope that her death might not have been deliberate; that perhaps the emotional strain of the leaving and the physical strain of the travelling could have triggered off high blood pressure and she might have suffered some kind of fit and fallen into the water. Certainly our doctor has suggested as much. But that was before the inquest and the news of the suicide note. It must have been a sensitive coroner to find a way to soften the verdict. I suppose there may be such a thing as too much guilt, too many people let down and disappointed. I can only imagine that that, along with the pressure to repay what was a large amount of money, and the fear that I might indeed pursue her and the baby, drove her into an action of despair. A despair which, I need not add, has since become ours.'

Beside him Mathilde was sitting still as a rock. He slid a long thin hand over hers and held it tightly. She didn't appear to register the pressure. They sat there for a while, statues of sorrow. He shook his head and sighed. 'When we heard what had happened I had to decide whether or not to go to the English police. Obviously what had taken place here was relevant to her death. On the other hand nothing I could have told them would have brought her back. Her or the child. And, given the nature of the circumstances, even if I had managed to keep it out of the inquest it would have been bound to become public eventually. It is ironic. The French, unlike the English, are not obsessed by the sexual misdemeanours of their national figures. A mistress or two would hardly be worth the cost of the ink on the page. But

[150]

illegal surrogacy leading to suicide? I have been in newspapers long enough to know it would have proved irresistible. The effects on my reputation I will leave you to imagine. But more important would have been how it would have destroyed the little time and privacy that Mathilde and I have left together. And that is something I would do anything to protect.

'You will now understand why I chose not to tell you the truth when I first met you. This business has brought enough heartache to my family without the risk of it being made public now. I had hoped you would be satisfied with my explanation. When you turned up this afternoon with the postcards it was clear that Daniel was right and you were not. As I'm sure you know, the postcards in themselves prove nothing. And should you be contemplating taking them to the authorities I could, of course, deny all knowledge of them. I probably don't need to add that my word against yours might be something of an unfair contest. However, it is not my intention to blackmail or threaten you. On the contrary. It is more a question of throwing myself on your mercy. The coroner's report was accidental death. It was, in the end, I think a fair description. And one that it would be kinder to all of us, particularly the memory of Carolyn herself, to leave unchallenged. Of course I appreciate you have a job to do, and a responsibility to your client. I understand I cannot force you into secrecy. All I would ask is that, in as far as you feel it possible, you and your client respect our desire for privacy. There will be little enough of it left.'

In the silence that followed the clock ate further into his life. He sat like a corpse in his chair, his hand still clutched over hers, her eyes still on the floor. I had come here predisposed to disbelieve him. Out-manoeuvred and used, it was in the interests of my bruised pride to keep him and his sexy, slimy assistant in horns and tails. On the other hand, I'm the one who's always telling Frank how women can sometimes get there quicker than men because they're not humping their inflated egos around with them. Everything he had said fitted with the facts as I knew them: the timing, the money, the motivations, the states of mind.

Even her *volte face* made its own kind of unsatisfactory sense. Pregnant women are supposed to be volatile beings. Even I knew that much. And nine months is long enough to change your mind. As the baby grew inside her, began dolphin-dipping its way around her womb, so the theoretical would have turned into the real. What had begun as any baby would have become her baby; mother and child, more binding than any legal contract. Which brought us to the very last mystery of all. Why this young woman, so apparently determined and so literally full of life, should run away from one trap only to catch herself in another, this time even more powerful and crushing. The high blood pressure story I could neither refute nor accept. A little research would sort it out, but my instinct was that if a post mortem hadn't found it, it was unlikely. What did that leave? Another seismic emotional shift? Had that last walk been, as Belmont claimed, a series of faltering footsteps in a fog of guilt and fear? Or could it have been a push from behind as punishment for a broken contract? I admit that one got me excited. If it had been a question of adoption rather than surrogacy it might have made sense. But even without the suicide note I couldn't make it fit. Revenge would have been an act of ultimate self-destruction. More than anything, Belmont needed her alive. She was – to use his own phrase – his last chance. Killing her was literally killing a part of himself. But discarding murder still didn't explain suicide. From whichever angle you looked at it, it didn't completely add up. Except in some ways that was what gave it its final credibility. Why go to the trouble of creating such an elaborate tale only to leave loose ends? Life is always messier than fiction. That's why we need stories to tidy it up.

Of course, mythically speaking, this is the moment where the private investigator steps in with the three subtle but penetrating questions which act as the litmus paper between truth and deception. I felt suddenly homesick for store detection and Mrs Van de Bilt's shopping sprees in duty-free ports. And good old English policemen, corrupt in the more predictable ways. I was adrift in a welter of facts. Question number one: was I really such a good private detective?

'Madame Belmont?' When in doubt over content go for strategy. She looked up at me. And her eyes were clear. Any pain there might have been in the story retold had passed away. 'Do you have anything to add? Anything that might explain what happened to Carolyn after she left here.' She shook her head. 'You spent a lot of time with her during the pregnancy. You must have noticed the change as it was taking place. Or have some idea what could have caused it.'

She glanced away, and I noticed she was careful not to look at him. I was getting a clear message from her reticence. The story had been told for both of them. She was just here as window dressing, to be seen but not heard. Except the last time we'd met she hadn't struck me as being the chronically shy type. After a small pause which might have passed for thought she said: 'I'm sorry. I can't help you any more than I have already. All I can say is that by the time she left I think she had come to see it as her child and not ours. And because of that what had once seemed possible was no longer.'

Belmont flicked a glance at her, a glance and a slight frown. Maybe it was just incomprehension. In which case that made two of us. As an explanation it was one for the birds, or the sybils. It occurred to me that Belmont might again be telling more of the truth than I wanted to believe, and that despite her perfect grooming the lady of the house might indeed have been turned doo lally by loss and the children she couldn't have. I shuffled around for a while in the darkness. The shaft of light when it came was weak and flickering. But it was all I had. Luckily it grew stronger as I got nearer.

'There's only one thing I don't understand. You said that if you adopted a child it would inevitably lead to some publicity and that was something you were eager to avoid. But when Carolyn had the baby and handed it over to you wouldn't the same thing have occurred? I mean people would have started asking questions about the baby anyway.'

He nodded, almost as if he was pleased by the question. 'I congratulate you, Miss Wolfe. You're absolutely right. There is one thing I omitted to tell you. When Carolyn conceived so did Mathilde. Officially that is. Of course, there had been too many disappointments for us to risk a full public disclosure. The few – and they were very few – people that we told knew the news had to remain a closely guarded secret. We made it clear that in order to minimize the chance of miscarriage Mathilde would be constantly supervised, and stay close to home for the duration of her pregnancy. It was hardly a great sacrifice. Our marriage has always been more private than public property, and since my heart attacks I have long ceased to be of much interest to the gossip columnists. Daniel is much more profitable fodder.'

Despite myself I let that one go. 'What about doctors? You could hardly fool them.'

'In terms of specialists, Mathilde had been seeing an American gynaecologist. That she did or didn't continue to consult him was nobody's business but her own. In fact throughout the process of AID and the pregnancy Carolyn was looked after privately by my own doctor. He has cared for myself and my family for over thirty years. He treated Carolyn with exactly the same expertise and attention he would have given to my wife.'

A faithful retainer? Recently blinded or just loyal and therefore very rich? 'So how did you explain an eight-month miscarriage? Or did you and the doctor just agree to forget the whole thing?'

'There was no need. The week after Carolyn's death we let it be known that Mathilde had suffered a miscarriage four months before, and that we kept the news a secret until she had had a chance to recover. As for our doctor – of course you will appreciate that the relationship between patient and practioner is confidential.'

As no doubt was his latest bank statement. I thought of old hatchet face at the front door and big Maurice who had managed to mislay the goose with the golden egg. Presumably they too had much more in their savings account than they used to. Meanwhile poor old Mathilde had become the scapegoat, the potential hysteric to be handled with kid gloves lest any mention of her continued barrenness push her over into permanent illness. It was not a role I would have agreed to play, but then no doubt she was better trained. From translator to Madame Belmont in one easy step; every promotion brings with it responsibilities. Maybe this was part of the contract. Either she loved him more than my imagination (dull and stubborn as it was) could conceive or she was biding her time. Presumably after he died she could do what the hell she liked, could adopt a whole slew of children that weren't his, fill the house with them like a latter-day Josephine Baker. The image was rather comforting: this huge mausoleum of restored good taste disappearing under the onslaught of jammy fingers and pen marks. I wound back the thread to get to where I'd come from and ran into the doctor and his confidentiality. 'I see. And your wife's medical records?' He gave an apologetic little shrug. Rather coy in the circumstances, I thought. 'Don't tell me. Unaccountably mislaid, of course. Along with the surrogate contract that never officially was.'

He smiled slightly. Of course. This has been the scam of a life as well as a lifetime. A businessman of his standing would have learnt how to cover his tracks. Except on balance it might have been simpler to do a Henry VIII. Chop off her head and marry a lady-in-waiting. Maybe he wished he had, now. Certainly this level of conspiracy left him all too vulnerable. And, as he himself had said, for a man committed to secrecy he had told me altogether too much. What guarantee did he have that I wouldn't walk out tomorrow and go straight to the police? His name might cut through icebergs in France but, as he himself had said, he was virtually unknown in England. No police buddies to hush it up there. And what wouldn't interest the French police would still fascinate the French press. He must have thought about it and considered it a risk worth taking. But then risks were something he knew all about. What were the odds against surviving the resistance in occupied France and then going on to make yourself a fortune or two? Maybe if you take enough risks you forge a different relationship with fate, start to write your own ticket. I wondered if he was afraid of dying. No bargain there. Except perhaps the one we were engaged in, allowing him to go with his reputation intact.

'I don't think I need add that I have taken a substantial risk in telling you as much as I have. As I'm sure you know only to well, a man like myself is not without enemies and there are people who would pay a good deal of money to learn what I have just told you. Which brings me to my last request. At the risk of alienating you further – and Daniel has made it clear that in his opinion I shouldn't say this – I would ask that if you should be tempted in any way in that direction I will freely and gladly pay you an equally large sum to protect myself and my family.'

It was not the most tactful way to end a submission, but it was, at least, sincere. What had he said about putting himself at my mercy? Maybe he wasn't such a bad judge of character after all. I let him sweat for a while, but the perspiration wasn't obvious.

'There's not much I can say. I've been employed to find out certain things. You've told me what you know. Now I have to tell that to my client. What they do with the information is their affair. Your nephew was right. I am not a golddigger, Mr Belmont. But more than that I cannot promise.'

He nodded. 'Thank you for your honesty, Miss Wolfe. I appreciate it. I am only sorry that you have been put through such distress and intimidation over the last two days.' And if there was any irony I didn't hear it. 'You are, of course, completely free to leave at any time. I would suggest that you do not return to your pension in Senlis. I fear the room may no longer be in perfect order. Your account and any damage will, of course, be settled for you. Should you wish it we can drive you to another hotel, or you can stay the night here and in the morning we will take you wherever you want to go. Now, if you'll excuse me, it's late and I think we could all benefit from a little sleep.'

CHAPTER FOURTEEN

I stayed, because I was tired and because I was fairly certain it wasn't in their interests to murder me in my bed. It was Maurice and not Daniel who was summoned to take me back to the summerhouse. No doubt the golden boy of Belmont Aviation was getting in his beauty sleep. Either that or he was needed for a conference after I had gone. I couldn't have cared less. Now I didn't have to think any more my brain had imploded in on itself. Everything else could wait till morning. This time he didn't lock the door. I heard him stomp down the stairs and out into the night.

Next to the bed was a thermos full of hot chocolate and an exquisite glass decanter half-filled with what looked like that best brandy. One could almost see the bubble coming out of the neck reading 'Louis XV drank here'. Chocolate versus Cognac. In fact, although I'd never admit it to Frank, I'm quite partial to a little hot chocolate but tonight, given the occasion, there was no contest. I poured a large brandy and swirled it around the glass enjoying the visuals. Considering how much he must have paid for it, it didn't taste as good as I expected – not so much the warm glow as the coal burn at the back of my throat – but then what did my plebeian palate know about vintage Cognac? I drank it anyway, then crawled between the clean smooth sheets and closed my eyes. I was lying where Carolyn Hamilton had lain for months as she grew into her body and away from the deal she had made. If I hadn't been so tired it would have been awesome. With any luck it would still be awesome in the morning.

Sleep turned out to be a good practice for death, instant total extinction with not even the slightest trace of dream. The first notice I had that they hadn't, indeed, murdered me in my bed was a very noisy opening of a door somewhere near by. I prized open an eye to see Hatchet Face hovering at the foot of the bed, tray in hand. From the way she was standing it was sort of clear this was the last call for breakfast. She put it down on the table, sweeping up the brandy decanter and thermos. I dragged myself up on to the pillows and looked at my watch: 9.00 a.m. I thought about making conversation. Now I had been accepted into the bosom of the family a few pertinent questions about that other English houseguest mightn't go amiss, but when I asked her how much she had seen of Carolyn during her stay she threw me her best Medusa look and was out of the door before the stone had had time to set. So much for the faithful old retainers.

I ate fast and was up and ready to go within twenty minutes. But no one came for me. I opened the shutters and windows and looked out on to the world according to Jules Belmont. A hazy sun was filtering through the trees. Off to the left I could just catch the shimmer of the glass-surfaced lake. I was caressed by a sense of timelessness and peace. She must have looked out over this view a hundred times, watched from her window as summer ripened and faded and the world grew dark into winter. It and her. Had she really been so happy about it at first? Sure she needed the cash. But no amount of money was going to have her on her points again, and without that she was still a young woman nursing a soured dream. Maybe with time laying heavily on her hands the memory of one failed career had made her decide to try another, this time less burdened by other people's expectations. After all, anyone can be a mother. I wondered at what point she had realized that – to quote Mathilde – what once seemed possible was no longer? It must have been an awesome moment. And she must have been frightened, of what she felt as well as what they would say. Discovering how much you love and want something can be as terrifying as it is exhilarating. I stretched my fingers across my flat stomach and tried to imagine the sensation, but all I could feel was breakfast disintegrating under the onslaught of gastric juices. There are some things that even female empathy can't reach. I could spend the rest of my life feeling for her but I would still never know how she felt.

I closed the window and gathered my things together. Now I had let the thought of her in, the room unnerved me. I wanted to be out of it, in a car, on a plane, anywhere where I could think clearly without her presence nibbling at the edges of my brain.

Outside the world was quiet and still, the back façade of the house shuttered up from the night. If the château had been mine, each dawn probably would have found me up and out counting the windows, just in case. Still, probably when you're that rich one room more or less doesn't matter.

I wandered over the terrace and through the rose garden. Then I made my way round to the front of the house and walked straight into Daniel, standing out on the front steps surveying the world. Maybe he was practising for the moment when all this would be his. He was dressed for work, the same scrumptious baggy suit that had been the cause of all the trouble. I realized I had never seen him in daylight. It made him a little older, maybe a little more ordinary. No doubt it did the same for me too. If I had given it any thought, and to be honest I had – just a little – I had expected the sight of him to rekindle my resentment. But now when I went looking for it, I couldn't find it. Even the magnetism seemed to have faded. As he said, we had both been doing our jobs. Simple as that.

'Good morning, Hannah. You look rested. I was on my way to get you. Maurice is ready with the car.'

Sure enough, at the edge of the drive sat the limo, gleaming and self-important. Daylight was kinder to it than to us. Maurice, I noticed, was tinkering under the bonnet.

'Jules and Mathilde have asked me to give you their apologies. Jules is not well this morning. They're waiting for the doctor.'

'Unfortunately he's out already. His wife says she's not expecting him back until lunchtime.'

She took us both by surprise, appearing from the door behind him so suddenly that one wondered if she hadn't been waiting in the hall until she heard our voices. She was wearing a pale-blue pleated skirt and a cashmere sweater, quiet but expensive. Her hair was held back in a bandana. But even she suffered under the morning sun, that perfect skin a little less firm and glowing. She walked down the steps over to me and held out a hand. It was a quick grasp, but the look stayed longer. 'Miss Wolfe. I'm grateful for all your time and patience. I realize this can't have been easy for you. I do hope you have a good journey home.' It struck me as slightly absurd, this arch politeness. Absurd and rather forced. 'Will you be flying her to London, Daniel?'

Her remark caused him a little trouble, although if you hadn't been looking for it you might not have noticed. 'I can't imagine that will be necessary. I'm sure Miss Wolfe has her own ticket.'

'Ah well, it was just a thought.' She smiled at me. 'We have our own private plane, you see, Miss Wolfe. Belmont Aviation, you understand. Daniel is always going to and fro. Sometimes it's hard to keep track of him. Well, if you'll forgive me, I must go to my husband.'

'Mathilde.' He waited until she was halfway to the door. And this time his voice was tight. 'Don't let him get up. He's not as well as he thinks.'

She bowed her head and a look passed between them. Don't tell me how to look after my husband, it said. If this had been a different kind of story, more of the Danielle Steele type, I would have had these two rutting their socks off in the gamekeeper's cottage, while the old man languished in the bathchair on the lawn. And after, as they shared the inevitable post-coital cigarette, they would weave their cunning plots to get rid of the girl carrying the heir that could potentially disenfranchise them both. Frank would have liked that version. But that was all that could be said for it. They might be the best-looking characters in the dramatis personae, but even allowing for great acting there was a good deal less than nothing going on between them. He watched her until she was inside the house, then turned to me.

'Maurice can drop you back at your Paris hotel or wait and drive you on to the airport – whichever you like.'

It was tempting, but even at this stage it didn't do to tell the opposition exactly what you were doing, even if it didn't matter that they knew. 'No. No, the hotel will be fine.'

Maurice emerged from the bonnet wiping his hands. I had the briefest of fantasies about the brake cable and a wild screaming bend at eighty miles an hour. But nobody in their right minds doctors a car with the victim standing right by it, particularly not when they're also the one doing the driving. He nodded at me, as if somewhat embarrassed at my change of status, then walked back into the house clutching the cloth.

In the warm still morning Daniel and I stood alone for the first time since last night's journey. It seemed a long time ago. He opened the back door and I slid inside. Here it comes, I thought, the long goodbye. If we were both still doing our jobs he needed to get as much out of it as I did. He leant on the open window. I held his gaze. Go on, buddy, you might as well go for it. After a moment he said, 'I think it must be hard for you, following in her footsteps but not really knowing who she was. If we had more time I could tell you what she was like.'

'Would it help me to know?'

'You'd have to decide that for yourself. They were very fond of her, you know.'

'So they said. And you?'

'I don't think "fond" is the right word. She always seemed a bit confused to me. Not really sure what she should be doing with her life. I don't think she ever understood the implications of what she'd taken on.'

'So you weren't surprised when she changed her mind?'

He paused. 'No, not entirely.'

'And, of course, you told all this to your uncle, but he went ahead regardless?'

He smiled. 'As you must have realized by now, in the end Jules does what he wants, which is usually the same as what he needs, but not always.'

[161]

I thought about what it must like, stepping into Belmont's shoes and running his empire. He wasn't the kind of a man to give up power easily, even to his own flesh and blood. It was my turn to make conversation. 'He told me he sent you to London to look for her.'

'I went, yes.' We both noticed the substitution of the verb.

'When did you go?'

'Saturday night.'

'What time?'

He smiled. 'Exactly or approximately? I believe I got in some time between 8.30 p.m and 9.00 p.m. But no doubt if you check with Heathrow flight control they could give you the exact timing.'

We both knew the post mortem had estimated death between 4.00 p.m. and 6.30 p.m. Which meant that had he arrived any earlier we also both knew he could have been a suspect. I pretended not to be interested in pursuing it. 'And from the airport?'

'I went to her house.'

'And?'

'She wasn't there.'

'Hmmn.' I counted to three. 'You must have been looking forward to having a cousin again, after all these years?'

He shook his head in mock exasperation. 'You don't give up, do you, Hannah? What are you after now? Motives? I'm sorry to disappoint you. But there was more than enough money to go round. Do you know how much Jules is worth? We could split it ten ways and we'd all still be rich. And by the time "he" – we always called him "he" – had been old enough to step into my shoes I'd already be taking them off for splendid retirement. So you see, even if she hadn't committed suicide there would still have been no reason to kill her.'

There was something catching in my mind, something that didn't quite fit, but I couldn't find it. Maybe later, when I was trying less hard . . . 'So, she wasn't at the flat. What did you do for the rest of the night?'

'Tried to find her.' He frowned. 'I hadn't really expected her to be there anyway. I mean it was the one place we were bound to follow her. I waited for a while, just in case I was wrong, then I went looking. Anywhere and everywhere. I even spent an hour or two on the embankment by Charing Cross. Right river, wrong place, eh? I think I knew what she had done even then. I kept thinking I might find her under the next cardboard box, with a bottle of pills in her hand. Poor kid.'

He stopped, rerunning footage of the homeless in his head. Luckily it hadn't stopped him coming home to his mansion. After a while he said, 'You know the real tragedy of this story, Hannah? She didn't need to kill herself. He would never really have forced her back. Despite what he might have said to her. I know this may not be the right time to bring it up, Hannah, but whatever his faults Jules Belmont is a remarkable man.'

'An old war hero who ought to be allowed to die in peace, you mean?'

He smiled. 'Something like that.' He left a second's pause. 'But then I'm hardly the one to be asking for favours. You'll do what you have to. I think we all know that. I just hope you make the right decision. *Bon voyage.*' He held out a hand. I hesitated, then took it. And just for that moment, just for that touch, the old flame licked up again, a sweet small burn in the pit of my stomach. I let go first. He withdrew his hand, slowly. 'As I told you, Hannah, it wasn't all lies. In other circumstances . . .'

'Yeah, well, work before pleasure. I gather it's becoming a European disease.'

'Perhaps some time when I'm in London . . .?'

But who wants to be just another name in the back pages of an executive's Filofax? A private investigator should have more pride. 'Yeah, perhaps.'

Maurice clomped his way into the driver's seat and fumbled with the ignition. It was time to go. I located the button and the window slid up noiselessly. I turned my eyes to the back of Maurice's head and kept them there until we were moving. Only at the last minute did I turn and look back along the drive to the front façade of the château. But Daniel had gone; back to the bosom of the family no doubt, and a scaly old man shuffling towards death. While I was *en route* for England and a lady with more grace but going the same way.

In the end I should have taken the offer of the lift to the airport. Time and transport meant more of her money and it took a while to gather up my belongings and get myself back to Charles de Gaulle. Waiting in my satellite gate while planes jumbo-danced into position on the runway I set my sights on a few French businessmen and engaged them in polite chatter. Eventually I brought the subject round to Belmont. In both cases I got the same story back: the miracle man who combined virtue with strength and had built up the national GNP as conscientiously as his own bank account. Consensus, or everyone wanting to believe in fairies? I was beginning to wonder at my own cynicism.

We left in sunshine and touched down to London grey. Back home I hadn't exactly been missed. Frank had called twice and my mother had left a message reminding me it was my father's birthday yesterday. Great. Maybe Kate had added my name to their present. First things first. I put a call through to Heathrow airport. Always cross the t's and dot the i's, Hannah. You'd be surprised what you can find in the small print. It took longer than I thought. Private jets mean public handling agents. British Airways put me through to Air France who put me through to the Operation Centre and finally the Operations Duty Manager. He found it eventually. Saturday 18 January, an 8.40 p.m. touch-down. It was not exactly public information and no passenger list was available, but he could confirm that the pilot was Daniel Devieux. Not so much what I'd wanted to hear as what I'd expected. At least I'd checked.

I sat at my desk and wondered what to do next. Outside it was threatening drizzle. I had this empty feeling in the pit of my stomach. I recognized it as the one that always comes at the end of a job. Except was this really the end? Certainly I'd done what I'd been paid for – the gap in Carolyn Hamilton's life had now been filled, and I had long since used up my advance filling it. If by any chance it wasn't the whole truth, then the client would have to be the one to decide if it was worth the money to keep me digging. I made myself a large pot of black coffee, propped up the picture of Carolyn on the desk in front of me and settled down to write a story for Miss Patrick.

Reports, the private eye's version of school essays, or in this case a game of consequences: Carolyn met Jules on a winter afternoon in a French château. He said to her . . . She replied . . . they decided to go ahead anyway. The consequence was . . . and the world said . . . I finished at midnight. I had tried my best to make it more than just the words. But it wasn't that easy. Somewhere over the last few weeks a seachange had taken place. The shiny-haired anonymity of Carolyn Hamilton had faded and, like a photograph developing under the wash of chemicals, another portrait had emerged. Except that when I tried to decipher this one I found myself looking at not one image, but two, superimposed under each other like a weird kind of double exposure. The first picture was simple enough. A young girl fed on dreams and other people's expectations had had to wake up to the fact that even talent couldn't protect you from bad luck, and so had begun the long fall from grace which led to Cherubim, an advert in a paper and from there, inexorably, to tragedy. I thought about Daniel's words: 'She always seemed a bit confused to me. Not really sure what she should be doing with her life. I don't think she ever understood the implications of what she'd taken on.' So, in trying to get herself out of one mess she had fallen into another, only whichever direction she turned this one had no way out. It was a tale to tickle the tearducts: life as a quicksand, with her own character supplying the fatal flaw. Except for one thing that kept niggling at me as I wrote. Had it all really been that inevitable? Had she really been that helpless? Of course it's all too easy to make the dead victims. They fit the role so well. So she was young, and had been disappointed. So had we all. Did that really make her so damned? The second Carolyn was harder to define, but she was there all the same. This was the 'bright, active girl with a sense of adventure' who had charmed Mrs Sanger into writing her a glowing report; the girl who had had the intelligence and the determination to lead a successful double life for six months, fabricating one reality for Miss Patrick while living the other for herself. And lastly this was the girl who Eyelashes had had so much time for. I thought of his tart, witty style, and how his anger kept him going when his optimism ran out. He just didn't seem like the kind of guy to hang around with one of life's wimps. Maybe Carolyn hadn't been such a loser after all. In which case the story I had written to Miss Patrick still didn't have a satisfactory ending.

I reread my report. Maybe I had made her a little too passive, a little too much used by life. Even though she had not played entirely straight with me, I had no wish to hurt Miss Patrick any more than she had already hurt herself. According to the rules, I should now call the solicitor and tell him it was ready. He would send someone to collect it and forward it to her. I would be paid any remaining fees by return of post. Case closed. Except if I were her I wouldn't want it done like this. There would be questions I had to ask, people I would want described, feelings I might need to experience. If I didn't owe it to her maybe I owed it to Carolyn. I decided to break the rules.

CHAPTER FIFTEEN

I suppose I could have called her to let her know I was coming, but she might have refused to see me. It was almost midday by the time I got there. Remembering how far the short walk to the cottage had been I took a taxi, on my expense account this time rather than hers. It dropped me at the head of the driveway. It was almost two months since I had last been here. It felt like two years. I had imagined Rose Cottage in spring bloom, earning its name with a mass of wild red roses crawling over the porch and tapping on the windowpanes, while inside she sat pouring out tea, that miraculously straight back putting the world to right. But spring comes late to the north. The roses were only just in bud, and when she opened the door it was clear that she too was still in winter. There was still the imperial posture and the soft parchment skin, but something was missing: something that was once sharp about the eyes had faded, and even her clothes looked less cared for, as if there was no one to dress for any more. She recognized me immediately and didn't look pleased to see me.

'Miss Patrick, I am sorry to disturb you like this. I understand that you probably don't want to talk to me, but I have found out some things that I think you should hear in person. I hope that's all right.' She stared at me, then stepped aside to let me in.

The parlour was colder than I remembered and the bone china stayed in the cupboards, waiting for a worthier guest. I sat down on the sofa, she opposite me, just like before. On the piano there was a space where a portrait of a young dancer had been. When it hurts too much maybe you just stop thinking about it. Especially when some of it was your own fault. I took the report out of my bag.

'I've come to you rather than your solicitor because I think you should see this first, and because I thought you might want to talk about it or ask me some questions.'

She looked at the folder. 'What is it?'

'It's my report. As much as I have been able to find out about what happened to Carolyn from the time she left Cherubim in May up until the day of her death. I have discovered who the father of the child was, why she stopped writing to you and why she couldn't tell you that she was pregnant.'

I felt rather than heard the long sigh pass through her. She sat very still, except for the slightest fluttering of the hands. After a while, when it became clear she wasn't going to move, I got up and laid the folder gently on to her lap. She stared down at it for a moment, then shook her head. 'I don't want to see it.'

'But – '

'I already know everything that I need to about what happened to her.'

I took a breath. 'No, Miss Patrick, I'm sorry, but you don't.'

She closed her eyes with a spasm of pain or maybe impatience. 'Miss Wolfe, I don't want to discuss this. Carolyn is dead. Your "report" will do nothing to change that. She was a talented young girl with a considerable future ahead of her and she threw it all away. I, of all people, do not need to be reminded of these facts. I'm an old woman and I have other things to do with my life. I am sorry. You have obviously put yourself to a good deal of trouble and expense on my behalf. I appreciate what you think you were doing, but it was never what I wanted. I thought I had made that quite clear after her death. I told you then that our association was over and that there was nothing more you could do for me.'

Sometimes I'm slow, I know that. Not everyone can be fast. But I usually get off the starting block before the race has ended.

[168]

Usually. 'Miss Patrick, I don't understand. Are you telling me that you didn't instruct your solicitor, Mr Greville, to employ me to find out what happened to her?'

'No, Miss Wolfe, I most certainly did not. I have never heard of a Mr Greville. My solicitor's name is Street, Edmund Street. He lives in Newcastle and, apart from a few questions about my guardianship, I have had no contact with him since the death.'

It was a little like living one's own personal earthquake, that physical shock as the earth opens up and your sense of balance crumbles into a wave of nausea. To counter the sickness I made a grab for something solid. I reran the solicitor's speech in my head. 'My client is, of course, deeply distressed by the loss. I think it's fair to say that they feel themselves to be in some way responsible for what has happened . . . But there is still the need for her to know.' '*Her*' to know. Mr Greville, or whoever he was, had known exactly what I would read from his choice of the deliberate pronoun. It was my turn to be distraught. I had not only been deceived, I had also been used. But if it wasn't Miss Patrick who was employing me, then who the fuck was it? And, more to the point, why?

'You seem in some trouble, Miss Wolfe – is there anything I can do for you?'

Oh, yes please. Pretend it was you, read my report anyway and let me go home to be a store detective again. Fat chance. I stood up and my legs didn't feel quite right. 'I . . . I need to use your phone . . . if that's all right?'

She showed me into the study. I stood staring at a wall and a dozen yellowing dance certificates from half a century ago, waiting for London Directory Inquiries to answer. Needless to say when I finally got through the girl couldn't find any record of solicitors Stanhope and Peters anywhere in her London computer. It was all tiresomely obvious really. I had had a phone call from a man who gave me a name and a firm's address. I went to a café in the city to meet him. I never saw his office, never talked to his secretary. In return for a couple of hundred quid advance I promised him utter confidentiality and that, should I need to get in touch either during or at the end of the job, I would use only the number he had given me. If not the oldest trick in the book then one that was distinctly greying at the temples. I could almost hear Frank laughing.

Back in the drawing-room I stopped in the doorway. I had been away longer than I thought. She was sitting with the file open on her lap, the last page still in her hand. Her face was set. Her distress filled the room.

'Miss Patrick?' She did not look up. I wanted to say something to lessen her pain, but I didn't know what. I had come to her because, despite her stubbornness, I had thought she wanted to know the truth; also because there were things in the story that might make her feel better, make her realize that Carolyn's final secrecy had been a contract rather than a desire to deceive, and that in the end her beloved little dancer had wanted life as much as money, but had got in too deep to get out. But seeing her now I knew it was all cold comfort. When push came to shove Carolyn had not come home for help, had not even been able to pick up the phone to the woman who had brought her up for almost twenty years. She had been feeding her guardian lies for so long that when she really needed her she couldn't tell her the truth. I thought back to all those dreary postcards full of performance dates and weather. They seemed so pathetic now. And so utterly make-believe. Especially for a woman as sharp as Augusta Patrick. It struck me then, standing there, looking down at her, that she had known all along that the fairytale had gone rotten. Long before she called the Cherubim company and spoke to the blowsy owner of a second-rate dancing school. And long before she called Frank. But would it really have made any difference if she had told me the truth at the beginning. Probably not. By then the story already had too many knots to be easily unravelled. Except she couldn't be sure of that. And that was what she had to live with. No. I had been wrong. My report couldn't help take away her grief. She needed it too much. To keep at bay the guilt.

'I'm sorry, but I need to ask you a few questions.' She gave no sign that she had even heard me. 'Aside from yourself and Frank

[170]

Comfort, did anyone else know that you had employed me?' She shook her head. 'What about Carolyn's mother?'

'You seem to forget,' she said quietly. 'I was her mother. In all but name.'

Surrogacy. This whole bleak little tale was riddled with it: women who couldn't have the thing they wanted most in their lives, using others to try to get it for them. So they didn't find me through her. No matter. If the police had managed to track me down then someone else could have done it too. I had left enough cards all over the place. Whatever else I needed to know, it better be now. She wouldn't answer the door to me again. But all I could think of was that new pair of ballet shoes tucked away in a box lined with bills. Cause and effect.

'Please don't get up,' I said softly. 'I can see myself out.' On the piano the Victorian father stared out at me in unrelenting disapprobation. Parents and children. I was getting sick of the pain they seem to bring to one another.

I took a mental cold shower on the walk back to the station. It didn't get rid of the dirt but it woke me up. The Hamilton family phone number was still in my book from the last time I had called. Once again it was the father that answered. And once again our conversation wasn't really worth the money. This time I told him my name, but it obviously didn't ring any bells. He'd had no contact with anyone since her death and his wife was not available for comment. She was staying with her sister, convalescing. Three weeks ago she'd been in hospital having a major operation, women's stuff. Of course that didn't preclude her from instructing a solicitor, but she didn't seem like the kind of woman to go behind her husband's back and it was clear he didn't know what I was talking about. I cut my losses and went south.

Back at King's Cross I used what I'd got. Greville's number turned out to be a paging service. Eventually we connected. He sounded pleased to hear from me, especially when I told him it was ready.

'Splendid. That was fast work. I'll send a bike round to pick it up straight away. Are you at home?'

'No, I'm at King's Cross station. And I'm not giving it to any bike rider. I want to see the client.'

'Ah, I'm afraid that's out of the question. If you remember – '

'I do remember. But I've changed my mind. If they want to read what's in the report they'll have to come and get it from me themselves.'

'Miss Wolfe, I don't think you understand. I must remind you we signed an agreement. You were paid a lot of money.'

'Not that much. And if I don't hear back from you in a couple of days I'll send you a cheque.'

The pause was so lively I could hear the wheels turning.

'I . . . er . . . I'm going to have to get back to you on this one. I must say I consider it rather shabby behaviour on your part. However . . . Will you be at home?'

'Me or a machine.'

Although it made me feel better, it was really a Pyrrhic victory. Until I opened the door to – whom? a face I already knew or someone I had never seen before – I was still the one being most used. Back to the question. Who apart from Miss Patrick and her real mother could possibly need to know enough to employ an investigator to find out? 'Her' he had said. But then he would, wouldn't he? So what if the 'her' had been only the bait to hook me. In which case who was the 'he'? Christ, the cast list wasn't that long, who else was there? Eyelashes? Surely not. He couldn't afford the fees. One of the Belmont *maison*? It was a delicious thought, juicy with possibility but fraught with contradiction. Why should everyone go to such lengths to keep me silent if somebody had instructed me to find out all along? Come on, Hannah, you know better than this. Don't waste time on questions you can't answer. Particularly when time itself might just do it for you. Go home and wait for the call.

It didn't come. Not that afternoon or that evening. Or the day afterwards. By the second evening I had got tired of waiting. The only thing worse than a plot that doesn't work is one in suspended animation. Maybe my attitude was wrong. Maybe the telephone was like the kettle: the longer I sat looking at it, the less likely it was to do its stuff. I had been working for too long. What I really needed was an evening off.

I bought a bag of popcorn and a large Coca-Cola and sat in the second row, where my mother always told me it would damage my eyes. More likely she was worried about me being so near to any naked flesh that might appear. The movie was pure Hollywood, well dressed and not unintelligent until the last ten minutes when it double-jointed itself to reach a happy ending. I imagined Carolyn standing on the wet grass by the river, poised for death, an orchestra of strings in the background while Belmont ran through the rain towards her. 'You don't need to do this. I shan't persecute you because – well, you better know the truth. It wasn't my baby after all. The sperm bank got their frozen vials mixed up. The father of your child is really . . .' but my imagination deserted me at the last slow-motion moment and she flung herself in anyway. Not a single member of the violin section put down their instruments to help. Bastards.

I walked back via the all-night pizza joint and jogged the last two hundred yards with a Four Seasons balanced in my hands. Despite myself I felt OK. The power of escapism. It lasted all the way home.

In retrospect I was surprised they'd bothered with the front-door lock. I had put a good deal of thought and professional advice into that one and it must have taken them some time. As we all know, if they'd come in through the back it would have been easy to force the loo window. Of course, girls with garden flats spend their lives waiting for this to happen. You either slap bars on every gap where the light comes in or do what you can and pray that they come when you're out and don't jerk off into your undies drawer. Up until now I'd been lucky. But this one, of course, had nothing to do with luck. I left the pizza on the step and went in slowly, just in case.

The air reeked of it, that sharp, static quality of intrusion. But atmosphere was all that remained. No one was there. Neither, I realized as I turned on the living-room light, was the video or television. Give unto the insurance people what is insurable. I hit the bedroom. The report had been in the bottom drawer of my desk, tucked away amid tax returns and National Insurance records. It was still there. I sat down on the floor and held it in my arms. Hannah with her unharmed baby. Kate would have found it poignant. When the relief had subsided my brain came back. I checked the answering machine. Nothing. Then I went into the bedroom. On closer inspection the desk didn't even look as if it had been disturbed. Certainly there was nothing to suggest a burglar with one aim and not a lot of time. Was I really looking at a piece of pure amazing coincidence? What do you think?

CHAPTER SIXTEEN

The police took most of the next morning and the locksmith the rest of the afternoon. I stayed in and watched the traffic go by. As far as I could tell no one was looking back up at me. Except someone had to have been there the day before, watching, waiting until I closed the door and disappeared off down the end of the street. The question was, had they also been at the station, or on the train north to Miss Patrick's? The fact that I hadn't spotted them didn't mean they weren't there, just that I wasn't looking. This time, though, I was. After the locksmith had been I went out to the local post office. Halfway up the street a man got out of his car and started walking behind me. When I went into the building he carried on walking. He was nowhere to be seen when I came out, but that didn't prove anything. In the time in between I had duplicated my report, sent the original to myself via Frank's office and the other to Kate's home. The car was still there when I got back. I took a note of the number. I had been away for only an hour. When I got back the little light on the message machine was winking joyfully at me. The cultured-pearl voice was Greville's.

'Miss Wolfe, I am sorry not to find you in. I have spoken to my client about your "conditions" and they have said they will think about it and get back to me. Obviously I can't predict when. Perhaps you'd be so good as to keep the report somewhere safe until we can discuss the matter further.'

Answering machines: a singularly great invention, except for the fact that they make everyone sound as though they're lying – something to do with trying to have a conversation with a piece of tape. This time the number he'd left was not a paging service. Instead I got a machine. Please leave a message. I didn't bother.

The evening passed without incident. Kate rang to welcome me home and tell me she had sent Dad a cashmere scarf on my behalf. If need be I could pretend it was a second present. I thanked her, omitting to tell her how pissed off I was that she always assumed the mother role, leaving me as the eternal child.

'You all right?'

'Yeah, I'm fine.'

'OK, don't bite my head off, I'm only asking. You want to come for Sunday lunch? Colin will be away. If it doesn't rain I thought I'd make a picnic and take the kids to the zoo.'

'Sounds great. I'll let you know.'

I had put the phone down before I realized I hadn't told her about the envelope due to drop through her letterbox next morning. She was engaged when I called back, probably talking to the family. I'd tell her tomorrow. I went to bed with a can of Mace, but it was more precaution than fear. You'd need to be a pretty dumb burglar to try again the very night after. I slept well. Next morning I woke up to the realization that, as far as the case was concerned, I was becalmed at sea and that until his or her client lordship decided to call me there was nothing else I could do. It just goes to show how wrong you can be.

It arrived through the door just after breakfast, plopping on to the mat along with a catalogue for bulbs and a chance to win £200,000 by opening the envelope. It had come first-class, franked West London last post the day before. Inside there were two pieces of paper folded neatly. I opened them up. They were photocopies, forms of some kind with dates on one side and comments and the odd figure on the other, all handwritten in a small cramped style and all in French. I had to put them down on the table to stop my hands shaking. It didn't help. The writing was appalling and even when the letters made sense the words they spelt often didn't. Jargon? Technical stuff? At least the dates were readable. Starting in May and going through to January. No, not technical stuff. Medical stuff? A doctor's report. On the other side of the dates one set of figures stood out: 130/90. What could it be but blood pressure? I sat down. What I was looking at was a copy of Carolyn Hamilton's pregnancy record that someone had sent me in the post from West London. A report that according to Belmont had gone up in smoke. So what had happened? Did he change his mind (so how come no compliments slip?) or was this someone else's *billet doux*? In which case – and let's hear it in chorus now – whose? For somebody who had this case all buttoned up and ready to go, I was becoming severely unravelled.

When in pain call a doctor. His wife gave me an office number. When I got through, his secretary said he was busy but then I knew that. When he called back he said he would make time. I knew that too. He'd meet me in an hour and a half at his office. I thought about ways of killing time constructively. Then I rang Frank. Funny. Half the time I'm not even sure I like him very much, yet when things get rough his is always the number I call. What does that tell you about my relationships to men? Kate would have a field day. Being Frank, of course, he wasn't exactly sympathetic.

'See what you get for not telling uncle what you've been doing. I could have you for moonlighting, you know.'

'Come on, Frank. I resigned, remember?'

'Yeah, but indirectly you got this job through me. I could be asking for a commission.'

'You're on. Ten per cent of the money for ten per cent of the work.'

'Yeah, well, I don't know if I can make it. I've got to see a man about a crime.'

'Please.'

'OK. I can probably get there by twelve o'clock. What's the name of the pub? Yeah, I think I know it.'

The car was still there when I came out. A guy with a peaked cap was standing on the corner looking in a shop window. I saw him again on the tube. He got out at Goodge Street. I let him take the lift, while I used the stairs. By the time I got to the top he had gone. I didn't see him again, but it was still the tail end of the rush hour and there were lots of people he could be hiding behind. I decided not to worry about him.

The entrance to the Middlesex hospital brought back broken nights. Hugh Galton, not so much a physician, more an old flame, where the embers had never quite gone cold. It was a long time ago, but I like to think of myself as the one who encouraged him towards his specialty, gynaecology. We were amateurs then, of course, relying more on enthusiasm than skill: altogether too young and too raunchy for true love. When the real thing happened she was prettier than I and much more dedicated to medicine. Doctors and nurses; a professional coupling, bringing forth a brood of anatomically perfect children and a rapid rise to a consultancy in one of London's best teaching hospitals. The teacher returning to the place where he had been a student. But for me it would always be associated with sex: sneaking myself in past white coats and black stockings to a bedroom like a monk's cell where we lay crushed together in a single bed, till the bleeper separated us and I was left keeping the sheets warm while he was off to resuscitate the dead. Sex was our way of being alive. We couldn't get enough of it.

From the look of him he still couldn't. Either that or his children had sleeping problems. It was good to see him. Over the years we had gradually lost touch, neither of us being the Christmas-card sort, but there are some memories that time doesn't wither. I still thought he was cute, but I got the impression he wouldn't appreciate hearing it. Maybe he was just a smidgeon embarrassed, being reminded of so much illicit past in the building of his official present.

'So, Hannah, what can I do for you?'

I smiled. Doctor-patient games. Didn't everyone play them once? 'I have something I need you to look at. A set of medical notes from a certain patient.'

I took them out of my bag and handed them to him. He drew them out of the file, glanced at them, then back at me.

'They're in French.'

'Yeah, I seem to remember you used to speak it quite well.'

'Yes, but that was a long time ago.' He glanced at them again. 'Hmmn. Should I ask where you got them?'

'Someone sent them to me through the post.'

'What about the patient?'

'She was a missing girl I'd been employed to find. She's dead now.'

'I see.'

'She died a few days after the last entry, when she was eight months pregnant. I need to know if there might have been any medical reason for her death.' I paused. 'I'm not asking you to do anything unethical.'

'No,' he said, looking at me, then looking down at the pages.

I waited. On his desk was a portrait of three little girls, giggling together on a beach somewhere. They looked cute too, although not in the same way. He was studying the last page, then he went back to the beginning. I could feel my palms getting sticky.

'Now I know how my secretary feels when she tries to decipher my handwriting. Let's see.' He shook his head. 'From what I can work out – and I must say that's not a lot – I can't see any immediate major problem. Though her blood pressure was on the high side towards the end. How did she die?'

'She fell in a river. The suggestion is she might have had some kind of fit and lost her balance.'

'Eclampsia?' He made a face. 'On first glance hard to confirm that one way or the other. The blood pressure would fit, but there would have to have been other signs. I think there may be a couple of urine tests here, though I'd need to translate the results to be sure of a protein reading. But you know the symptoms of pre-eclampsia are pretty hard to miss. Most doctors spot it long before it gets to the serious stage, make their patients rest, even take them into hospital if necessary.'

[179]

'Yes, well, in this case hospital would have been very much a last resort and she might just have disobeyed advice.'

'Silly girl. Hmmn. Eclampsia? I assume the fact that you're here at all means that the PM didn't show up anything.'

'No, although they didn't have the medical report.'

'No, but they had the corpse. Chronic eclampsia would probably show up in the foetus. Still, I suppose it depends on how hard they were looking.'

'Probably not that hard. She left a suicide note.'

'I see. Or rather I don't. Curiouser and curiouser, eh? Well, all I can say is if eclampsia was the problem it'll be in here somewhere. Let's see. Otherwise everything seems pretty normal. Except, of course, for the blood type. She was Rhesus neg.'

'Rhesus neg? What does that mean?'

'Not a lot, normally. It's not exactly rare – something like fifteen per cent of the population are negative. But under certain conditions if the father is Rhesus positive, well, you want the long explanation or the short?'

'Let's start with the short.'

'Basically it can cause problems for the baby. If the foetus is also rhesus positive, of which there's a good chance, and the woman has developed antibodies either from a previous pregnancy or a termination or a mixed-match blood transfusion, those antibodies will start to attack the baby's blood. In the old days in extreme cases a baby could die *in utero* from erythroblastosis foetalis – sorry, anaemia and heart failure. If it was born alive it would be badly jaundiced and have to be given an immediate exchange transfusion to get the antibodies out of its system. Fifty years ago, before it was properly understood, rhesus disease was a killer. But now it's no big deal. Here in Britian most rhesus-negative women are given a shot to prevent antibodies anyway. And if not we can do safe blood transfusions *in utero* after 22–23 weeks.'

I wondered vaguely what the long explanation would have been. 'And what about in Carolyn's case?'

'Well, as I say, it doesn't seem to have been a problem. At

least not as far as I can tell. She was young. If this was her first pregnancy the chances are it wouldn't have been relevant anyway since she would never have developed the antibodies. And they would have monitored her throughout anyway. But this is all off the top of my head, you understand. If you want me to confirm it you'd have to give me time to study the notes properly, get to work with a medical dictionary.'

'One more question. Would it have made any difference if the child had been conceived by artificial insemination?'

'None at all. Of course since the process is anonymous they wouldn't know the blood type of the father –'

'Actually in this case it wasn't anonymous. She knew him.'

'Really? Well, maybe his blood type is in here somewhere too. AID but not anonymous, eh?' I nodded. 'Well, I don't suppose I should ask what the story behind this was.' He smiled. 'I seem to remember you always got very hot under the collar about secrecy. What was it? – "the public's right to know". You must have changed your mind about some things.'

'Oh, you know, growing older.'

He shook his head. 'Never heard of it.'

I used to love his sense of humour. It had been one of the most attractive things about him. That and the touch of his body in the cold young hours of the morning. Across the desk my old lover smiled at me, the same crooked smile I remembered as being such a turn-on. For years after we split up I'd harboured this fantasy that we had unfinished business, him and I, and that some time in the future we might share a moment of erotic reminiscence, powerful enough to make us think of getting back on the couch. But sexual memory can do strange things to the psyche and like most things anticipation is often all the pleasure. When it came to it, we were no longer twenty-two any more. I was neither as invincible nor as invulnerable as I had been and he, alas, was no longer as irresistible. The moment slipped away. I don't know whether he even noticed it. He leant forward in his chair, gathering up the notes. 'I'm sorry to rush you, Hannah, but I have a ward round with second-year students in ten minutes.'

[181]

I wondered if they looked younger than traffic wardens, but didn't ask. He walked me to the door. I held out my hand for the file. 'Leave it with me. I'm at the Hammersmith later today. There's a consultant there whose wife is French, he worked in Paris for a couple of years. I'll see what he says. Maybe I can come up with something a bit more useful.'

I had remembered the name of the pub on the corner perfectly. Frank wasn't there, but then it was only 11.15 a.m. At the bar a young man in a houseman's coat was sitting propped in front of a pint of beer smoking a cigarette. The end of the day and the night shift. Poor things. No wonder nurses want to look after them. I ordered a Bloody Mary and a cheese roll. Elevenses. Frank would be proud of me. As he's only too eager to tell you, the new licensing laws have done a lot for the image of private investigators in Britain. In the old days when you had something to thrash out you had to go to a café and sit playing with your teaspoon and rock cake. I took a swig of the drink. Too much Worcester sauce and not enough lemon. I decided to leave it for Frank who probably wouldn't notice.

He called an hour later. The place was already filling up for lunch as I made my way to the phone. The barmaid told me not to be long. 'You know, Frank, people are going to think you're just a figment of my imagination.'

'Listen, there's nothing I can do. He's doing me a favour, all right. If I'm not here when he gets back I won't get another chance. You I can do on the phone. Come on, tell me what you've got.'

So I did. He listened carefully all the way through. And to give him credit he thought a bit before he went to work on it.

'So where's the report now?' I told him. 'Good. And the medical records?'

'Copy with me, copy with Hugh.'

'You think he'll find anything?'

'I don't know. Except why else would someone send them to me?'

'How about if Belmont was looking for a way to convince you

he kept his side of the bargain: a couple of sheets on care and concern of the pregnant wouldn't go amiss.'

'So why not give them to me then, why go to all the trouble of having them posted in London three days later?'

'Maybe he changed his mind. Got worried that you might not see it his way after all.'

'Maybe. But that still doesn't help explain who the client is. And who broke into my house two nights ago.'

'Yeah, well there you gotta decide whether it's coincidence with a big C or a little one.'

'Meaning?'

'Meaning you could be making it more complicated for yourself than need be. You know how it pains me to kick you when you're down, but you know it wouldn't be the first time. Remember the Pollack case.'

'Frank, I was wet behind the ears. And I still say the car could have belonged to his wife.'

'Sure. As long as Sierras always look exactly like Citroëns. Anyway, I only bring it up to serve as a reminder. Look at the facts. You've got a client who wishes to remain anonymous. Why? Obviously because she or he feels bad about what she or he has or hasn't done but doesn't want to have to admit it. I tell you where I'd go. To the real mother. Paralysed by guilt and grief after fifteen years of neglect. Desperate to find out what really happened to her baby. What more do you want?'

'Do me a favour. It's tabloid stuff, Frank.'

'And that, little lady, is sometimes just what makes it true.'

'Anyway, I've told you, it's not her. She was in hospital.'

'Doesn't prove a thing. Listen, I'm not saying it *is* her, I'm just making a point. This client stuff could have nothing to do with the medical report.'

'Or with the break-in?'

'What did they take? The television and the video. What did they leave? The report.'

'There's such a thing as a hand-held photocopier, you know,' I said, thinking about it for the first time.

[183]

'Don't tell your grandfather how to suck eggs, Hannah. It's one of my favourite toys. But if Greville had already got the report, why bother to call you about it?'

'So I would think he hadn't?' But even as I said it, it sounded weak.

'Hmmn. And what about this guy in the car? You sure it's not just your imagination?'

'No, of course I'm not sure. And it wasn't the same guy as on the tube, but who knows, maybe there's a whole army of them.' I looked around the pub. It could have been anybody. 'Christ, Frank, do you always know for certain when you're being followed?'

'Yeah, but then that's why it's my name on the door and not yours. That and other things. Listen, you want my advice? Sit tight and wait to see what Dr Kildare brings home.'

'Great. Well, thanks a lot, Frank.'

'Wait. I haven't finished yet. You got a buzzer to get back into your answering machine at home?'

'If I need it, yes.'

'OK. Stay away from home for a bit. Take the afternoon off, maybe spend some time buying some underwear – that'll make it easy to spot 'em. Then go out and get yourself laid for a night or two. And stay at their place, just in case. You can check your phone from there.'

'In case of what?'

'In case coincidence is more than coincidence. Now, you still want me to bust a gut to get over there?'

'No. Thanks.'

'All right. I'll give it a bit more thought and get back to you. Call me with a number where I can reach you ... Oh, and Hannah?'

'Yeah?'

'Ten per cent, remember?'

I decided to defer to the expert. They've even got whole shops devoted to the art of the undy now. If it hadn't been work I would probably have quite enjoyed it, slipping myself in and out of a variety of lace corsets and boob-enhancing bras. The girl in the changing-room next to me spent a hundred and twenty quid. Maybe she had someone special to show it all to. After the third shop I was pretty sure I was alone. Thanks, Frank. Then I thought about all the people I could spend the night with. It wasn't exactly a rich choice. I ended up going to Kate's. They were in the middle of a tea party when I arrived. Six mothers and what felt like twenty-six children. The kitchen was awash with orange juice and chocolate-chip crumbs, most of which Benjamin was attempting to hoover up with his nose while Amy was locked in mortal combat with a curly-haired boy who was trying to get on to her tractor. Kate sat sipping tea watching the scene with admirable detachment. Of course she was surprised to see me, but being Kate didn't mention it. She simply pointed me in the direction of the teapot, and said they would all be leaving soon.

When they did, Amy went with them, clutching a small overnight bag and exiting with theatrical hugs and waves. Back in the kitchen Kate pulled out a bottle of gin from the kitchen cupboard and poured two hits, then drowned them with tonic.

At my feet Benjamin was making a noise. He had pulled himself up until he was clinging to my knees, and was letting out a series of fierce guttural explosions. Kate's voice reached me from behind the freezer door.

'You'd better pick him up. He wants to be held. It's the only way you'll get him to stop.'

I leant over and put my arms out. He moved himself inside them and I lifted him up. He stood up on my lap, bandy legs like little pile drivers stomping into my thighs, practising for the Big Walk. He had cheeks like powder-puffs and a chin like Buddha, and he smelt of slightly sour milk and baby powder. I couldn't decide whether it was pleasant or repellent. He poked around my eyes for a while then flopped down on to my lap and sat, apparently content. I kept my arms around him to stop him falling off. I thought about all the women in this story and the babies they'd never had or let someone else take away from them. Was this what they'd all hungered for, the aroma of rancid milk and handfuls of chubby flesh?

Kate placed a glass in front of me and a bottle in front of him. He grabbed it and began sucking, instantly mesmerized by pleasure. Don't grow up, little nephew. It's cold and dark out there, and there's never a tit when you need one. I took a swig at the gin. It was stronger than it looked. Whatever happens I musn't get drunk.

'Well, and to what do we owe the honour?'

'Oh, I was just passing.'

'Just passing?'

'Yeah. Where'd Amy go?'

'To Polly's. She's staying the night.'

'Nice. By the way, thanks for sending Dad's present. I'll leave you a cheque. Did he like it?'

'Well, it would be you he'd call, not me.' She was right. And he hadn't. Maybe this time he'd spotted the handwriting. 'OK, let's try again. What's up, Hannah?'

'Nothing.'

'You come here voluntarily during a tea party, sit with twelve kids under five and their nannies and mothers and then say nothing is wrong.'

I smiled. 'I wanted to tell you something and I happened to be passing.'

'Yes.'

'I've sent something in the post. A big brown envelope. If you haven't got it already, it'll arrive tomorrow morning.'

'And? Are you going to tell me now, or should I wait till tomorrow?'

I shook my head. 'It'll be addressed to me and I don't want you to open it. It's work. Just something I need kept safe.'

She frowned. 'Should I ask from whom?'

'To be honest, I can't tell you.'

'Of course not. I'll put it in the laundry cupboard. Underneath the bibs and facecloths. Will that be safe enough?'

'That's fine. Thanks a lot.'

On my lap Benjamin was moving from bliss to waking slumber, eyes wide open, mind disengaged. Outside it was a winter twilight, a gentle but swift slide into dark. Soon we would be turning the clocks forward. People would start sitting out in their gardens. I imagined Colin with a beer in one hand, fanning the barbecue with the other, while Kate lugged saucepans of hot water out to the paddling pool. Playing at being mums and dads. There were worse ways to spend a summer.

'Listen, Hannah, I have to ask you something.' I should have spotted it already. That slight tension that comes between sisters before the storm clouds break. 'What was it happened to you in France?'

'In France? Not a lot.'

'But you were working on the dancer's case, yes?'

'Yes.'

'So. Did you find out who the father was?'

'Um . . . No, not really.'

'Oh come on, Hannah, I don't mind being used as the domestic fantasy to make you feel better about not having children, but I do object to being treated as educationally subnormal.' Kate's temper. A rare and wonderful thing, spiced now with adult humour but still to be taken note of. 'You arrive here out of the blue, make small talk for half an hour, then ask if I'll keep something safe for you, and I'm supposed to oblige you without the luxury of a single question. If you don't want me to know then why didn't you take it to Frank?'

I closed my eyes. 'I did as well. I'm sorry, Kate, I didn't mean to sound patronizing. It's just a long story. And I'm not even sure I understand it.'

'Fine,' she said, but didn't mean it.

'I know who the father is. What I still don't know is why she died. But I've found some medical reports. I'm hoping they'll tell me.'

She nodded. 'And that's what's in the envelope?'

No, actually, but it was too complicated to explain. 'Yeah, that and other things.'

[187]

'But you'd prefer it if I didn't read them?'

'Yes.'

'And it's just work?'

'What does that mean?'

'I mean you seem different, agitated. I felt it when you called from France too. I wondered if there was something more.'

'What more could it be?'

She hesitated. Then decided to say it anyway. 'I wondered if there was a man involved.'

It was my turn to get exasperated. 'Christ, Kate, I'm strung out, and you immediately assume it must be because of some guy.'

'No,' she said quietly. 'It was not immediate. I gave it some considerable thought.'

I shook my head. 'Honestly, it's nothing serious. I'm just tired and touchy, all right?'

She nodded. I looked down at Benjamin. Out for the count. I opened my mouth to tell her to change the subject. But she did it for me. Sort of. 'Colin thinks you're afraid of men, you know.'

Colin. Mr Psychoanalysis 1991. Give me a break. 'You mean he thinks I'm gay?'

This time she laughed. 'Oh Hannah, he's not that much of a fool.'

'No,' I said begrudgingly. 'He's not. What else does he think?'

'That you liked Joshua more than you were willing to admit and that you use your job as an excuse for not sorting out your personal life.'

'I see. And what do you think?'

She paused, choosing her words. 'Well, I suppose I think he's not that much of a fool.'

Great. If you can't trust your sister who can you trust? But nobody else tells you quite as much truth. We sat silent for a moment. Then she said, 'You're in trouble, aren't you?'

'I don't know.' I thought about it. 'It's possible.'

'Can I help?'

I thought about it some more. 'Yeah. I might need somewhere to stay for the night.'

She looked at me for a moment, and we both read the disappointment in her eyes. 'Of course. The spare room's made up.'

'Thanks. I won't get in the way. And anything you need me to do . . .'

She got up and turned her attention to the sink, maybe so I wouldn't register how the disappointment had turned to anger. 'Yes, well, as a matter of fact there is. I didn't manage to get out to the shops today. Colin's due home in a couple of hours and I need to buy some stuff for dinner. It would be easier if I didn't have to take Ben with me.'

The little man himself was still comatose, eyelids fluttering on dreams of lactose sucked from giant breasts. Interesting how as they grow older the milk dream dries up but the other fantasies remain. 'Of course. Be as long as you like. You know, if you want I'll babysit. The two of you could go out for the evening. See a movie, have a meal.' You could tell she was tempted. 'It's all right. I've done it before. He knows I can change a nappy and make a bottle.'

'Yes, but what if he wakes up later?'

'Then I'll pick him up and sing to him. He'll go to sleep immediately to get away from the noise.'

She smiled. Pax. Like exchanging toys or Barbie-doll clothes when we were little. 'I'll ring Colin, see what he says.'

Colin, of course, said yes. Anything rather than have to share the dinner table with his sister-in-law. They agreed to meet in town. Together we bathed Benjamin and put him in his nightsuit. Of course he sussed something was up, clung to Kate as soon as she started to get dressed. By the time the cab came they were inseparable. I put my hands out. 'Come on, give him to me. You know he'll stop screaming the minute you're out of the door.' But behind her reticence I read something else. Something she didn't quite know how to say. 'Kate, don't even think about it. Nobody knows where I am. We'll be quite safe. Do you really think I would have asked to stay in the first place if it was any other way?' Put like that it made both of us embarrassed. I gave her a gentle push. 'Go on, get out of here. You know you want to.'

We went out together to see her off, Benjamin a screeching windmill in my arms. She waved all the way down the road from the back window of the cab. It was more traumatic for her than for him. As soon as he sussed that his screams wouldn't bring her back he treated the whole thing with admirable pragmatism, aided and abetted by the odd digestive biscuit in my pocket. Silence fell. We went back and sat together in the living-room watching *Sesame Street* on the video, after which we both crawled round the carpet in pursuit of each other. Eventually he got tired and lay on the floor. I was tempted to join him. I went into the kitchen and heated up some milk. He took the bottle and allowed me to carry him up the stairs to the bedroom. He whimpered a little when I put him down, so I sat by the cot and stroked his back. He rooted himself down in the bedclothes, bottom up in the air, eyes wide open watching me through the bars. I told him a story. About the last few days. He fell asleep before I got to the end.

I sat with him for a little while, just in case. His sense of peace was seductive, so complete, so contagious, so simple. A bottle of milk, the odd biscuit and an endless supply of love and attention; when it comes down to it that's all they require. And in return they make you feel indispensable. Until, that is, they can do it for themselves. After which it's just a matter of time and bloody battles until they decide to leave home. I did it to my family, he would do it to his. The mistake is letting yourself feel like a parent when all you really are is a guardian. Of course, you can see it all so clearly from the outside. Yet ask Kate or my mother about the sense of loss, and both of them would no doubt swear it was all worth it, that the pleasure far outweighed any pain. But then they could hardly say anything else, could they? Sometimes I think motherhood is really a form of religious conversion: faith taking you places where reason cannot follow. But as we all know, even atheists sometimes find themselves wondering what all the fuss is about.

See what happens when you spend too much time watching sleeping cherubs? Downstairs I turned up the baby alarm until I could hear him breathing, made myself a strong cup of coffee and went back to work. There was only one message on my answering machine at home. But it was worth waiting for: Hugh's voice sounding just a little excited. 'Hannah, I've done some work on this stuff. You'd better give me a call. I don't know if it'll help but I think I've found something. I'll be at home after eight.'

I looked at my watch: 8.14 p.m. I redialled.

CHAPTER SEVENTEEN

'I'll go through it point by point, all right. Stop me if you don't understand.'

'OK.'

'The first thing you should know is that there were definite signs of pre-eclampsia. The blood pressure started to rise around week thirty and there were traces of protein in her urine. Also some swelling of the ankles.'

'You mean you think she could have had some kind of fit after all?'

'No, that's not what I said. I know it's important, Hannah, but it'll be easier if you just listen rather than jump.'

'Sorry.'

'OK. The other thing the report says, quite categorically, is that the AID donor was rhesus negative too. Now since you told me that she knew the donor I would assume that that information comes from a blood test done by the doctor.' Of course. He had treated the old man for long enough, must have punctured a thousand holes in that liver-spotted skin. Rhesus negative, eh. Both of them. It had indeed been a coupling made in heaven. What was the rule? Two rhesus negatives cannot make a positive . . . I bit my tongue.

'Now what that means, of course, is that since two negatives can't make a positive the baby would have automatically been rhesus negative too. So far so simple. Medical fact.'

'Which also means that even if the mother did have antibodies the baby would have been safe?'

He sighed. 'You know you never could be quiet for more than five minutes at a time. I always found it extremely irritating and very attractive at the same time.' Did you? How come you never told me? Ah well, too late now. 'Anyway, you're absolutely right. Rhesus antibodies can only work against rhesus positive blood. The mother *did* have antibodies though. The report shows a blood test taken just after pregnancy was established. The titre is very small, but they are there.'

'Titre?'

'Sorry, jargon. It's how we measure antibodies.'

'Right.'

'Now comes the more complicated part. With a rhesus negative woman most doctors nowadays would monitor the antibody levels throughout the pregnancy. Maybe once at twenty-eight weeks, again at thirty-two. That's more or less automatic practice now. However, this doctor didn't do it.'

'I see.' Except I didn't, quite. 'But I mean why should he? – you said yourself that the baby was rhesus negative. In which case there was no chance of the antibodies harming it.'

'Yes, that's true. And no doubt that was exactly what this doctor thought too. Even so, precautions are precautions. And if he were my houseman he'd be looking for another job.'

I had this image of the faithful old French retainer skulking out of the hospital, under the never-darken-my-doors-again finger of the shining young consultant. 'I think it might have been more a question of retirement than redundancy. I gather he'd been around for a while.'

'Yes, well maybe that was his problem. Anyway, let's get back to the pregnancy. According to the report the first six or seven months went fine, no problems. Then around thirty weeks the patient starts to develop the first signs of pre-eclampsia with a rise in blood pressure. As far as the doctor ascertains everything else is OK. Her weight appears perfectly satisfactory, no excessive gain as usually happens with pre-eclampsic mothers, a basic

[193]

external examination shows the baby to be growing well and the patient says she's feeling regular movements. He advises her to take it easy, to rest. Fair enough. High blood pressure can often cure itself. Two weeks later her urine starts to show traces of protein. Sign two. Six days later – she's now thirty-four weeks – he notes that she is very anxious, although still insisting that she's feeling fine. However there is now swelling occurring in fingers and feet, although by thirty-four weeks that could be happening anyway. He orders her to bed for three days. But then the blood pressure is still high, the urine still has protein, the swelling is slightly better. According to her there are no other symptoms, no headaches or problems with vision. He decides to keep her in bed and monitor her. For the next ten days nothing changes. By now I would have had her in hospital, but he's hanging on.' He paused, but it was more for breath than effect. That silence was still to come. 'Then – and I must say not before time – he sends off a blood test.'

This was it. I could tell from the sound of his voice. 'And?'

'The result shows a massive titre of antibodies.'

Yep, definitely it. But what? 'Wait a minute, I don't understand. You mean more than before?'

'I mean massively more.'

'But how is that possible? I mean I thought the whole idea of a rhesus-negative baby was that the mother wouldn't produce more antibodies.'

'Not wouldn't, Hannah, couldn't. It isn't possible. That's the point.'

'So what does it mean?'

'It means that the baby can't have been rhesus negative.'

'But I thought you said that two . . .' Holy shit. A positive baby. 'You mean that the father can't have been rhesus negative after all? The donor wasn't the real father?'

'You got it.' Next to me the baby alarm exploded with noise. I almost dropped the phone with terror. 'Hannah, you still there?'

'Yes . . . er . . . it was just a child coughing. It's OK. My God, Hugh, but would *she* have known? I mean could she . . .'

'You're in a better position to answer that question than I am. Assuming she knew that the father wasn't the father – and since all AID candidates are told specifically not to sleep with anyone else at time of insemination, she must have been aware of the risks, and assuming she understood the significance of rhesus disease – and most textbooks spell it out pretty clearly – then at some level, yes, she would have known.'

I heard Belmont in his tell-the-truth voice describe again those idyllic middle few months. 'She seemed very happy with her decision. She even became quite interested in the process, reading a lot about the pregnancy . . .' Until the change. Yes, she had known. She must have done. But there was no one she could tell. No wonder she'd become withdrawn. No wonder she'd asked to leave. Except . . . except if Hugh had worked it out, then so, eventually, must everyone else.

'Hugh, when did you say the doctor did that final blood test?'

'Just under thirty-six weeks.'

'No, the date, what was the date?'

'Hold on, I'll have to look it up.' I waited, smelling my own sweat on my skin. 'Boy, this guy's writing is terrible. Here you are. It's the last entry – 18 January.'

18 January? The day after she phoned Eyelashes. The day that, according to Belmont, she went out to buy Augusta Patrick's birthday present and never came back. 'And when did the result come through?' I think my voice might have been shaking.

'It's not dated differently, so I presume that same day. Presumably for once in his life he used a bit of medical science and sent it out to an emergency lab. Maybe he was suspicious. In which case depending on how far the nearest lab was he could have got the result back in what, a couple of hours?'

'And the doctor would have realized, I mean about the father?'

'Of course. It would have explained everything. There was, I'm afraid, a certain medical irony to all this. You see, in extreme cases pre-eclampsia can be one of the signs of rhesus disease. But you hardly ever come across it because it doesn't usually get to that stage. As I said, normally the doctor would know

[195]

immediately because of the increased reading of antibodies in the blood tests done earlier in the pregnancy. But because of the donor's blood group, rhesus disease was the one thing this doctor wasn't looking for. For him the signs of pre-eclampsia were just that.'

Boy, I wouldn't like to have been in his shoes when he discovered his mistake. Maybe Belmont didn't need to pay him off. Maybe he offered his silence as an alternative to a malpractice suit. Saturday 18th. It must have been one hell of a day. Confrontation versus flight. No contest. But if Daniel followed her, was it really in order to bring her back? Hugh was talking, but I was already standing by the riverbed listening for footsteps behind me. 'What?'

'I asked when she died?'

'Er . . . later that day. Some time between six and eight thirty.'

'And when was she found?'

'Two days later. The body got caught in some weeds.'

'Hmmn. That may explain why the post mortem didn't show it up. Of course I'm not a pathologist, but depending on the stage of rhesus disease the foetus would probably have been rather swollen. On the other hand a body in the water for two days . . .'

Rather swollen. I sort of didn't want to think about that. Except I had to. 'Do you think the baby was already dead?' And I was surprised to hear the break in my voice. Maybe here it was, after all this time, the real reason for suicide.

'I very much doubt it. And for her to be sure it would have had to stop moving a while ago. In which case that *would* have shown up on the PM. No, not dead, but it would have been in trouble. By thirty-six weeks the antibodies would have been crossing through the placenta and attacking the blood supply for some time. The baby would have been becoming progressively more anaemic. It might even have stopped moving. In order to cope it would be frantically pumping what little blood it had left around the system. Eventually the effort of pumping would have caused the heart failure. Technically that's what would kill it.'

He stopped. I couldn't think of anything to say. Next to me the sound of Benjamin's short, loud breathing filled the room. 'Are you all right, Hannah?'

'Mmn ... Yeah, I'm fine. Listen, er ... thanks a million. I mean I really appreciate ...'

'It's OK. You sure you're all right?'

'Of course. This is my job.'

'Yes, well it's mine too, but it doesn't stop it being a bitch sometimes.'

'Yeah.' A memory suddenly washed like driftwood into my mind. Him and me outside a cinema, his arm around me as I sobbed into his shoulder. Even he wasn't completely dry eyed. I couldn't even remember the film any more, but I was glad that the years hadn't thickened both our skins that much.

'Well, Hannah, if there's nothing more I can do ... You know you can call me if you need more help.'

'Sure.'

'Do I assume you'd like me to put this report in the shredding machine?'

'Please.'

'Fair enough. And listen, take care of yourself, all right? Maybe we could get together for a drink some time? Talk about something other than work.'

'Yeah, some time.' What is it people say about never going back? 'I'll call you,' I said, but it wasn't him I was thinking about.

I didn't have time to dwell on it. The front door opened with a bang. I was up and on the balls of my feet heading for the doorway when I heard Colin's voice in the hall. I caught up with it at the bottom of the stairs.

'God almighty, Hannah, don't you think it's about time you developed more of a sense of responsibility? I just hope for your sake he's all right.' But he didn't wait for an answer, just thundered up the stairs two at a time.

'Who?' I called up after him, just because I knew it would enrage him further. So Kate had told him about work. I would have thought she had more brains. I heard her come in behind me. The door slammed a second time. When I turned it was hard to tell which one of them was the most furious. She saw me and shook her head, at a temporary loss for words.

'It's all right,' I said. 'I know. You mentioned I was in trouble and he freaked out about the baby.'

She used some words I hadn't heard from her for a long time. From upstairs Benjamin let out a wail. 'Well, if he's crying at least he's not dead,' she yelled up the stairs. 'And since you've woken him, you can bloody well get him back to sleep.' She flung off her coat and stood at the bottom of the stairs. It was a while since I had seen the maternal caring Kate so blazing mad. 'I swear sometimes he can be such a stupid old woman. We're sitting in the cinema waiting for the film to begin and I just mentioned it, that's all, and he blows his top. What does he think? I'm really going to leave Benjamin with you if I believed there was any chance of trouble?'

'Listen, don't worry about it. He'll be so ashamed he over-reacted that he'll have to be nice to me for weeks. It could be the beginning of a whole new relationship. As it happens it's perfect timing. I have to go anyway.'

'Now, don't you start –'

'Not just because of this, I promise. I've had a phone call. There's someone I have to see.'

She sighed, as if it were all too much for her. 'So when will you be back?'

'Don't worry. I'll stay somewhere else tonight.'

'No you will not. I'm not letting him getting away with driving you out. He'll use it as an excuse for being right. It'll take us a couple of hours to get Benjamin back down and finish the row. We'll probably still be up when you get back.'

I shook my head. 'Maybe not.'

'So take a spare set of keys. You'll need our car anyway. The tubes are buggered and there are no taxis to be had.'

'Colin'll go mad.'

She smiled for the first time. 'Why do you think I'm offering it? The keys are hanging up by the door.'

We looked at each other. I gave her a quick hug. 'Thanks, Kate. You're a real older sister.'

'I know. That's what worries me. Should I ask you if you'll be all right? On second thoughts just do me a favour, will you? Have an adventure for me while you're at it.'

As I closed the door she was heading upstairs to the sound of fury.

CHAPTER EIGHTEEN

Finsbury Park doesn't make a great impression at any time of the day, but it's at its worst around the time when the pubs close and people realize there's nowhere to go but home, even though it's the last place most of them want to be. No wonder he hadn't wanted to invite me back to his flat that night in February. Just as well I'd found an address anyway. He wasn't in. But that was hardly a surprise. If he was dancing, then the show had either just come down, or not yet gone up, depending how bad a job it was. I was willing to wait.

I stayed in the car. It was warmer that way and more of a deterrent for people who might feel tempted to run their pound coins along the side for a lark. Good thinking, Batwoman. Good strategy too. Start with the questions you can answer and maybe the others will give themselves up in gobsmacked admiration. OK, so on the surface Eyelashes might be an outside choice, but he wouldn't be the first man to swing both ways, and if he didn't want me to know, how better than to play it more camp than he really was. That he had been fond of her had shone through even his exaggerated cynicism. When it became clear, after three months of trying, that the Belmont sperm wasn't capable of making babies, why not go to him? Certainly it had been his number she had called eight months later when she'd really needed help, even though she'd never arrived at his door to collect it.

The taxi pulled in at 11.45 p.m. I had to move to get to the door before he was inside it. I caught him by the gate. He whirled round. I think, for a second, he thought I might be a mugger hiding in the bushes. I put my hands in the air to show him I had dropped my knife.

'Hi. Remember me?'

It took him a few seconds. 'Yes. Wish I could say I didn't.'

'I need to talk to you.'

'Don't you always? Well, sorry to disappoint you, dear, but much as I'd love to invite you in I've got an audition in the morning and I must get my beauty sleep.'

'Don't worry, it won't take long, if need be we can do it out here. Just a couple of questions. Tell me, are you exclusively gay or do you sleep with girls?'

'We-ell . . . Now is this meant as an offer or an insult?'

'Or maybe that's not the right way to put it. Maybe I should ask if you're bi-sexual?'

'ACDC, darling. Get the jargon right.'

The camper he got the more I was sure. 'Next question. Where were you between the nights of 29 April and 2 May? Your bed or hers?'

'I don't know what you're talking about.'

'Oh come on, Scott. I wasn't born yesterday. And I know a good deal more than I did when you last lied to me. What happened? Did she ask you or did you offer?'

He seemed so well protected that I was almost surprised when it hit home. Even in the street light I could see the face crumple. If this had been a happy-ending type of story I would have thrown my cap in the air and yelped for joy. As it was, I just closed my eyes for a second. 'OK. At last. Now I've got some things to tell you. Do you want to hear them out here or invite me inside?'

It wasn't big, but it had style – Habitat filtered through a couple of interiors magazines, ideas rather than money. You could see he had put a lot of energy into it. The drinks cabinet was an old safe painted matt black. He clicked the code while I made myself comfortable in a tubular chair. He hadn't looked at me since that moment on the street. I decided not to rush him.

He poured a generous measure. Among his many jobs he'd probably been a bar tender. I waited. He sat down on the sofa and put his elbows on his knees cradling the glass between his hands. He still wasn't looking.

'It was no big deal. I mean we'd messed around the odd time before. It was just a nice way to spend a night, that's all. She was a good-looking girl. And yes, I like them both. There's no crime in that.'

'Except when you're setting out to deceive and defraud.'

'Listen, I don't know anything about that. She just came round one night and offered. I accepted.'

'Bullshit, Scott. And I tell you I'm getting tired of coming back to hear the things that you don't tell me first time round. Except now I'm not the only one who wants to know, and I can always flash my address book open on your page. My suspicion is they won't be as understanding as I am.'

He looked up and you could see he was frightened. It was a bit cruel really, but fuck it, I had had enough of him getting away with it. 'I swear that was all she said. Of course I had a good idea it wasn't the truth, but when I asked, she told me it was better if I didn't know. She just wanted a favour. If I didn't give it she could always go elsewhere.'

'And if you did?'

'She said when she was rich she'd take me on a Mediterranean cruise.' He laughed even though we both knew it wasn't funny. 'I always knew she'd find some way of getting out of it.'

Boy, if I'd known then what I knew now. 'So why didn't you tell me, Scott?'

He lifted his glass to take a drink but it was too fast a gesture and Scotch splashed on to the carpet. He scowled. 'I don't know. I was scared, I suppose.'

'Of what?'

'That she'd done something wrong and that they'd come look-ing for me. She sounded pretty freaked out on the phone. I've thought about it a lot since.' He looked up. 'It was some kind of surrogacy deal, wasn't it?'

'Yes, some kind. Only it was the sperm that was the really important bit.'

He nodded. 'So what happened?'

'It's a long story. And most of it I don't think you'd want to know.'

He looked at me for a moment, then dropped his eyes. 'They found out.'

'Of course, they found out. Jesus, Scott, what did you think? Come to that what did she think? That someone was going to just hand over sixty thousand pounds and not check the merchandise?'

'Sixty thousand?' he whistled through his teeth.

'If they hadn't discovered it when they did, they would have found out later, after the baby was born. They would have tested for paternity. She must have realized that.'

He was silent for a moment. Then he said quietly, 'I think she thought she could get away by the time that happened. Or that they would want it so much it wouldn't really matter.'

At last, after all this time, I could hear it, Carolyn's voice secondhand in my ear. So, I had been right. She wasn't just a victim. All along she had had her own scam going, her own game plan. Except in the end she just hadn't been smart enough, had only been one jump ahead when she should have been three. Still, you could see how it had happened. Such a lot of money. How could she not have been tempted? 'Yeah, well, under other circumstances she might just have been right. But not with this family. This guy wasn't looking for *any* child. He was looking for his. Nothing else would do.'

'So he checked it out while she was still pregnant?'

'In a manner of speaking, yes.' Why tell him? He'd thought he was being a friend to her. Wasting my time wasn't really crime enough to deserve carrying this one around with him for the rest of his life.

We were both silent. I imagined her sitting here, that long

shower of hair cascading down a slender naked back. Had it been a quick fuck, duty over passion, or had they squeezed some long slow pleasure from it? Maybe it made you a better lover, knowing how to be the woman as well as the man. He had a good body. Let's hope for her sake it was one when the earth moved. That was one secret he could keep for himself.

'Listen, I know you think I lied to you about the baby, but she never told me, I swear. She didn't say anything that morning on the phone. Just that she needed a place to stay and she'd be coming soon. That was all. When she didn't turn up I suppose I knew that something had gone really wrong. I kept calling her flat, just on the off chance. Late on Saturday night someone picked it up. But it wasn't her.' He looked up at me. I nodded. 'Yeah, that's what I figured. Bet it scared the shit out of you too. Christ, I wish she'd told me. I mean I'm not that much of a shit. I would have helped her, you know. I would have looked after her.' I let him play with it for a bit. There was nothing I could say to help anyway. Eventually he let it go. 'What happens now?'

I stared into my glass. It was a good question. I had a frightened woman carrying an ailing foetus on the run from the man who had just lost his last chance to buy shares in earthly immortality. I had a nephew who could pilot his own plane to London, but had a flight report that said he couldn't have got here in time, a wife who probably took too many anti-depressants to care one way or the other and a housekeeper, a doctor and a chauffeur, all of whom were being paid to keep their mouths shut. I also had an anonymous client, and – and this wasn't just coincidence any more – a set of medical notes that one of the aforementioned five people had decided I needed to see. And just to really screw things up I had a suicide note that claimed full responsibility. None of it made any sense at all. Back in the car I tossed a coin. Tails I give up and go home for the night. Heads I keep on trying. Queen Elizabeth as a young girl stared up at me in profile. I decided to behave like a policeman.

According to Frank, some of his greatest triumphs had come

from getting inside the criminal's head. 'Imaginative reconstruction, Hannah. You go where they would have gone, do what they would have done, think what they would have thought, and eventually fuck up where they fucked up. And in the end they do, you know. There's always something that gives it away, it's just a question of finding it.' It was the kind of Frankism that was probably only half bullshit, but it had always sounded too like a TV cop show for me. Still, when you've got nothing else to do . . . She wasn't exactly a criminal, but she was all I had got.

It took me just under an hour to get to Kew. I passed through Kilburn on the way, just to double-check the time from her house. Of course she might have taken public transport (certainly no cab driver had come forward to give evidence, but then neither had any bus or train driver) and the traffic would have been a lot heavier. Let's call it an hour and half door to door. It was getting on for 2 a.m. when I got there. Anyone still up was certainly not on the roads. I drove over Kew bridge, parked the car on the other side, then walked back. At the middle of the bridge I hoisted myself up on the side and sat there, staring down at the black water below. The place was deserted, not a soul to check if my solitude was pain or pleasure. Not at all as it would have been at five o'clock of a Saturday afternoon. Then it would have been jumping. She would have had to pick her way down to the river bank and walk until she found a spot where the people and the lights had died away. And while the rest of the world was using its credit cards and making restaurant reservations for the evening she would have been loading the stones in her pocket and searching for the right place to throw herself in. Returning to the scene of the crime. I looked up river to where the towpath lights ended and the darkness began. But where exactly? Maybe Frank would have gone to look. But not me. This story had already seeped its way in through the cracks of my defences. No point in scaring the shit out of myself for nothing. Or maybe there was a point. I swung my legs over the outer edge of the parapet and edged forward until there was just a few inches between me and the drop into the water. The bridge lights dappled the surface, picking out veins of running silver. Pretty in a cold kind of way. I thought about the times in my life when failure had far outstripped success, when I had been alone and feeling as bad about myself as I did about the rest of the world and when there hadn't been any practical, let alone any philosophical, reason for getting up the next morning. But it wasn't enough. The water still looked cruel, not at all like any kind of way out. Maybe I just wasn't trying hard enough. Once again I tried to slide my way under her skin, burrow into her brain. Whatever her spirit she was still just a young girl in deep financial trouble who'd taken one hell of a gamble and lost. Having set out to save herself from debt she had ended up even worse, as a thief taking money under false pretences and not able to give it back. And not just a thief: very possibly a kind of murderer also. Her own child. Even if she hadn't wanted it, how could she let it die and stay alive herself afterwards? It or her. Her or me. Fifteen feet below, the water winked at me. I took one hand off the parapet. Then the other. Then I put them both back. She must have been braver than I. Or driven stupid by more despair. If I had been her I might have just come here to torment myself, but I would never have followed through. Instead I would have hailed the first cab and fled to a hospital, saved both it and me and faced up to everything else when it came looking for me.

Which, of course, is what she must have been planning to do when she had called Scott that Friday. Otherwise why bother to get in touch? Needing somewhere to stay presupposed being alive long enough to stay in it. And choosing the father of your child as your host showed at least some sense of coherence in the midst of despair. Coherence and strategy. She had been careful enough to warn him that someone might come looking for her, had told him to keep quiet about it. As late as twenty-four hours before her death she had been ready to fight to keep them off her back. Did it really change everything when she realized they had found out? It was still the same baby, still hers, still slowly sliding into unconsciousness. Despite or more likely because of

[206]

that she'd still been plucky enough to get the hell out of there and make her way to London. It just didn't make sense to get this far only to give up. What she needed was a doctor whose first oath was to medicine rather than Belmont, someone who would help first and ask questions later. Except who and where? When the police had plodded their way around the emergency clinics and gynae wards nobody had remembered a long-haired young beauty, eight months pregnant, coming in off the streets that afternoon in the kind of trouble you wouldn't forget. And one thing was certain: once she'd got in there no doctor in their right mind would have let her out. So she hadn't gone for help. Could she really have been too scared even for a hospital? But in which case why go all the way home just to write a suicide note? If she was looking for the nearest piece of river why not come straight here from the airport? Equally, if she was at home why the hell travel all the way here when she had her own perfectly good black water just down the road at Westminster or Waterloo.

Welcome home to the old problem. What was Frank's resident cliché? If you can't find the answer then you're not asking the right question. Back to the facts. Even a slipshod pathologist can tell fresh from sea water diatoms, and the contents of her stomach showed only one sort. She had died swallowing water which had not come into contact with the sea. Given that and given how long she'd been in the water she must have gone in somewhere around Kew or Hampton Court. Science doesn't lie. Her stomach proved she'd gone in up river. Her note proved she'd been home first. But as Daniel had said, home was the first place they would go looking for her. And home, was indeed where he had gone. He had arrived at Heathrow at 8.40 p.m. From there, according to him, he had driven straight to her house. Assuming VIP treatment through airport bureaucracy and customs and Saturday night traffic, Heathrow to Kilburn would have taken what – an hour, hour and half. Let's say 10.00 p.m. No, let's say later. Let's say it took longer and that he arrived nearer 10.30 p.m. By which time I was sitting back in my car thawing my hands back to life after the ice of her living-room. And, as I sat, I was watching the figure of a tall man in a trench-coat walk in through the front gate and up to her door. Except he didn't need to ring the bell, or even fiddle the lock. Because he had a key. Of course. How else could they have collected her mail over the last eight months? And then I saw the empty table in her room as it had been half an hour before, illuminated by the brief light of a naked bulb and then the more methodical sweep of my torch beam. And last of all I thought of the suicide note, that sad little litany of words. With the rumble of the river in the background I recited it out loud, the prelude to a final act of contrition. Holy Mary, mother of God, forgive me for I have sinned . . . 'By the time you read this you will know the truth. I am sorry for all the deceit and the trouble I have caused. Also for all the money which I cannot repay. It seems the only thing I can do is to go. Please, if you can, forgive me.'

. . . For these and all the sins of my life I am very sorry. But most of all for the sin of stupidity, Hannah. 'The only thing I can do is go.' But a debt to Miss Patrick isn't the same thing as the money owed to the Belmonts, and the deceit of a concealed pregnancy isn't the same thing as deliberately picking the wrong father for the child. And most of all, leaving France isn't the same as leaving life, although, given the circumstances, you can see how a coroner might just have been fooled into believing it was.

I got down from the bridge and walked slowly back to my car. She had written the note and left it in the summerhouse. Which meant they must have found it after she'd gone. But for Daniel to bring it with him to England they must already have appreciated its ambiguity. Yet facts are still facts and forensics is still a science. According to the pathologist she had died between 4.30 p.m. and 6.30 p.m. Daniel touched down two hours later. So let's say for the sake of argument that death was the automatic punishment for betrayal in Belmont's post-resistance world. Let's even assume, however much it hurt, that Daniel had the stomach as well as the strength to drown an eight-months pregnant woman just because his uncle asked him to. The question remained – how could he possibly have thrown Carolyn Hamilton into the

Thames at a time when he was still on the other side of the Channel? And if it wasn't him then who the hell was it? How many times do I have to tell you, Hannah, it's not the answers but the questions . . . I tried again. And again. And eventually I got somewhere. This time I drove to Kilburn via Heathrow, just to check the time. It worked. Shame it was too late to thank Frank personally.

If it hadn't been for Colin's car I would probably have gone straight back to the airport. It was nearly four when I got to Islington. In the kitchen the only paper I could find had Amy's abstract doodling on one side, but sometimes art has to suffer for the sake of history. It took me the best part of two hours to write the report out twice. By that time Benjamin had decided it was time to get up and Kate didn't have much option but to agree. When she came down to fill up his bottle she looked more weary than I did and I'd been up all night. He on the other hand was radiant, all smiles and top-o'-the-morning-to-you. She slumped in the kitchen chair and plugged him in, while I made a pot of tea. We sat together and chomped our way through a plate of custard creams and chocolate digestives – midnight feasts postponed from childhood.

I think now that most of my childhood had been spent trying to catch up with Kate, trying to narrow that eighteen-month gap that meant she did everything before I did. And even when I'd managed it, had gone more places, done more things, slept with more men, I could still look back and find her in front of me. Three weeks ago I had sat on her staircase, hearing her lecture me about how it couldn't have been suicide, regardless of what any note might have said. If I'd listened to her right from the start, I could have saved myself a lot of time and trouble.

'I went to Finsbury Park,' I heard myself say, 'to see a dancer she used to work with, the father of her child. Then I went to the river. And now I have to go back to France.'

She studied me for a moment, then said, 'You don't have to tell me, you know. I didn't ask.'

I nodded, then pushed one of the small piles of Amy's drawings across the table towards her. 'Maybe if you get a moment you could read this before you stash it in the airing cupboard.'

'What is it – a whodunnit?'

I shook my head. 'More a how than a who. It's gripping stuff as far as it goes. Unfortunately it doesn't have an ending.'

'Is that why you're going to France?'

'Sort of.'

She smiled. 'What happened? Did you fall for the bad guy?'

Yesterday it would have made me mad. Today I allowed myself to give it some thought. Without the luxury of sleep to fortify my defences it was a little easier. She was right, of course. Something had gone down between us. I could continue to dismiss it as the attraction of dress sense, adrenalin over vocation, or I could look at it for what it was: the break-up of the iceberg, even the first sign of spring. Hannah 'Self-Sufficient' Wolfe comes out of hibernation to test the air. Admirable stuff if it wasn't for the timing. And the man. Still, it never stopped Humphrey Bogart from shopping Mary Astor. But then she really was one of the bad guys. Whereas Daniel . . . well, not one of the good guys, certainly, but further than that . . .

'I don't know,' I said, after a while. 'I think that's one of the things I'm going to find out.'

She nodded and shifted Benjamin to her other arm. She looked down at him for a second, then back up at me. 'You know the first six months after Amy was born I used to have this recurring nightmare. I was locked in this room. I had gone in there voluntarily and closed the door behind me. But then I couldn't get out. There was a tiny window up high. If I climbed up I could just see out of it to a long stretch of road. And there was this figure walking along it, away from me. It was you.' She laughed. 'Pretty basic stuff, eh? I was so ashamed of its literalism that I could never tell you. Well, that and other reasons. After a while it faded. Amy got bigger, I found I could cope better, found that, as well as loving her so much it scared the wits out of me, I even quite enjoyed it. And now it seems altogether possible that having children doesn't end your life. So now I only envy you some of the time.' She paused. 'Funny thing is I get the impression you could say the same about me.'

I thought about the witty things I could say to deflect her, about how it was hardly the kind of thing a private investigator could admit to, undermining, as it did, the image. But in the end I didn't say any of it. In fact in the end I didn't speak for a while. I think it took me more by surprise than it did her. Eventually she dug a tissue out of her dressing gown pocket and pushed it across the table. It smelt of baby. I blew my nose. 'I haven't slept,' I said after a while, maybe by way of an apology.

'Don't worry. You'll find it good practice.'

I shook my head. 'I might not want a child, you know. Not every woman does.'

'I know that,' she said gently. 'I just think you should give yourself the chance to choose. Isn't that what you would have wished for your little dancer?'

And, of course, she was right. On the wall the kitchen clock read 5.45 a.m. I stood up. 'I have to go.'

She nodded. 'So, back to criminal proceedings. Do you want me to leave this thing in the airing cupboard after I've read it or what?'

'No. Maybe you should duplicate it and send it to Frank under my name.' I screwed up my mouth into my James Cagney impersonation. 'And if you don't hear from me within twenty-four hours, kid, tell him to open it.'

CHAPTER NINETEEN

I was lucky. At Heathrow the Duty Operations Manager was the same guy who'd been on shift that Saturday night. Of course he didn't want to tell me anything, but a bit like Deep Throat he was willing not to deny it. I caught the 9.00 a.m. flight. No messing this time. I had hired a car from London and it was waiting at Charles de Gaulle. The trip to Villemetrie lasted 34 minutes on the autoroute, but then I wasn't sure of the road and it wasn't the latest model. In a private plane Daniel would have flown out of le Bourget, but he would have been in the BMW and could easily have made up the extra distance in speed. My whole journey took under three hours, or two, discounting British summertime. For Daniel it would have been shorter. I parked fifty yards or so from the main gate, in the entrance to a field. Outside the house two big black cars were waiting. I thought about leaving it until after lunch, but to be honest I couldn't wait. I went in over my favourite piece of wall, on through the forest and parallel to the polluted little river that ran along the edge of the garden. It was six days since I'd been here. Spring had already made a difference. The grass had sprung up and the foliage was denser. I crossed the dirty brown river at the same point, the lake on my right. On the long patio at the back of the house a trestle table was set up covered in a white tablecloth with a few round smaller tables near by, with chairs. Not so much a business lunch as a party: a birthday or celebration of a young/old marriage and a golden position in French society? I made my way across the lawn not bothering to conceal myself. Even if they threw me out now they would have to let me back in again. I was halfway to the house when a figure appeared on the terrace, tall and willowy, dressed in black with that shining cap of fair hair. If I could see her, then she must also be able to see me. I kept on walking. She stood there for a moment, very still, looking towards me, then turned and sat herself at one of the tables. She opened her bag. I caught sight of a red spark and then watched her settle herself in the chair, cigarette gracefully in hand. She made an elegant figure, silhouetted against the rich brickwork and symmetry of windows. Is that what Belmont had seen ten years ago, an aesthetic complement to an architectural folly? It was more convincing than the image of Mathilde as a child-breeder, a torrent of ruddy-faced babies gushing forth from those slender loins.

The last twenty yards was pure theatre, or rather film. The prop girl had placed a chair at right angles to her, the sun slicing on to it. I sat down. She let her head fall back into the warmth of the sun. Close to she looked particularly stunning, the cream skin against soft black crêpe and a single row of pearls around her neck, sheer stockings and shiny black shoes. Six days ago I might have labelled her silence as some kind of damaged eccentricity. Now I was pretty sure it was confidence.

After a while she looked up at me and nodded. 'Hello, Hannah.'

'Hello, Mathilde,' I said because I felt I had earned the use of her first name.

'How long did it take you to get here?'

'Oh, about five days, I think. But then I wasted some time on dead ends.'

She made a comforting face. 'Well, anyway, you're here now.'

I looked around at the tables. 'I'm sorry if this is an inconvenient time.'

'Not really. In fact in some ways it may even be quite appropriate.' She paused. 'If Jules were here I'm sure he'd offer you a drink.'

I shook my head and smiled at her. In the end it had been obvious. I mean who else had recourse to the doctor's report and a solicitor, fake or otherwise in London? Come to that who else could afford the fees? Except Daniel, of course, and whatever fantasies I may have harboured in the past, last night had watched them tumble into the river. It was time to be realistic. She smiled back. It was a warm moment, girls together on a ripe spring morning with the prospect of a party to come. I was almost loath to break the spell. From my bag I pulled out a folder. I handed it to her.

'I think this belongs to you.'

She hesitated just for a second, then took it from me. She held it on her lap, her fingers playing over the cover as if they were reading Braille. Even the physical presence of it seemed to make her uneasy. Wanting to know is not the same as finding out, as I knew only too well. 'We've never had much of a chance to talk to each other,' she said after a while. 'Why don't you tell me what it says?'

'Because I don't know how much you know. I wouldn't want to bore you.'

'How much? Well, I know that the child was not my husband's and that in some way she died because of that. I also know it wasn't suicide.'

'He didn't tell you?'

'No,' she said softly. 'He didn't tell me.'

'Why not?' Although I suspected I already knew the answer.

'As you yourself once said – I wanted a child very much. It was less important to me than to him who the father was.' She paused. 'I assume he felt he couldn't trust me.'

'So how did you get hold of the medical report?'

She took a long drag of her cigarette. Interestingly I couldn't remember her smoking before. Even now it seemed more of an affectation than a need. 'The doctor had kept a copy, just in case he needed to prove it wasn't his fault. So I blackmailed him, told him I would make public his part in the deception unless he gave me it. It was a risk, but it was clear you needed help and it was the only help I could give without entirely giving myself away.' She cast a quick glance behind her, up to the house. Then back at me. 'We don't have a lot of time, Hannah. I need to know.'

I took a breath. Here it was, the moment every private investigator dreams of – the truth, by Hannah Wolfe. 'You were right, she didn't kill herself. The so-called suicide note wasn't written in her flat after all, it was written here in the summerhouse before she left. Daniel took it with him to London and planted it there for the police to find. But it wasn't the only luggage he brought from France. There was also a trunk. Full of company reports apparently. Although, of course, no one opened it to check. As you suggested to me that day on the steps, there are some distinct advantages to being Belmont Aviation. Like being able to arrange your own flights at the last minute. Like having preferential treatment coming in and out of airports, knowing you can move fast and that no one will question you. They touched down in the private jet at 8.40 p.m. He arrived in Kilburn at 10.25 p.m. – I know because I was there. In between he had just enough time to get himself and the luggage down to the river.

'Carolyn died by inhaling fresh river water between 4.30 p.m. and 6.30 p.m. on that Saturday evening. When the river police found the body two days later they jumped to the obvious conclusion. The PM and the inquest backed them up. The approximate time of death, the contents of the stomach, the suicide note, it all fitted. Given the facts there was no reason to suspect that the fresh water diatoms in her hadn't come from the Thames. Except that at the time of death, of course, she was nowhere near the Thames. She was still here.' I paused, looking out over the grounds to the glisten of water at the edge of the forest.

'It's a beautiful lake. Very old, I imagine, and fed directly from the river. Not such a clean river, alas, but pollution is a fact of life these days. Still cleaner than the Thames, but luckily the pathologist wasn't checking for levels of pollution. Or for the differences between one river and another. To do that he would have had to call in a marine biologist, and why bother? As I say, everything fitted just as it was.

'Carolyn wrote her note, waited until dark and then tried to leave. What happened next maybe you would know better than I. Maybe she didn't see the edge of the water, fell in the dark and panicked, thrashed around until she couldn't swim any more then opened her mouth to the water. Or maybe someone helped her in and made sure she stayed there. Whatever the explanation, I think Carolyn Hamilton drowned in your lake somewhere around 5.30 p.m. to 6.30 p.m. Then they – probably Daniel with a little help from Maurice – scooped her out, packed her up and flew her, post haste, to London. It was an act of pure bravado. But a clever one. Of course they were lucky to get away with it. A better PM might have gone in search of questions that the body couldn't answer. As it was they found only what they were looking for.'

The ash on her cigarette had grown dangerously long. Her hand trembled slightly and it slipped silently on to her dress. I wondered how she was going to get it off without smudging the divine hot black of the crêpe. Had she paid for me with her husband's money? Rather ironic really, him indirectly financing his own destruction. Even though I had known it for a while I was still somewhat awed by the magnitude of her disloyalty. No wonder traditionally women were absolved from testifying against their husbands. It just meant they had to employ someone else to do it for them. She looked down at the ash and employed a small perfect nail to flick it deftly away. Nevertheless a faint grey shadow remained. She looked up at me and you could see that whatever else she was feeling she was also pleased.

'I was out that afternoon. Buying nursery furniture,' she said with a hollow little laugh. 'She had told me about the baby the day she asked Jules to release her from the contract. I told her it wouldn't matter. I assured her that when the time came to test for paternity I would protect her from his anger. I thought that would be enough. Of course what she hadn't told me was how she knew for certain that it wasn't his. Do you think the baby was dead?'

'Not according to the expert I talked to. I think she was leaving in order to try and save it.'

She shook her head. 'By the time I got back here it was after seven o'clock. She had already gone.'

'But Jules was here.'

'Yes. Jules was here.'

'How was he?'

'Beside himself with anxiety. Daniel was already on his way to London. Agnes was flitting around him with a dozen medicine bottles and there was no sign of Maurice. Jules told me he was out looking for her.'

'Out yes, but not looking. Every executive needs a chauffeur, and someone to help carry the trunk. I think it's called "keeping it in the family". He's Agnes's son, isn't he?'

She nodded. 'She's been with Jules since the war. He and his first wife took her in after her parents were killed by the Germans. When she married, her husband came to work for the company. When he died the son took his place. They would do anything for him. All of them. All except Carolyn, of course.'

'When did you learn about the blood test?'

'That evening. Jules told me.' She looked down at her hands for a moment. 'You know there's a story told about Jules during the war. That he uncovered an informer in the resistance group he was leading. It was a woman. She'd been responsible for six people falling into Gestapo hands. Jules took her out on a mission with him to blow up an armaments store. He came back alone. Her body was found in the remains of the warehouse.' She paused. 'Do you think he killed her?'

I wondered how many times she had asked herself that question since the night Carolyn disappeared. 'I don't know. Why don't you ask him?'

And for the first time she laughed. 'You're right, I should have done. The trouble is I don't know if he'd have told me the truth.' Finally the tense registered. Had it been there all along and I been too caught up in my own triumph to notice? 'You took one too many wrong turnings, Hannah. Jules had another heart attack two days ago. A big one. He died an hour later, never having regained consciousness. What did you think all this

[217]

was for?' She waved an elegant hand over her dress and beyond, to the sea of white tablecloth. 'The vultures are gathering to pick over the corpse. I came out to get a little fresh air after the reading of the will.'

I have to say my primary emotion was disappointment. I suppose I had been looking forward to seeing his face. I didn't like the idea of him going to his grave believing he had fooled me. She on the other hand didn't seem to mind at all. In fact, despite her immaculate costume I was having just a little trouble adjusting to Mathilde Belmont as the grieving widow.

'What will you do with the report?' I said after a while.

'I don't know.' She looked up. 'I haven't really thought. I've been a married woman for seven years. I've rather lost the use of my brain. No doubt it'll come back. Tell me, how much of this can you prove?'

'How much of what?' He must have come out through the open French windows, soft footfalls on hard stone. Or maybe he'd had training, listening outside other people's doors. The black suit was just as striking, but then this time I had done some mental preparation. He walked over and stood between us. A dangerous position to be in. Near to, he looked tired, much more the worse for wear than her. When it was clear she was not going to answer his question he turned his attention to me. I kept my eyes on the floor. 'Hello, Hannah,' he said quietly. 'I didn't expect to see you again so soon.'

'No, well I just couldn't keep away.'

He smiled, then went back to his aunt. Funny, I'd never thought of her like that before. It must have been a little incongruous for both of them. 'They've gone into the library for an apéritif, Mathilde. I think they're expecting you to join them.'

'So, let them wait. I'm in mourning, if you remember. That makes my eccentricity acceptable.'

'Not to mention your dry handkerchiefs,' he added softly. We both waited for her to respond but she said nothing. After a while he glanced down at the folder on the table. Then up at me. 'It looks like you've been working. May I?'

I met his eyes: that old mixture of the serious and the mocking. I wondered how far I'd have to go before I hit the granite. I shrugged. 'You'll have to ask my client.'

And from the way he looked at her it was clear he hadn't had a clue. I already knew they didn't like each other, but even I was surprised at the little darts of hatred now singing through the air between them. She broke the gaze first, but it took a while. He picked up the report. Neither of us moved while he read it. Even the air seemed to freeze. Eventually I stopped watching my fingernails and started watching his face. Now you know what it feels like, buddy, I thought, being the last kid on the block to learn that everyone else knows it too.

He closed the folder and put it down carefully between us. Then he said, 'Well done, Hannah. It's a lot of work.'

'I can't take all the credit,' I said. 'I had help.'

'Yes, so I see.' He was silent for a moment, then turned to her and smiled. 'Well, what comes now, Mathilde? You want to call the police straight away or would you prefer to talk about it for a while? Couldn't be better timing. We've got a house full of lawyers. You just tell me what you want and they could have the documents drawn up by the time lunch is served.'

'Don't be crude, Daniel. You're the one in trouble, remember.' And her voice was ice cold. 'Why don't you try and save your own skin? Try to convince us that you didn't kill her.'

'Of course I didn't kill her.' And if she was looking to provoke anger she was disappointed; he sounded almost amused. 'Neither did Jules or anyone else for that matter. But I wouldn't let that concern you. You've probably still got enough here to put me behind bars for a while. Assuming, of course, you can prove it. But you can always cross that bridge when – or if – you come to it. You know we really shouldn't be wasting time talking. You get this to the police today and it might make the first edition, along with the details of the will.' She glowered at him, but she didn't move. 'No? Hannah, why don't you persuade her? After all, this is a quest for the truth, isn't it? What's a cut of the Belmont estate put against a righteous hunger for justice? Wasn't

[219]

that why you employed Hannah? So go for it. You've got nothing to lose. It surely can't matter to you that if I go to jail the money goes with me. It still wouldn't end up in your pocket, however much you might think you deserve it.'

She stood up. It was an abrupt movement. 'Don't give me this shit, Daniel,' she said between clenched teeth. 'You're the criminal, not me. I don't have to listen to this.' She held his gaze for a second then turned to me, sweeter now, more like the loving widow. 'Miss Wolfe, I'm so sorry. Maybe you and I should conclude our business indoors.'

'Oh, nice one, Mathilde. Except I suspect "Miss Wolfe" isn't that stupid, are you, Hannah? In fact I bet she wants to hear the truth even more than you do. Come to think of it she's probably the only one who does. But then she's also the only one without a vested interest. Sit down, Mathilde, and I'll tell you both what happened that night. Then you can tell me what you're going to do about it. I said sit down.'

My God, but you're lovely when you're angry, I thought. Mathilde was less impressed. But she sat. I could hear my heart in stereo in my ears. Except which one of us was I nervous for – him, her or me? He didn't speak for a while. Maybe he was looking for the right words. When he found them I was reminded of defending counsel addressing the jury, that same kind of intensity, that same apparent, shining sincerity. Except that was the jury's job. To sort out the truth from the rhetoric.

'I was at the office that Saturday afternoon. I got a call from Jules just before five. The results of the test had just come through and the doctor had told him about the baby. Of course he was upset, and he was also angry. But as much because she hadn't been able to tell him as because of what she'd done. I think it made him realize how frightened of him she must have been, and for that reason he wanted me there when he confronted her. I got here as soon as I could. Nevertheless it was dark by the time I arrived. Agnes let me in. She was in tears. She led me out into the grounds. They were down by the lake. Jules, Maurice and the body. It had been Maurice who had found her. He'd let the dogs out just after dusk. Then heard them barking furiously down by the lake. He hadn't taken any notice for a while, thought it was a rabbit or a shrew. But they kept on and on. He called to them to come in but they wouldn't budge. So he went out to them. They were standing by the edge of the lake, howling at the water. The body was about twenty yards out, caught in the weeds. They must have heard her, thought she was an intruder. It was pitch black and she was off the path. With the dogs on her heels it must have been easy for her to miss her way and fall in. It was bitterly cold that night. By dark the temperature was already well below freezing. I think that would have done it as much as the water.'

He stopped, letting the picture linger in our minds. To his credit he could have milked it more. There were details he could have used to colour the images: those delicate ankles, for instance, swollen by the signs of pre-eclampsia and weakened by operations. How easy it would have been for her to lose her balance and fall panting into dark water and weeds. While I of all people had good reason to remember the terror the dogs could induce, and how panic can make one careless and crazy. I could see it all. But equally I could see something else, a split screen version of another truth: a young girl rendered weak and clumsy by fear as well as a blighted pregnancy, and an old man, stronger than he looked, energized by fury and the need to save his Othello-like 'reputation', holding her down until that golden hair was matted by slime and there was no life left, either in her or her stomach. In the end believing or not believing Daniel had nothing to do with it. This need not be a case of defence counsel lying, but rather of his client never having told him the truth. And that, of course, was the final irony. Because what was not known now would never be known. The real story, whatever it was, was already being eaten by worms in the Belmont mausoleum. The cunning old war hero had won the final battle. Except he had paid a high price for the silence. Maybe it was nature's way of evening the score. When the monarchy had been restored to power in England in the seventeenth century the government had disinterred the bodies of the king's enemies and had them hung, drawn and quartered anyway, just to show that justice can pursue you even beyond the grave. But that was English law, and they had had proof. I, even after all this time, had nothing but theories. Daniel was watching me carefully.

'I know what you're thinking, Hannah. And you're right. We'll never know for sure. But you shouldn't let that cloud your judgement. It made absolutely no sense for Jules or anyone else to harm her. All she wanted was a way out. She wasn't threatening blackmail – she had already promised that she would tell no one, she wasn't even asking for anything, just to be allowed to leave. And even if she had been it would have been easier and cleaner to pay her off and get her to a hospital before it was too late. She was a pregnant young woman, a little lost, a little screwed up, but nothing more. Whatever she had done she didn't deserve to die. And whatever anger he might have felt Jules wouldn't, couldn't, have killed her. I told you once, Hannah, that he was a remarkable man. You didn't really believe me. I suspect he had too much money and power for your liking. But that still doesn't make him a murderer.

'Of course I can't prove to you he didn't kill her any more than you can prove he did. All I can tell you is what happened. When I arrived it was clear we had to do something. Even for Jules the police couldn't have kept it quiet. The scandal would have destroyed him. Him and the company. He asked me for advice and I gave it. And if you're looking for a villain this is where you'll find him. I persuaded him not to go to the authorities, but to let me handle it instead. I told him that not only would the scandal destroy him, but it wouldn't do her any good either. She was dead. Nothing we could do would bring her back. This way she would just be a talented young girl who'd made a mistake and couldn't cope with the consequences. A tragic accident, someone for us all to pity. You know as well as I do that she would never have been treated so generously if the truth had come out.

'Except Jules couldn't let it rest. If Mathilde were honest she

[222]

would tell you the same thing. I think he was almost half-waiting to be found out. Or informed upon.' He glanced at her. 'As it is he did what he could. I don't think he was under any illusions that the money would make any difference. But at least it would keep her name alive. You look puzzled, Hannah. Let me guess? Mathilde hadn't got round to mentioning the details of Jules's will. So you wouldn't know that it includes an anonymous donation to set up a bequest for young dancers. To be named the Carolyn Hamilton bequest. Really quite a lot of money. He asked that Miss Patrick be approached to administer it. I don't know whether or not she'll accept. As I said, nothing he could do could bring her back. But in the end she was already dead. All we did was move the body. It just felt better for everyone that way.'

He stopped. I felt a little like a Roman emperor called upon to decide which Christian the lion would get for dinner. My thumb was itching but I couldn't be sure it would point the right way. I knew what I felt, but I also knew better than to trust it. When it came down to it I was tired of peeling this onion, tired of trying to decide if the tears were real or just a reaction to the spray. Maybe my client held the answer. She, after all, had been the one who was willing to pay to uncover the truth. Except, contrary to cliché, the pursuit of truth is not always the same as the pursuit of justice. And right at this moment she wasn't looking so good. I could see the rage building up in her, but could I also detect apprehension? Having Daniel here with us now had not been part of the plan. She was gathering herself up for an assault when he cut in on her. And for Daniel it was an unexpectedly bitter tone.

'No, wait a minute, maybe I should rephrase that last thought. It wasn't better for everyone. There was one person who didn't gain anything from hushing it up. I wonder, amid all the stories, did Mathilde ever tell you the one about her and Jules? About how they got together in the first place? No? Shame. It's a deeply romantic little tale. She was seeing another man at the time, quite a passionate affair I gather, but then she just kept having to deliver translations to the boss's office and one day – well, it was fate really, he had to notice her sooner or later. Of course he wasn't entirely stupid. A much older man and a beautiful younger woman. He knew it probably wasn't mutual love at first sight. He also knew what a financial catch he was, particularly since it was clear even then he wasn't going to live very long. But he'd fallen for her and he'd also fallen for the idea of a child. Nevertheless he was persuaded into protecting himself just a little. Before they married he asked her to sign a pre-nuptial settlement. She didn't mention that either? It must have slipped her mind. It said that if they had a child she would inherit a third of his fortune. The other two thirds would be split between myself and the child, with the two of us as equal guardians of his or her portion until he or she came of age. However, if there was no child the bulk of the money would go to me. She would get a small, but not by most people's standards inconsiderable allowance in perpetuity. But it didn't quite work out as she planned. For what I imagine must be the first time in her life her body let her down. Never mind. Jules was still besotted. He came up with an alternative. And this was where Carolyn came in. She was employed to have the baby for both of them and then to disappear. The world would think it belonged to Mathilde and Jules would go along with it. When he died the money would go to her. But if there was no baby, then, alas, we revert to plan B, and Mathilde would become just a well-heeled English translator with fantasies of luxury. Of course when it did go wrong she did have something on her side, something to sell. Information: the sort of story that a newspaper would love to buy. But she was not exactly an innocent bystander herself, and even she didn't have the nerve to try to blackmail her own husband. However, after he'd gone, and if the story could be made juicy enough, then there might be someone willing to pay to keep it quiet. Someone who would by then have a great deal to lose.

'And that is where you come in, Hannah. You were employed to squeeze some more juice out of the orange. To get Mathilde what she needed. Well, now she's got it. As of an hour ago, with the exception of generous bequests to herself, Agnes and Maurice and a lesser one to the family doctor, Daniel Devieux inherited most of the Belmont fortune.'

He paused for a moment. Beside me I felt Mathilde shaking, but whether with fury or fear it was hard to tell. Certainly if she had anything to say in her own defence now was the time to say it. The silence lingered. Daniel snorted softly. 'Which, as you can see, brings us neatly back to where we started. So, what do you want to do, Mathilde? Phone the police or talk about what it's worth? Because with this report in your hands it's all up for grabs. You too, Hannah. Don't let yourself be cut out of this. It's your information as well, you earned it. This could be your big chance to get out of security. Don't be squeamish about the morality. Your employer won't be, believe me. As I said, she has an unerring eye for where the money is. I can bear witness to that. Because I was where the money was for a while. Before she walked into Jules's office and saw the light dance up in his eyes. Come on, Mathilde. It never suited you to be the demure wife. Let's start talking.'

Now, at last, I turned and looked at her. The trembling had ceased. She was sitting instead like a statue of serenity, those lovely legs crossed into a long slender line, her hands clasped together on her lap. Whatever was going on inside, it was now safely under lock and key. She glanced up at me and gave me a big smile. It was the action of a pragmatist, not a woman to be troubled by moral ambiguities. 'I'm so sorry you had to listen to all that, Hannah, I'm sure you have better things to do with your time. You've done a marvellous job. You should be very proud of yourself. If you just let me know how much we owe you, you can be on your way.'

She was still smiling, so I smiled back. In the end it was altogether fitting that the one woman who claimed to be desperate for a child didn't really want one at all. So what did you expect, Hannah? That someone somewhere in this grimy little tale would really turn out to be a hero? Or, more importantly, a heroine. Instead it was more a question of degrees of corruption, morality as a rubber band, with everyone rejoicing in its elasticity. Carolyn had needed eight thousand pounds, but she'd been willing to take sixty if she could get away with fraud. Belmont didn't see why he shouldn't buy anything and everything he couldn't legitimately have. And in the end Mathilde wanted to be in on the deal too, so that she could use it to carve out her own empire. Agnes, Maurice and the doctor could be explained by a mixture of loyalty and greed. And Daniel . . . well, Daniel had watched from the sidelines and then moved in to clear up the mess. Sure he was fond of his uncle, grateful for all the things he had done for him. But it was also in his interests to inherit a company free from scandal, and he must have known that he'd be well rewarded for his pains. So there they were, the complete character list, untarnished by moral principles. Which left me sporting my threadbare idealism like a pair of flared trousers. But everyone has to grow up some time. How much could I ask? What did I need? A new car? An apartment? All I'd have to do was not think of her each time I put the key in the lock. Because Daniel was right. She was dead, and nothing I could do was going to bring her back. You know what, Hannah, Frank's voice sighed like the sea in my ear, either way this could be the biggest mistake of your life. 'My bill is in an envelope inside the folder,' I said quietly.

She stared at me for a moment, then pulled out the envelope and glanced inside. 'This seems altogether too modest. You're sure there isn't something you've forgotten?'

Like a couple of noughts, you mean. I tried again. I parted my lips to say something, to construct some suitably shadowy, ambivalent sentence that would lead me later to dazzle my bank manager and buy Frank that gold nameplate he's always dreamed of, but the words wouldn't form and even if they had I wouldn't have been able to get my tongue out from the taste of bile at the bottom of my mouth. Damn it. Not so much a moral problem as a physical one. Principles as a Pavlovian response. God help you, Hannah. It's good you're freelance, because you'd never make a cop. It had even got to Frank in the end. Yeah, well, there had to be some reason why I worked with him, didn't there? 'Thanks,' I said, the bile sliding away with the saliva. 'But I'll just take what I'm owed.'

'Of course,' she said quickly. She stood up and smoothed down her dress, then held out a hand towards me. 'If you'll excuse me, I think I am needed inside ...' I left the hand floating there, five perfect little nails flashing crimson in the sunlight. She didn't seem to mind. She turned. 'Daniel – perhaps you'd settle up with Hannah and say our goodbyes. I'll see you later.' My last view of her was that gorgeous figure gliding its way inside the French windows on the way to charm a few more ageing professionals. Despite it all you had to admire her confidence.

Which left Daniel and me. He picked up my bill where she had let it fall on the table, looked down at it and up at me. And it was a very warm look, no curtains across it. Something in my stomach curdled. 'I'm surprised. And you led me to believe that you practised a sliding scale, at least when it came to expenses.' I shrugged. He took a small wad of naked-breasted notes out of his pocket and handed them to me. It seemed altogether too crude to count them. Then he leant over, pulled the report out of its folder and started slowly to tear it into small pieces. It made a rasping angry sound. And as he tore he said, 'Of course, we both understand that what I'm doing is just theatre. That you've already made copies of this, and that those copies are somewhere safe in case anything should ever happen to you. That way you are protected from me, although not necessarily me from you. But that's a chance I just have to take.' He gathered up the bits and let them fall back into the envelope which he handed to me. This time our fingers touched. 'I said this once before to you, Hannah. You didn't believe it then, so there's no reason for you to believe it now. I'm sorry. If we could have done it any other way ... As you probably know now, I've not always been the greatest judge of women. However, this time it feels like my loss.' And then at last he smiled, a big wide grin devoid of any guilt or restraint. 'I'm sure I don't need to add, but if you ever need a job ...'

[227]

And it was so exquisite, so much the stuff that myth is made of that I knew it to be both true and at the same time a gross lie. Like the rest of this whole bizarre tale. It didn't matter that much anyway. Happy endings were not what we were talking about.

I think I may have smiled back. Then I gathered up my bag, got up and walked away. Only this time I went out through the front gates. They clanged shut behind me. In the distance I heard the dogs barking in their kennels.

The news of the bursary hit the papers six weeks later. Miss Patrick, to my surprise, agreed to be the administrator. I wrote a note congratulating her. She sent me a short, polite reply. The French press spent a while speculating on the future of the Belmont empire now the dashing young Daniel was at the helm (with rather more shares than many thought good for him, certainly more than they had expected Belmont to leave him) but in general the business consensus was that it was in safe hands. They were a little more excited when two weeks later it was announced that Daniel had given a half of the Belmont estate to Jules's widow, the very lovely young Mathilde Belmont. There were some photographs of her looking positively scrumptious in some very expensive outfits, but, alas, she was not available for comment.

As timing goes that would have been the moment; such sweet symmetry. Well, you didn't really think I'd let sentiment get completely in the way of business, did you? But in the end you can't accuse an international tycoon of being an accessory to possible murder or his beautiful young aunt of covering up for him when you don't have any proof at all. And the saddest thing of all was that I didn't. Even assuming that Agnes and Maurice could be persuaded not to perjure themselves to keep alive the flame of the dead hero, the medical report could have belonged to anyone, Carolyn Hamilton's body had been cremated two days after the inquest and the pathologist's samples, in particular those darling little French water diatoms which could have brought down an empire, had all been chucked down the sink a week later. I can't say I was surprised. How disappointed I was I've yet to decide. Interesting I wasn't the only one to have checked. Apparently a man with an American accent had been making inquiries a couple of weeks before. So he had known all along. Well, I would hate to have thought he was more stupid than I. Or less diligent. What do they say about relationships? That the best ones are based on equality. And fantasy.

Frank refused to give me another job until I told him what happened. So I gave him a version of the truth. He seemed satisfied. I was about to go shopping with an Israeli heiress when I got some free vouchers through the post. Apparently my name had been picked out from a thousand others and I had won fifteen thousand air miles with any company of my choice. It was postmarked West London, no address. What was it a good-looking man in a suit once said to me? That every airline owes something to Belmont Aviation. I must admit I found it harder to refuse than money. In the end I compromised. I ditched the princess, tore up half the vouchers and booked myself a round trip to the Galapagos Islands. Well, I had earned a holiday and a woman in evolution needs to be reminded of what happens when you get stranded in one place too long . . .